Princess
Juniper
OF THE
HOURGLASS

Princess Juniper

OF THE HOURGLASS

AMMI-JOAN PAQUETTE

PHILOMEL BOOKS

An Imprint of Penguin Group (USA)

PHILOMEL BOOKS

Published by the Penguin Group
Penguin Group (USA) LLC
375 Hudson Street, New York, NY 10014

USA | Canada | UK | Ireland | Australia | New Zealand | India | South Africa | China
penguin.com A Penguin Random House Company

Library of Congress Cataloging-in-Publication Data
Paquette, Ammi-Joan, author.
Princess Juniper of the Hourglass / Ammi-Joan Paquette.
pages cm.—(Princess Juniper)
Summary: Tired of all the rules of comportment at court, Princess Juniper asks for, and receives, a very small country of her own for her thirteenth Nameday, one she can set up and rule with less formality and more simple friendship—but there is trouble at home and she has to find a way to thwart her distant cousin's ambitions.
1. Princesses—Juvenile fiction. 2. Kings and rulers—Juvenile fiction. 3. Cousins—Juvenile fiction. 4. Friendship—Juvenile fiction. 5. Conspiracies—Juvenile fiction. [1. Princesses—Fiction. 2. Kings, queens, rulers, etc.—Fiction. 3. Cousins—Fiction. 4. Friendship—Fiction. 5. Conspiracies—Fiction.] I. Title.
PZ7.P2119Pr 2015
[Fic]—dc23
2014030626
Printed in the United States of America.
ISBN 978-0-399-17151-2
1 3 5 7 9 10 8 6 4 2

Edited by Jill Santopolo. Design by Siobhán Gallagher. Text set in 12.5 pt. Perpetua.

For Lauren:

Let's have lots more of those coffee shop days, shall we?

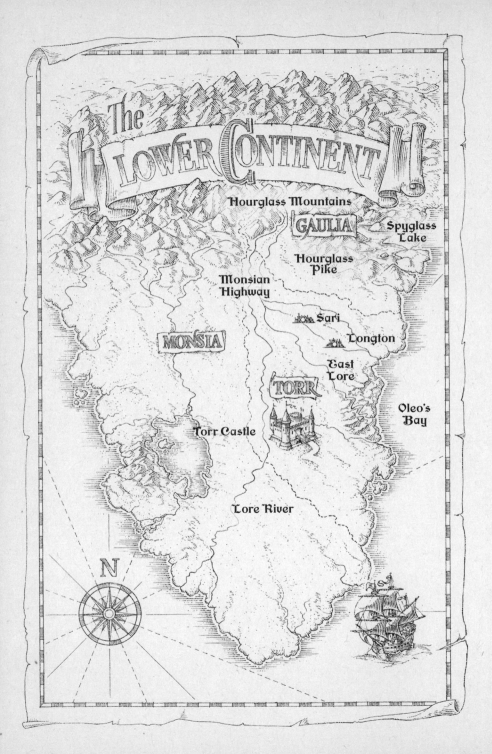

The

LOWER CONTINENT

Hourglass Mountains

GAULIA

Spyglass Lake

Hourglass Pike

Monsian Highway

Sari

Longton

MONSIA

East Lore

TORR

Oleo's Bay

Torr Castle

Lore River

N

The Official Daily Schedule of Princess Juniper

5:00	Rise
5:10	Bathe
5:25	Dress
5:40	Morning Grooming
6:15	Harpsichord Practice
7:15	Breakfast
8:00	Political Discourse
9:00	Studies
10:30	Outdoor Constitutional
11:00	Studies
12:30	Luncheon
1:30	Midi Rest
2:30	Croquet / Fencing / Polo
3:30	Equestrials / Dance / Comportment
4:30	Tea
5:15	Needlework
6:30	Supervised Reading and Devoirs
8:00	Dinner
9:00	Leisure (unless required in state matters)
10:00	Nightly Grooming
10:30	Retire

1

PRINCESS JUNIPER WAS RUNNING LATE. THIS was not only unusual, but quite nearly unforgivable.

In her own mind, anyway.

Oh, she knew there was no servant following her with a timepiece and a lecture, but today's croquet lesson had gone so abominably long! Now it was six minutes past the start of her riding lesson, and she was *still* in her chambers getting ready.

Juniper kicked aside her croquet tunic and crushed her riding cap onto her windswept curls.

It would have to do.

She dashed out of her bedchamber, through the vaulted midroom, past the dressing room—no time, no time!—skidded across her parlor, and yanked open her suite doors.

Where she ran directly into her maid.

Elly toppled onto her backside, still managing an apologetic half curtsey. Juniper only just kept her balance, grabbing hold of the door frame at the last moment. "Oh, filch—I'm sorry, Elly!"

Juniper reached out a hand, but her maid ducked and leaped back to her feet, scrabbling for the fallen silver tray, her face sunset red.

Juniper snatched her hand back, hoping she hadn't shamed the girl by her forwardness. How many times had her Comportment Master lectured on this very thing? *Your royal gratitude is best expressed by your silence. A ruler can make no error, and to suggest that one has been made only heaps confusion and shame onto the listener.* She knew this, but always seemed to forget it on the fling of the moment. No matter how many lectures she sat through or notes she took or resolutions she made, Juniper could never seem to act quite regal enough.

For a girl who had been a princess her whole life, this was a problem.

Composing herself, Juniper motioned to her maid. "What is it, Elly?"

"Your Highness, I have brought a message from His Majesty," said Elly. She raised the silver tray, upon which rested a sealed parchment letter. Juniper sighed. Her father had been in meetings all day, right through breakfast *and* luncheon. Was he really too busy to come tell her this news in person, whatever it might be?

"Thank you, Elly," she said, then winced as she realized she'd boggled propriety yet again. She jammed the note into the pocket of her fluted overdress, clapped a hand to her riding cap, and took off down the hallway.

Juniper reached the stables panting and disheveled. The white gravel courtyard surrounding the Equestrian Gate gleamed in the midafternoon sun, and the stable boy awaited her arrival with one hand ready on the latch. On the other side of the fence, the horses stomped and whinnied in anticipation. To her relief, the timepiece mounted on the outer stable cornice showed that she was barely fifteen minutes late, which seemed a fair exchange for the sacrifice in appearance.

Nevertheless, she paused to fluff her curls and crisp her collar as she neared the gate. When she looked up, the stable boy was studying her with interest. "What do you think? Do I look presentable?" she asked, tilting her head to each side. She paused a moment. "You're Toby, right?"

The boy's eyes went wide. He looked over his shoulder toward the main corral, where Master Rolf sat astride his mount. Shaking his head ever so slightly, then casting his eyes down, Toby swung the gate wide. Juniper's shoulders slumped. Master Rolf was every bit as strict as his beaky nose and high arched brows suggested. He made her Comportment Master seem mild, and that was saying something. She certainly didn't want Toby to get punished on her account.

Dejectedly, Juniper lifted her riding skirts and swept into the exercise yard.

From high up on Timber, a magnificent silver stallion, Master Rolf bowed his head at her approach. "Your Highness," he murmured, "at your pleasure." He said nothing about her late arrival, of course—said nothing at all, in fact, outside the scripted greeting—and Juniper sighed. By the goshawk, she was tired of being treated like some unapproachable royal figurehead! Another Comportment gem popped to mind: *A princess does not mingle, unless there is some opportunity for profit.*

On its heels came a thought she'd curiously found herself

thinking in recent days: *Why?* Did things really *have* to be that way?

Then Juniper's fingers touched Butternut's flank, and all other thoughts flew from her mind. She tugged off a riding glove and reached under his mane to scratch the length of his silken neck. Butternut stamped a hoof, dancing about in clear delight. Here was a creature who didn't care a fig for position or rules of behavior, who loved her for herself alone. Juniper dug into her pocket and pulled out three hard lumps of sweetcrystal. Butternut whinnied with anticipation, eyes on her hand, nostrils flaring. Juniper held her flat palm out for him to nuzzle with his velvety lips and gravel-scratch tongue.

Looking up, Juniper saw Master Rolf was staring off into the distance—a touch impatiently, she thought with satisfaction. She glanced toward the gate. To her delight, Toby seemed to have noticed Master Rolf's distraction, too. The boy caught her eye, lifted both thumbs up, and flashed her a huge smile. In a half second his correct posture was back—arms straight, chin lifted, face blank.

But it was enough. Juniper's insides glowed warm. For once in her day, she'd been seen. *Just as if I were a regular person.*

Giving Butternut's nose a final scratch, Juniper did a quick inspection of her tack to be sure all was in working order, then she replaced her riding glove and pulled herself up into the saddle.

As she did, something crinkled in her pocket. The note from her father! She'd almost forgotten it.

Ahead of her, Master Rolf led Timber into the warm-up pace they'd take around the exercise yard before beginning their ride. Butternut followed the familiar routine easily. Shifting the reins to her left hand, Juniper pulled out the parchment with her right and tugged until the purple wax seal gave way. She shook the letter open and ran her eyes over the ornate script, written in the royal scribe's best hand.

My Darling Daughter:

I deeply regret missing you at breakfast and luncheon today. How fast time has flown, and it is your thirteenth Nameday already! I am sure to see you at teatime, and of course this evening at the ball in your honor. But I hope you have been giving thought to your Nameday gift. What can you give the princess who has everything? Ha, ha!

All my love,
Your father

Juniper smiled. That was her father all the way: a formally dictated and sealed parchment, with a goofy note inside. It was a side of the king only she ever saw, and she loved him for it. Butternut slipped into a canter, and Juniper shoved the letter back into her skirts, gripping the reins in both hands. With the warm-up finished, Toby the stable boy reopened the Equestrian Gate, and the two horses set off down the lane bordering the hedge maze.

In truth, today didn't feel much like her Nameday. When she was younger, Juniper had looked forward to this day all year—a time filled with treats and surprises, gifts and good-ies. Her mother had delighted in surprising her with a whole array of simple joys: releasing a cloud of ruby butterflies in the greenhouse, climbing to the top of a cherry tree with a spyglass and a storybook, teaching her how to bring her hands to her mouth and whistle such a loud, piercing note that the chande-liers trembled. Each adventure was a doorway out of Juniper's formal, structured life, turning her—whether for minutes or hours—into someone completely different. Juniper knew that being a princess was a glamorous and privileged position. And she loved it, she did. She understood the responsibility and ac-cepted the need for her every waking hour to be packed with training and skillswork and learning and refinement. But all that had been a lot easier to bear when she knew that just around the corner lurked that *other* Juniper, and she could slide into those carefree slippers every now and then.

Juniper had been young when her mother died—young enough that she hadn't been allowed to attend the public mourn-ing ceremonies. But not so young that she couldn't remember these whispers of another, freer life all those many years ago. By now, her mother had been gone so long that the missing was nothing more than a quiet pulse deep in her chest. And truth be told, Juniper's daily schedule kept her so busy that there was very little space for personal reflection, about her mother or elsewise. Which was, all in all, quite a good thing. But on days like this one, days when she felt the need to wish and dream and reach, days when the world opened up to offer her anything she wanted—anything at all within the power of King Regis of Torr—she couldn't help but wonder.

If her mother had still been alive . . . what would *she* have thought Juniper should ask for?

2

NO SOONER HAD JUNIPER'S RIDING LESSON ended than her afternoon shifted into its own quick-step canter. Teatime was a rushed affair, her father doting but distracted, his mind clearly fixed on the night's festivities. Next, Juniper was packed off to her grooming chamber, where six maids devoted the next hours to pampering, beautifying, and dressing her in the most gorgeous gown she had ever seen. Its pale pink bodice was crisscrossed with deep burgundy ribbons and swathed in leagues of creamy Gaulian lace. The skirt swept out in a lacy waterfall wide enough to keep all tedious diplomatic admirers at arm's length. Juniper studied herself in the tall looking glass and grinned in delight. Then she frowned. Just behind her reflection, a little round head hovered reprovingly over her shoulder.

"Comportment Master," she murmured, swinging around into a respectful half curtsey, as he came the rest of the way into her room.

He had a name, she knew: Master Tobbo—a name extraordinarily well suited to his perfectly symmetrical head and bulky sausage body. Still, he was only ever called by his title, as though he was more status than person. Which said a lot about him, actually.

"Your Highness," the Comportment Master replied, his bow bringing his face to a perfectly correct knee level. "I know it is not the day for our lesson, but I came by for a final inspection and conduct check, in advance of your Nameday ball this evening."

He paused, and in her mind, Juniper filled in the unspoken gaps. The importance of the ceremony! Transitioning to adulthood! Her uncertain ability to follow correct procedures, which required a last verification! She glanced toward the timepiece. "That is so generous of you," she said demurely. "But I fear the time has all but run out. Perhaps we could speak . . . as I walk toward the ballroom?"

The little man puffed out his chest. "Your Royal Highness should *never* appear in public less than an hour behind schedule. A two- to three-hour delay is vastly preferable. *Vastly!* Anticipation, Your Highness—*that* is the stock and currency of monarchy. Anticipation breeds awe, and awe grants power, and power is strength."

Juniper suppressed an eye-roll and—where were all those maids when she needed them?—opened her own door. She glided out of her suite and headed down the hallway in the direction of the ballroom. She kept her body tilted toward the still-prattling Comportment Master, but her mind was a million leagues away.

This is me showing anticipation for the end of your lecture and awe that you have so much to say, she thought. In truth, although she would never have told him so, this "be as late as possible" mandate was one she didn't even try to keep. There was little Juniper loved more than time: knowing the time, having time, being on time. It was one of the few things in her world she could actually control—how she planned it, how she moved within it, where she chose to put her attention and when. She liked to keep busy, and she *would* be on time.

Whenever possible, anyway.

They swept along the hall, nearing the wide atrium that opened onto the palace library. Just ahead, a boy came out holding three fat leather-bound volumes, one open and the other two clutched to his chest.

". . . your royal arm must *always* stay at a three-quarter angle from your waist, fingers evenly spaced—*evenly spaced,* that is *so* important—but the last finger should be slightly raised, like *this*—"

"Erick!" Juniper called, a little frantically. "Erick Dufrayne!" She had hardly spoken to the boy before, but she was desperate.

Now Erick jumped, blushed scarlet, and slammed shut the volume he'd been reading as he walked. A cloud of dust mushroomed over his face and he immediately began to cough, dropping the other two books and doubling over to catch his breath.

Juniper's hand was halfway to picking up the nearest volume, which had fallen near the hem of her dress, when she caught her Comportment Master's horrified look. She straightened, lifted her arm to the specified angle, and splayed her fingers out evenly. *Just posing, that's all I was doing,* she thought angelically.

"Your Highness," said Erick uncertainly, "my apologies for the interruption."

"Nonsense, I called out to you," said Juniper, then coughed and inclined her head. What *was* the correct response again? Her brain hurt. She turned suddenly, offering her Comportment Master a proper royal-student-to-respected-teacher curtsey. "Comportment Master, I sincerely regret that I must now absent myself. I have something I must discuss before the ball, for which I believe I am now very nearly properly late. I trust we may resume our lesson at a later time?"

Without awaiting a reply, she swept her skirts around, cocked her head at Erick, and dashed down the hallway. She didn't stop until she'd rounded a corner, chest heaving inside her tightly laced bodice.

"Your Highness?" Erick said from behind her, obviously still unsure what was going on.

"I just *had* to get away from that man," Juniper gasped. "You saved the day."

Erick looked surprised. Then he grinned at her, and Juniper wanted to shimmy in place. That was twice! In one day! She considered the boy in front of her: tall, lanky, straight-nosed, and warm-eyed. His father was the captain of the guard, but Erick himself seemed fully content in his official role of boy-of-all-trades around the palace. Obviously this fit well with his need to have a book with him at all times. In fact, Juniper didn't think she'd *ever* seen him without at least one dusty old tome in his hand.

"Well, it's my pleasure," he said. "Do you need an escort to the ballroom?"

Juniper waved a hand. "I'll be fine." There was a question on his face, though, so she waited a moment, then finally asked, "What? You're wondering something?"

Erick scuffed at the marble floor. "It's only—this is your thirteenth Nameday, right? A big deal."

"The biggest," she agreed. Thirteen meant fully grown in Torr, the skip-step from child to adult, the time for choosing an apprenticeship or profession. For Juniper, that meant taking her place as crown princess, fully able to inherit the throne of Torr upon her father's passing. Which wouldn't be for a very long while, of course. But still.

She studied Erick, considered his wrinkled shirt and patched-up pants. "You're not going to the ball, are you?" He shook his head, and she glanced at the volumes in his arms. "But you've read all the histories and"—she paused—"are fascinated by the ceremony?" He grinned sheepishly. Juniper tilted her head. "I've just had an idea. Would you like to see something?"

It was the quickest of detours: Right before the ballroom, a door opened into a lush coatroom. Off the coatroom was a smaller hat closet. In the hat closet was an alcove hung with shelves and hooks and bars. It was so tiny that Juniper's billowy skirts filled nearly the entire space. "No one ever uses this room," she whispered. "I discovered it years ago when I used to come here and play house." She bent down, grabbed one of the waist-high hooks, and twisted. It swung up to reveal . . . a peephole. From its other side, they could hear the buzz of ballroom music and the chatter of guests.

Erick's mouth dropped open. "But you—but I—I couldn't—"

"Tosh," said Juniper. "Why shouldn't you? If it were up to me, this is where I'd spend the evening. All the fun of observing without having to play the role. What could be better?" She jogged him on the shoulder. "Enjoy the ball!"

At the heavy doors of the ballroom, Juniper paused as the herald called out her name to announce her arrival. All movement stopped for a heartbeat, each face turning in her direction, before the room erupted into a hearty applause.

Juniper felt her cheeks warm as she inclined her head in the proper three-quarter dip. The crowd was even larger than she'd expected. The sliding walls on either side of the long, narrow Throne Room were gone, tripling the space in the hall and turning it into a Grand Ballroom. This vast room was packed with guests. Juniper knew only a handful of them on sight, but their official costumes told her a lot—there were nobles and dignitaries from all the main cities of Torr, as well as dozens of representatives from Gaulia, their neighbor to the north. Juniper didn't see anyone from Monsia, their much-larger neighbor to the west, but that wasn't surprising. The Monsians were rude and ill-mannered, and the frequent butt of tales ranging from the colorful to the mildly alarming. Juniper was glad they weren't at her party.

The crowd parted as Juniper glided down the center of the room toward the carved dais. In a gap between swishing skirts, she caught sight of Erick's eye at the barely visible peephole and suppressed a grin. Up ahead, her father sat on his tall, ornate throne, with her mother's slightly smaller throne empty, as usual, to his right. But at the base of the marble stairs, she paused, uncertain. The fancy cushioned stool that always rested to her father's left—her seat whenever she attended royal functions—was nowhere to be seen.

An attendant materialized at her side. "Your Highness," he murmured, offering an arm to guide her up the stairs. Pointing the way to her mother's throne.

Juniper looked up and met her father's gaze. He smiled. "Happy Nameday, Junebug."

Feeling quite giddy, Juniper let herself be guided up the dais. She lowered herself onto her mother's throne.

Or . . . she tried to. Instead, to her mortification she found that trying to sit down made her lacy skirts balloon up in every direction. She wobbled and would have fallen if the attendant hadn't caught her. Aware of every head turned in her direction, Juniper took a deep breath, mashed the back of her gown, and tried again. She caught herself this time on the velvet armrest.

There was a mild cough behind her. "May I?"

Face flaming, she looked up and saw her father standing next to her, holding out an arm. The court musicians had launched into "Belle and the Moon," one of her favorite songs, and Juniper gratefully let herself be swept onto the dance floor.

"That is *some* gown," her father whispered, and she socked him on his meaty royal arm.

Keeping her head up, back straight, and feet light as her Dancing Master had taught her, Juniper kept her gaze on the twinkle in her father's eye. How did he do it? He was every bit the ruler, playing his role for the critical masses that lined the room. Yet some tilt of his chin, some roguish look in his eye that perhaps only she could see told her that he took all of this only so seriously. This may have had something to do with her own bouffant dress, which wobbled between them like a third partner. Still, the many years he'd been doing this had clearly taught him a thing or two.

After the song ended, her father put an arm at the small of her back and propelled her toward the central pillars. "There's someone here you'll want to see," he said into her ear.

The bystanders parted around them, and Juniper saw her father's chief adviser, Rupert Lefarge, bow low in greeting. A small cluster of others standing with Lefarge sank into bows and curtseys as well. Including a skinny beanpole of a boy with slicked-back hair and a sardonic smirk.

"You remember your cousin Cyril?" the king boomed. "He's back on a visit from the academy. Isn't that grand?"

Juniper remembered Cyril, all right, though *grand* wasn't the word she'd use. Two years her elder, Cyril was her cousin in only the most distant sense of the word, someone she had to tolerate because of his father's position in court. One of her earliest memories was of Cyril dropping her headfirst into the fountain, and things hadn't improved from there. The day Cyril had left for the academy, five years before, had been a high point of her life.

Still, a person could change a lot in five years.

"Your Royal Highness Princess Juniper," Cyril said smoothly, sinking into a bow so low it was almost an acrobatic feat.

"Cyril Lefarge." Juniper curtseyed in return, accepted his outstretched hand, and let him sweep her onto the dance floor.

No sooner had they spun out of the adults' earshot than Cyril's nose lifted visibly. "Quaint old Torr," he sniffed. "So darling and antiquated. One does have to readjust one's expectations simply to get by . . . but one does what one must."

Apparently five years was not long enough after all. Juniper fought the urge to bash her forehead into Cyril's snotty upraised nose.

"Of course," he went on breezily, spinning her out and then back toward his tasseled suit coat, "I shouldn't expect my gormless little cousin to be aware of these things. You did have so very much *heritage* to overcome. Quite admirable you can get by, really."

Juniper narrowed her eyes. The jibe did not hit her in the chest, as Cyril clearly intended. Instead, it hit her in the gut, sharpening her senses. It made her *mad.* Her mother had not been a Torrean noble, nor any kind of a royal member of the continental dynasty. She'd been the daughter of a chieftain of the Anju, a roving tribe of obscure origin and uncertain habitation. Tribal representatives had come to the palace requesting talks of an alliance; they had left two months later, one daughter short and hopping mad. The whirlwind courtship had left all of Torr in shock. It wasn't entirely clear why the Anju had taken such offense to the match, but the tribe had never been seen in Torr again. Any desired negotiations were completely set aside. Queen Alaina, for her part, had integrated well

16

into her new role; her dubious bloodline and lack of pedigree were well known by all but referred to by none.

Well. *Almost* none.

Juniper knew better than to risk making a scene here, in the very center of the ballroom, with all eyes fixed on her and her partner. If she opened her mouth even a crack at this point, she would lose control entirely. So she concentrated on ignoring Cyril's taunts and avoiding his heavy stamping boots, which seemed dead set on connecting with her slippered toes.

Unending though the dance seemed, finally it was over. After that, the party improved greatly. Juniper put Cyril firmly out of her mind, was swept up by another partner, and spent the next two hours spinning and twirling across the mosaic tiled floor. She loved the swing of the beat and the swell of the notes. She even managed to get her dress to behave, for the most part. Her partners—young and eligible noblemen, visiting dignitaries, and other carefully selected candidates—were suave and skillful, and each dance step was perfectly executed. Everything was the same as always: elegant and polished and *just right*.

But Cyril's needling had raised in her a sort of ghostly nostalgia that only grew with the passing hours. For the first time in years, she missed her mother keenly. Suddenly, nothing around her seemed quite *enough*. Tonight of all nights, her thirteenth Nameday celebration . . . she was officially an adult, the future ruler of Torr. But it was almost as if something was missing. She kept catching herself scanning the crowd as though seeking something just out of reach, lifting an ear as though to catch some strain of wild music.

And then . . . suddenly, she *did.*

It was a single sustained note, caught between the end of one dance and the beginning of the next. It didn't last. No sooner had she heard it than it vanished, and then the next dance began and swallowed up all other sound. But Juniper's interest was piqued. She curtseyed formally to her partner, made excuses to the next waiting noble, and, fanning herself extravagantly, moved across the hall to the far balcony.

Stepping outside, Juniper pulled the door shut behind her and moved to the railing, placing both hands on its polished top. She closed her eyes and let the breeze cool her overheated cheeks. And then she heard the sound again. It *was* music, barely audible over the lively and polished gambol from the ballroom. The new melody came from somewhere down below.

If she went back into the ballroom, she would be ambushed immediately by eager partners seeking favor. It was only to be expected as part of the official duties of her Nameday celebration.

But . . . what if she *didn't* go back inside? Juniper didn't think her presence had been missed yet. And there was still a full hour before the speeches and formal Nameday ceremonies were set to begin. This daring impulse—sneaking off alone, in the dark, boldly shirking her duty—both thrilled and terrified her.

And still the foreign music called.

Juniper made up her mind. She pulled her skirts in as tightly as she could and hurried down the long, narrow balcony. Peering through the glass to make sure she hadn't been spotted, she slipped down the curving staircase that led to the ground floor.

The rough music grew more distinct the farther she got from the ballroom. It was coming from the far end of the palace. Juniper let her ear guide her until she turned a corner.

Eyes widening, she ducked behind a pillar.

There was *another* party going on, right in the lower patio off the kitchens. Far from the stiff, formal elegance of the Grand Ballroom, this was a motley crew of servants, palace workers, and village kids. Yes, *kids*! Some were older teenagers, and some were visibly younger, but most looked right around Juniper's age. In the far corner, Toby the stable boy puffed away on a battered trumpet, while a roundish girl Juniper recognized from the laundry rooms twanged at a rusted harp. Three or four others kept time on various pieces of musically appropriated dishware. Patched skirts were swishing and mud-crusted boots were kicking and faces were red and out of breath. The air crackled with life and pulsed with energy.

Despite herself, Juniper could feel her toes tapping to the rhythm. She didn't dare show herself, though. She knew what would happen if she did: That musical magic would go out like the snuffed flame of a candle as everyone returned to their proper formal roles, following the unbreakable behavior rules of Torr.

Was it like this in other countries? Did there *have* to be these kinds of boundaries?

Juniper scooted farther back into the shadows. And as she looked around at this all-kids gathering, suddenly she knew exactly what she wanted for her Nameday gift.

And she had a feeling that her mother would have approved.

3

THE NEXT DAY CRAWLED BY. JUNIPER'S PLAN took shape slowly in her mind, growing more defined with each passing hour. Everything hinged on the all-important first step: her request—and its answer.

Her father had invited her to dine with him that night, just the two of them. "I've started to forget the shape of your face," he'd grumbled playfully, then had instructed Lefarge, "Have a buffet set up for the rest of the court. I've got a date with my daughter."

It was a rare treat, and Juniper enjoyed it to the fullest. She also kept a sharp lookout for the right moment to ask her question.

Sitting across the long mahogany table from her father, she waited out the cheese puffs, and the aubergine bisque, and the crispy oven-roasted root vegetables with thin-sliced pheasant breast in a mulled wine sauce. Her father should be comfortably full, she decided, before receiving any unexpected requests.

And hers was as unexpected as they came. Finally, after the second helping of pheasant and roots but before the fig pudding, the gleam in her father's eye as he stretched back in his seat told her that the time was right.

Juniper clasped her hands under the table. "Papa," she said. "I have been thinking about my Nameday gift."

"Ah, excellent," he said. "It is one of the great pleasures of my year, and I have been awaiting this request with particular interest. It is your thirteenth, after all!"

Juniper nodded. "It *is* an important year. And so I wondered . . ." She just had to come out with it. "May I have a country for my Nameday?"

"A *country*?" King Regis lowered his fork and studied his daughter with concern.

"Yes! A very small country, but one that's all my own. I could find subjects to settle it, other kids probably, and I should rule it all myself. To practice being queen, don't you see? I'll get to make up my own rules and such."

Juniper's heart hammered out a galloping beat, but she kept her face smooth and focused on sawing the pheasant breast with her ivory-handled game knife, the very picture of a calm, unruffled royal daughter.

"A very small country," her father mused.

"Oh—well, yes! If you have any to spare, that is."

"Just sort of lying around."

"That's it exactly!" Juniper opened her mouth to say more, to tell him of her wishes and longings. Then she stopped. How could she put any of that into words, here in the formal dining room, over rutabagas and roast? She settled for a tentative smile. "I could set up court there over the summer. Think of all the time you've spent instructing me in rulership! This could make a grand sort of test, to see how well I've taken to it."

Sensing she'd given her father enough to think about, Juniper picked up her gold-hemmed napkin and dabbed at her lips. She glanced around. Three staff members stood at attention on the edges of the room, ready to leap to any dinner-related assistance. The first two looked suitably blank and disinterested. The third was a tall, wispy girl with a turned-up nose and bright, smart eyes. This girl's eyes were wide with excitement, and her fingers, when she refilled Juniper's goblet, trembled just a little. The king's attention seemed to have been equally captured by her request; Juniper soon realized that she wouldn't get much more conversation out of him this evening.

"If I may be excused, Papa dear?" she murmured, and he nodded absently. This was the time to give him plenty of thinking space. She'd planted the idea seed and now he would go about watering, pruning, and harvesting it into a perfectly executable plan. Or so she hoped, anyway.

Meanwhile, she had her own planning to do. A great deal of it.

When Juniper entered the dining room the next morning, she started with surprise. "Why, Papa dear!" she cried.

King Regis was bent over the table, still wearing his outfit from the night before, only crumpled around the middle and

22

with a suspicious dark stain at his elbow. His graying hair stood up in more than one place. Juniper was earlier than usual—breakfast was her favorite meal of the day, and watching the empty table pile high with food was nearly the best part—but she had never seen a morning table like this one. No food was in sight; no dishes or silverware, even. The surface was fully strewn with papers.

Her father looked up and beamed. "Ah, Junebug! There you are. I've been waiting for you to be along. I believe I have found the very spot for your little adventure!"

Juniper's mouth dropped open. "Truly, Papa?" She'd known her father to get feverishly attached to new plans and ideas, but this was extremely fast, even for him.

"Your idea took me by surprise," the king said. "But the more I thought it over, the better I liked it. A testing ground, as it were, yes? Controlled setting, not too far off from society. Put to the proof all this booklearning you've been packing in. Test of adulthood, if you will. Yes." He nodded sagely, and Juniper could almost see this entering the record books as a rite of passage for future Torrean heirs.

The door swung open, and in came a girl carrying a platter of sizzling pork belly strips. It was the same wispy girl from last night, and she took a tentative step in, blinking curiously at the state of king and table. She had the kind of face that spoke of ideas, and Juniper half wanted to invite her to pull up a chair and hear what the king had to say.

Juniper shook herself. What a peculiar thought!

23

"Ah, breakfast," said the king distractedly. "Set it up in the morning room, would you? The delegates and other nobles will be along shortly, and this room is in no fit state."

"Certainly, Your Majesty," replied the girl, managing to bow low without spilling a single pork strip.

"Wait," Juniper said quickly. "What is your name?"

The girl ducked her head. "Leena, Your Highness," she said. Then, with a last glance toward the papers on the table, she vanished through the door, the savory scent of breakfast fading in her wake.

"Now, here we have it." The king's voice was triumphant as he jabbed a forefinger at the map of the Lower Continent spread open in front of him. Sidling closer, Juniper saw he was pointing toward the coast. "What do you think of this spot, eh?"

"Oleo's Bay," she read.

"A country, just as you say. Or a parcel of land, at any rate. It's in need of development. You've got plenty of coastline there, a few gentle hills. Two or three towns within an hour's ride, in case anything goes wrong. The soil is sandy—you won't get much in the way of crops. And it wouldn't do in the cold season. But for this summer country of yours, I can think of no place better. What do you say?"

Juniper's heart leaped. Her very own country!

Then she hesitated. Was this *really* the best spot? She wished she might learn a little more about the location before making things official. "It sounds marvelous, Papa dear!" she exclaimed. "Only . . ."

"Only?"

She paused, thinking fast. A summerland kingdom, right on the beach. What could be better? But . . . did she really want her country *only* for the summer? What if they wanted to stay longer, or wanted to set things up to return at another time? Winter storms along the coast were fierce and destructive; it was probably why the land lay undeveloped to begin with. Further, the king's mention of the nearby towns, instead of being reassuring, felt somehow stifling. "Only don't you have anything a little more . . . *away*? I'm terribly grateful, Papa, please understand. Just, I'd hoped to start something more off on my own. And it must be a venture that will last."

"Something that will last . . ."

Juniper slid into a chair and studied the map, from Torr's stretch of coast clear up to its borders with Gaulia in the north and Monsia all along the far west.

Her father's voice went uncharacteristically hazy. "Well, there is the Basin, but no, that would never—"

Juniper perked up. "The Basin? Oh, please do tell!" His finger had begun moving away but now snapped back up toward the Hourglass Mountains, which stretched like a ribbon across the neck of the Lower Continent, with Gaulia up above them and Monsia and Torr below.

"It's quite unthinkable," he murmured. "A hard day's ride or more from here, and that's if all goes well. Right in the heart of the Hourglass. It's not a place on any map I'm aware of. Bit of a secret hideout, if you want to know the truth." The king leaned back in his seat. His face took on a soft, looking-back quality that made Juniper's eyes widen. "I had a summer off myself—I was far older than you, mind, nearly out of my teens. But I persuaded my father to grant me two fortnights alone. He was a hard man, but he agreed. Off I went, with only two guards for companions, and what a grand adventure we had! It was the only time in my life I was fully free from obligations, all the pressures of court . . ." He trailed off, apparently registering Juniper's gape-mouthed stare.

"In any event, we happened upon a series of tunnels, and after losing ourselves for a while, we came through to a fully enclosed valley at the heart of the range. We called it the Basin, for that's how it seems inside—up the high mountains, you are, but you'd never think it. There's a sun in there that glows like its own bit of heaven."

Juniper didn't need to hear any more. A secret kingdom at the heart of the Hourglass Mountains? "Oh, that's it, Papa. *Please!*" She raised a hand, seeing the refusal already forming on his lips. "It's neither too far, nor too dangerous, nor at all improbable. Haven't you always said how capable I am? It wouldn't be the same to set up a country only a league away from other townships, with my sub-jects running about here and there and dashing off whenever they like. This way, we'd be a real kingdom, a country off on our own. Think of that!"

"Off on your own?" The wistful note was gone from the king's voice, and now he was all business. "I can't support that idea, Junie. No, I don't like it one bit. Those are high mountains, and not two skips from the Monsian border. Thirteen may be an adult as far as so-ciety goes, but it's hardly so in actual fact. Oleo's Bay will do nicely."

"Oh, Papa!" Once again, she wondered whether she might not

tell him more. But Juniper had long since learned that her father avoided talk of her mother at all costs, and her own feelings about the all-kids dance party were vague at best. She didn't even know if it *could* be put into words—this odd need, this longing for something more. Her father's story had only crystallized it further; his tantalizing glimpse of the Basin had changed things yet again.

She opened her mouth to try once more, but a rap came at the door, and her father's chief adviser pushed his bulk through the door frame.

"Your Majesty," said Rupert Lefarge. To Juniper's surprise, he was panting, with visible sweat dotting his brow. "If I might beg your pardon for the interruption. There is a matter of greatest urgency requiring your attention. It positively cannot wait."

The king rose at once, delivered a distracted kiss to the top of Juniper's head, and followed Lefarge out of the room.

Left alone, Juniper began gathering her father's papers into a pile. She had gotten her kingdom, and she was grateful. Oleo's Bay would be adequate, she knew, would be fine. But, oh, it was hard to let go of the other!

Now she had breakfast to eat, and a kingdom to plan, and a mountain dream to push fully out of her mind.

It turned out that setting up a new kingdom was a *lot* of work. To her relief, her father's business went long and he canceled that morning's Political Discourse session. All the free hour did, however, was reinforce the scope of the job Juniper had taken on. She'd put a great deal of thought into *getting* her kingdom.

What happened next—what needed to happen now—was a lot less clear. Where would her subjects live? What would they eat? What would they all *do* every day? Not to mention, of course, that she needed to find those subjects to begin with.

Juniper needed help, and she needed it fast. She thought of Rupert Lefarge. He kept her father running, pretty much! Well, that was what she needed: a chief adviser of her own.

Settling on the perfect person for the job took barely a moment's thought. Hardworking, always busy, able to do a little bit of everything that needed doing . . . she couldn't think of anyone who read more or knew more than Erick Dufrayne.

The moment she was released from her morning studies session, she set about tracking Erick down. Cornering him in one of the small ground-floor reading alcoves, Juniper launched into a full and complete explanation of how the day—and her new country—had unfolded.

"So." She wrapped up her speech with a zesty wave. "What do you say?"

Erick tilted his head toward the fireplace stoop, as though asking permission to sit down. Juniper nodded, and the boy sank into a thinking pose. "Let me see if I understand this all right. You're gathering a group of kids to take off someplace in the mountains, where you're going to build your own settlement."

"Not the mountains—that's the place my father told me about, but we're not going there. Even though it's a far better spot. We're going to the other place, down by the coast. That's where my kingdom will be. Oleo's Bay." The name was slightly stale on her tongue, like it knew it was the weaker choice but couldn't do a thing about it.

Erick nodded. "And you want my help to organize this kingdom."

"I wouldn't call it 'help,' precisely," said Juniper, falling automatically into her Comportment training. "Think of it more as filling a role. The queen cannot do everything, after all."

Erick raised an eyebrow, as if he was trying to take her seriously but wasn't quite succeeding. Juniper struggled a moment, then sighed. If she was starting her own country, did she really need all those pesky Comportment rules?

"Oh, very well," she said. "I really *do* need some help. I've been working at this planning effort all morning, trying to figure out supplies and jobs and travel details. I had no idea that making up a kingdom would be so complicated! What on earth am I to do?"

"You could ask your father for advice."

Juniper groaned. "*Even* if I wanted to," she said, "he's got something big going on. It's been meetings and messengers and dictating urgent letters since daybreak. He didn't even come back for breakfast."

"I've been hearing some strange things, too."

"Oh? What have you heard?"

Erick's face grew bright red, as though he'd said more than he intended. He shook his head.

"Go on," Juniper coaxed.

"It's nothing, I'm sure," he stammered. "Only, the court seems very hectic all at once. Everyone frowning and rushing about like the world might break in two."

"You're right. Lefarge looked positively frantic when he interrupted us this morning. There must be some mischief afoot. But what could it be?"

"Need to be ready for anything, that's what I'd say." Erick aimed his gaze back to the ground.

Juniper smiled. "Ready for anything . . . I like that. And I happen to feel the exact same way. Whatever's going on here, my father will handle it. What *we* need to be concerned about is getting ourselves moving, and quickly. I'd hate for something to happen that changes Papa's mind about letting us go. I'm stuck with Oleo's Bay—well, all right. That's better than nothing. Now we need to get our team together and head on out double-quick."

"Er . . . *we?*" Erick's eyes were wide with sudden panic.

"You will be my chief adviser," she blurted out. Erick looked up. "That is to say, I'm to be the queen, obviously. But I need you to—that is . . . I'm putting together this kingdom, and I've got to have somebody with me I can trust. For making decisions and all that. Along with me. And I desperately want you to join me in this role. Would you?" Juniper knew she was breaking just about every Comportment rule in the book right now. To her surprise, she found she *liked* how that made her feel. *A brand-new kingdom,* she thought, *with completely new rules.*

Erick shook his head. "Oh, no. I couldn't! I'm just . . ." His shoulders slumped.

"Erick Dufrayne," Juniper said gently, "what are you trying to tell me?"

"The other night, at the ball. When you showed me the peep-hole. What made you do it?"

Juniper thought about this. "I'm not sure. Only . . . that place has been my secret forever, and I've always wanted to show it to someone. You seemed like the right person. And you're right for this job, too. I just know it."

Erick still looked unconvinced. "I do a bit of everything around the palace—that's my job, even: boy-of-all-trades. They had to invent the role for me, did you know? But there's no one skill I'm really tops at. My father tried to train me in the guard, and I simply could not make it stick. I suppose I'm more . . . more of the inkpot and parchment type?"

"And a very fine type that is," said Juniper firmly. "It's perfect, really. You know a little bit about a lot of things. You know how to fill a need. You're quick and smart and dependable. *And* you know book stuff, while truly, I should be happy if I never had to lift another cover till the end of my days. Don't you see now why I need you?"

There was a long silence.

"You *are* in, aren't you?" She knew her voice was unbecomingly pleading for a crown princess. But at the moment, she didn't feel especially princesslike. She felt like a girl on the edge of a cliff facing a vast, dark ocean; she felt like a girl barreling headlong into her greatest opportunity and her greatest challenge and her greatest risk. She felt, on the whole, a good deal less sure of herself than she had expected. And this was a leap she could not take on her own.

She looked up and met Erick's eyes. He smiled tentatively.

"Would there be room on this journey for a few books? Or . . . more than a few, perhaps? I find them to be quite a part of my everyday routine, you see."

Juniper waved a hand. "Consider it done."

"All right, then," said Erick, and held out his hand. "I'm in."

With a deep relieved breath, Juniper reached out and clasped it firmly in her own. "Good. Now let's get started."

Princess Juniper's List of Essential Personnel for Her New Country

(Draft 1)

Filled Positions

Queen—Juniper Torrence

Chief Adviser—Erick Dufrayne

Positions Pending

Queen's Maid(s)

Royal Guards (2–4?)

Head Cook, Plus Undercook and Serving Girl(s)

Seamstress and Personal Groomer

Sweeper (for the mud—there will be lots!)

Activities Director (parties!!)

To Do:

Ponder What Positions a New Country Actually Needs (?!)

4

"I HAVE BEGUN PUTTING TOGETHER A personnel list," said Juniper the following day, as she and Erick sat huddled in a copse of trees in the outer gardens. Back in the Music Room, her harpsichord tutor was surely wondering where she was, and it grated on her to keep him waiting. But this business could not be delayed. "All we need is to outline the necessary roles, then go about filling them. It should be quite straightforward."

"What have you got down so far?" Erick asked. Having accepted his role as Juniper's adviser, he'd sunk into it with relish. He was still one of the quietest people Juniper had ever known, but he didn't seem gobsmacked by royalty the way most palace inhabitants were. Clearly he had never spent time with her Comportment Master. She thought back to the day before, when they had shaken hands like genuine partners. There was something refreshing about Erick's lack of pretension, she decided. And hers was a fully new country, after all.

"We shall have no Comportment Master, that's for certain," Juniper said.

Erick nodded. "I'm not sure I actually know what that man *does*."

This was so obvious from the way Erick acted that Juniper actually giggled. Her hand shot up to cover her mouth. Where was this new relaxed attitude coming from? Then she heard a distant voice calling her name, a voice better suited to harpsichord instruction but that was now searching the grounds for wayward princesses.

She had to hurry.

"I've started out by listing the essential positions," she said briskly, handing him her list. "It was harder than I expected, and I might have missed some. Along with this we'll also want any number of villagers and courtiers. There . . . might be some overlap in here." She glanced at his face.

Erick looked like he had a live frog in his mouth. His lips turned up, then down, then his face got bright red. Finally, he burst out laughing. He laughed so hard that little tears sprang up in the corners of his eyes.

"What?" Juniper demanded.

Erick's laughter dried up and he looked mortified. "Um," he stammered. "Well, er, Your Highness . . ." He looked unsure how to continue.

"Oh, do call me Juniper," she said. "This is going to be ridiculous otherwise. At least"—she looked side to side, as though the bushes might be listening in—"at least when we're alone. I don't think my father would approve. So go ahead."

"All right, Your——Juniper." He seemed to be trying out the name, then smiled as though he liked how it fit. "Juniper. Well. That is to say, do you really want my advice? Not only for me to say 'that's a fabulous idea' so you can act on your royal wish?"

"I said so, didn't I?"

"All right." He swallowed, then plunged on in a single breath: "You've got some good stuff to start. But you're thinking about *your* everyday life, here at the palace. If we're going to make a country, even a little one, we'll need to have the right sort of people. We'll need builders and farmers and people who can, you know, do things with food. Care for animals, if we're having some along. At least, that's the way they do it in the stories. There's an awful lot to think about." He let out a little puff of air, as though suddenly overwhelmed.

"Oh!" Juniper exclaimed, glad to not be the only one feeling that way. She flipped her page over and made a fresh mark on the other side. "You *are* good! Give us a list, then."

"There's a groom who works in the stable——he's really good with animals. His family's got a sheep farm on the banks of the Lore. We could ask him——"

Juniper raised a royal hand. "This groom, is he all grown?"

"He'll be eighteen at the least."

Juniper nodded. "Well. I've come up with my first decree as queen."

"Your first?" Erick said with a raised eyebrow, and Juniper waved the comment away with a grin.

"I've just had my thirteenth Nameday. And since I'll be ruler,

I don't suppose it would be very nice to have all my subjects be older than me. So. We shan't have any recruits who are older than thirteen."

"I'm older than thirteen."

"You *are*?"

Erick pushed out his chest a little. "I turned fourteen two months ago."

Juniper groaned. "Of course you did. Well, you shall be the exception. My second decree is that you must never tell anyone your true age. You may say you are thirteen. Do you agree?"

Erick shrugged.

Juniper turned back to her page. "Your points are valid, however. We need recruits, the type who know how to do real things. And what does my father do when he has need of something? He writes up a proclamation." While she'd been talking, her stylus had been scratching away, and now she leaned back and held up the page for Erick to see. "I should think this will do nicely—what do you say?"

Seeking Young Recruits!

Are you brave, fearless, and thirsting for
adventure, fun, and the summer of a lifetime?
Then look no further! Princess Juniper is gathering
an expedition of like-minded explorers to establish
a settlement at a location to be disclosed (to
accepted candidates only).

Applicants shall be received at one hour after
noon, in the Small Gardens (Royal Palace), for
the next three days. Come prepared to show your
skills! Especially seeking those capable at building,
farming, animal care, and soldiering.

PS: Please ensure your parents are in
agreement before applying.

PPS: Only candidates of age 13 and younger
will be accepted! (Don't even try!)

"I'm not sure you need that last sentence," said Erick. "But it's
very good overall."

"I *do* need it. I have to show I mean business. Now I'll give this
to the scribe and have copies made. We shall put the notices up all
over the palace, for I know there are many subjects around who
are of the right age." She thought back to that dance party she'd
stumbled upon. Surely some of those energetic partygoers would
like the idea of a summer escapade!

"Shouldn't we send some copies in to town, as well?" Erick
asked.

Juniper shook her head. "There's no time. I wish to be gone
within a week, or as near to that as we're able. If we start recruiting outside the palace, who knows how much time that will add?"

Erick's eyebrows went crooked.

"It will have to be long enough," Juniper said firmly. "Summer
has already begun, and I have a country to fill."

The sound of crashing footsteps nearby broke into their conversation. Juniper jumped. "I can't let Master Hemlock find me here," she said. "Deliver this paper to the scribe, will you?"

Before she could give him the notice, however, a boy burst through the shrubs and tumbled into them. The boy was unfamiliar, and as soon as he saw them, he squeaked and scrabbled backward. Juniper reached out and grabbed him by the collar. The boy's long, pin-straight hair stood up in all directions, and his brown eyes bulged with shock.

"Paul Perigor," said Erick, "what in the storms are you doing?"

Paul let out a stream of unintelligible gabble. Waving Juniper back, Erick took the other boy by the arm and settled him down on the grass. He patted him on the back. "There, now. It's just us. Um . . ." He looked up. "Her Highness and myself, we're having a bit of a conference here. Are you recovered enough to tell us what's going on?"

"Oh, nothing at all, nothing at all!" Paul wailed, wringing his hands. He was wearing a groundskeeper's uniform, Juniper noticed, though the knees were stained dark brown and green. "Only, I'm meant to be patrolling the grounds, and I'm afraid I was, er . . ." He looked at Juniper, face quivering.

"I shan't tell a soul, whatever it is," Juniper said.

"It's my father," Paul said, slumping in defeat. "He's the proudest soldier alive, and he thinks there's no other career for a true man. But me . . . I just don't see it. I love soil, you see. I love the green, the way life starts so small and reaches out to grasp and grow and blossom, all in a day. It hits me right here, the outdoors does." He thumped his chest, even as his face darkened.

"My father won't ever understand that. I thought groundskeeper would be a good compromise, but I just can't keep myself from sneaking off . . ."

For the first time, Juniper noticed that the little copse of trees looked rather . . . cultivated. She'd assumed that the round stones so perfect for sitting had come there by chance. But these flower beds were, upon inspection, far too perfect to be wild. "This is your secret garden," she exclaimed.

"Oh, Your Highness!" Paul's eyes brimmed. "I shall tear it apart with my two hands, shall never touch dirt or seed again, only I beg you not to tell my father what I've done. He'd think it the worst of betrayals."

"Paul Perigor," Juniper said solemnly, "your secret is safe with me. On one condition: that I may come here from time to time, when I need a place to sit and think or plan. And I won't breathe a word to your father. Speaking of which," she said grimly, "I'd better go find Master Hemlock before *my* father gets involved."

And with that, Juniper whisked away, leaving Erick to patch up the thwarted gardener. She would deliver the notice to the scribe herself . . . right after her harpsichord lesson.

Whoever had named the Small Gardens must have had a skewed sense of size. Juniper's seat had been set up next to the glossy marble fountain, and from her perch, she could see in all directions: along the ornamental maze to the edge of the fruit and nut orchards, down the long parallel hedgerows that lined the path from the main gate into town, and back around the wide curving sweep to the palace's main entrance.

There was not a recruit in sight.

She'd finished her luncheon in minutes in order to arrive well before the appointed hour. But here she sat, alone but for Elly at her side and Erick scuffing the dirt next to her seat. She wished she'd thought to have a chair brought out for him, too. But then Elly would be standing alone, and how odd would that be? The whole thing made her head hurt.

"You're certain this time is correct?" she asked, glancing up at the fountain's peak to check the embedded timepiece. The year before, the king had had the newfangled timing devices set up all over the palace and grounds, and Juniper had found it the absolute best way to organize her life and maximize her efficiency. Now, however, the pink-tinged sand was half expired; the numbered lines along the base put it well past the first hour of the afternoon and edging fast toward the second. In another quarter of an hour at the most, she would need to ready herself for her croquet lesson, a fact which irked her greatly. How could she be expected to plan a country under these conditions?

"The timepiece is definitely correct, Your Highness," Elly replied. "The head gardener sets it himself every evening, and has a boy check it by the high noon sun every third day. That was yesterday, ma'am."

Juniper scanned the grounds again. Still nobody.

"Other palace timepieces may not be as accurate," Erick offered. "And there are still two days when recruits can come."

Juniper wouldn't worry, she wouldn't. She just wished there was *something* she could do to help the process along. She shifted her gaze and focused on her maid.

"Elly," she said slowly.

"Yes, Highness?" said the girl.

Juniper studied her, an idea sparking. "How old are you, Elly?"

"Sixteen, Highness."

She caught Erick's eye and sighed. Then Erick cleared his throat. "Don't you have a sister, Elly?"

"I do," she said. "Tippy's a spry little thing—she's only just turned nine, but she's got a yen for action, that one. I would think she might like this adventure of yours, Highness, if I were to tell her of it."

Erick looked doubtful. "She's not too young?"

"Oh, I shouldn't think so. Our ma's been gone for years, and Tippy and I are right good at caring for ourselves. That is—it *is* to be a safe expedition, is it not? No dangers of any sort? Begging pardon, Your Highness," she added hastily.

"Tippy sounds perfect!" Juniper said. "Please do go and fetch her for me. Yes, right now would be marvelous. And don't worry— it will be perfectly safe. After all, what harm could possibly befall us in our own settlement?"

Tippy was every bit as enthusiastic as promised. She was small for her age, wiry as a flax bean, with large floppy hands and feet and a mop of tousled hair. Her face was lit by a giant sunbeam smile.

"Your Princessness!" she exclaimed, throwing herself at

Juniper's skirts and clasping her around the ankles. "I shall be honored to join your traveling party, if you will have me!"

Elly prodded her sister with a slippered toe. "Tippy Larson! Get up on your feet, you goose. You're to make a proper curtsey, as I showed you. None of this toppling-over nonsense."

Tippy leaped up and executed a perfect curtsey, with a zesty twirl at the end. "Right you are, sis. Your Highness Princess Juniper, I ain't too much of a lady, and I haven't been no lady's maid before. But I watch my sister like a lizard, and I can heartily tell you that anything she can do, I can certainly do also. Probably a good deal quicker and more elegantly." To demonstrate, she stood on her tiptoes and dashed off a pirouette that was spectacular for its utter lack of any grace or elegance whatsoever. Elly cuffed the back of her sister's head, and Tippy resumed her normal position.

Juniper couldn't keep down her smile. "You're in!" she exclaimed. "Our first official recruit, and my lady's maid to boot. Welcome to the royal expedition!"

"And there's another coming now!" Tippy chirped, bobbing up and down on her toes.

Juniper jerked her head up, and sure enough, a dark-haired girl was marching determinedly down the long gravel-strewn path toward them. A glance at the timepiece told Juniper that she needed to leave this very moment if she wanted to be on time for her lesson. With resolve, she shifted so the timepiece was out of view. Just this once.

A moment later, the newcomer reached them. The girl stepped up to where Juniper sat and curtseyed awkwardly. Tippy giggled, and Elly quietly cuffed her again.

"My name is Alta, milady," the girl puffed, reaching up to smooth her straggly hair. "Alta Mavenham. My father's the baker in town, and I was delivering bread to the kitchen here this morning when I saw your notice. I should like to join you on your journey."

Juniper sat up straighter in her seat. "Come closer, Alta. We are glad to have you apply. You're a baker, you say?"

Alta started shaking her head, then seemed to see something in Juniper's face that made her hesitate. "Ye-es?" she squeaked.

"Excellent!" Juniper clapped her hands. "Do you cook other things also?"

Alta's shoulders slumped.

"She's good at baking, but she don't like to," chirped a voice from behind Juniper's seat.

"Tippy!" Elly yelped and dashed for her, but Alta's look gave Juniper pause.

"Is this true, Alta Mavenham?" she asked. Then she made her tone as soft as she could. "Please tell me true. I wish to have recruits who see their work as a passion, not a chore."

"It's true, milady," Alta admitted. She scuffed the gravel with a sandaled toe. "Every morning I must wake at four hours after midnight, well before the cock crows. I make dough and knead it and roll it out, and I toil in the heat of those blasted ovens. It's not that I begrudge my pa the work, exactly, but . . ." She bit her lip.

"And what is it you *do* want to do, then?" Juniper asked.

Alta looked up, her eyes blazing with a sudden fierce light. "I wish to be a soldier, Your Highness. Oh, I know what you'll say," she added quickly, cutting right through the surprise that was clearly visible on Juniper's face. "I know I'm a girl, and I look all dainty and delicate-like. But I've trained every day for years. I've fought boys twice my size, and I've never been beaten. Not for ages, anyway," she amended.

"I . . ." Juniper didn't know what to say.

Alta looked miserable. "I know it's a foolish dream. My pa says so all the time, says I should be happy with the work I've got here to hand. Torr's army isn't what it used to be, back in the day when all youths were required to put in their fighting years. Females barely even join up, these days. But then I saw your notice—well, it's the talk of adventuring that caught my eye, honestly. I'm a baker, and my pa's a baker, and my grandparents both before him, and on through the generations. There's flour and not steel in these here veins. And yet"—she paused, then continued in a rush—"I thought if it was somewhere new, made up all of boys and girls our age . . . well, why should we have to follow all the rules we leave behind? Why shouldn't we be any way—or any*one*—we please?"

Juniper sat up straight in her seat. It was like having the thoughts pulled right from her own mind. "What about your father?" she asked suddenly. "You *have* talked to him about this?"

Alta nodded eagerly. "I've been there and back this very morning. The truth is, my pa's none too happy, Your Highness. But he loves me so and said I might have a spell away. Stretch my wings, he said. I reckon he thinks it'll make me homesick for the family ovens." She grinned wickedly, as if to emphasize how wrong he was.

Something caught Juniper's eye. "What is that around your waist?"

Flushing, Alta pulled her cloak shut. Then, hanging her head a little, she opened it to show a roughly crafted leather scabbard. "'Tis my sword, Your Highness." Her voice was scarcely a whisper, but it glowed with pride. "I've saved up every penny I could for the last three years. I finally bought it two fortnights ago . . . The blacksmith's apprentice made me a special offer on a reject." She pulled out a sword with no defects that Juniper could see: a slim, strong blade with a skillfully worked handle.

"That is a fine piece," Juniper said approvingly. She considered the girl for a moment, then clapped her hands together. "Alta Mavenham, you *shall* come on our expedition. You are to be my royal guard."

Alta's face flushed a scarlet sunbeam as she slid her sword back into its scabbard. While quite unable to form any words, she seemed on the verge of kicking up her heels and sidestepping across the yard. Then a blur shot out from behind a nearby shrub. Tippy tore over to grab Alta's hands and prance about her in jubilant circles, all the while chanting loudly, "Four! Four! Now we are four!"

They were four—but no more. The following days clipped briskly by, but though Juniper waited patiently, with Erick, Alta, and Tippy checking in when they could, no other recruits came to answer her notice. It was enough to tempt even Juniper's stubbornly sunny spirits to flag.

"We're nowhere near enough," she told the others, having

taken the occasion of her outdoor constitutional to squeeze into Paul's secret garden for a quick emergency meeting. "There's ever so many roles to fill."

Erick nodded. He should know; he was the one who had suggested most of them.

"Maybe people are too busy," said Alta. "Or maybe they haven't seen the signs, with whatever else they've got going on."

"Yes," Erick agreed. "Maybe you've got to go to *them*."

"Go to them?" Juniper said slowly. "But who?" Her strict Comportment rules kept her firmly away from any "mingling" with palace workers, young or otherwise. It had always been that way. Juniper considered. Well . . . it *had* always been that way—until the last few days, when she'd begun pushing at the edges of those boundaries.

She leaped to her feet. "You're both brilliant!" she shouted, and galloped off through the bushes. She stopped only when she reached the edge of the woods to calm her breathing, smooth her gown, and compose a suitably regal face.

Then she set about to poach herself some subjects.

The plan was as simple as it was perfect. *Follow the passion,* her mother had loved to say, *for it will never steer you wrong.* And that certainly proved to be the case here.

Her country needed a good gardener—and who loved plants more than Paul Perigor? He actually fell over his own feet in his eagerness to sign up. The face of Leena the serving maid grew as bright and sharp as a carving when Juniper showed her the flyer and told her about the plan. She claimed immediate control of the kitchens, which she confided was a long-held dream. And Toby Dell, equestrian gatekeeper, only let her get as far as "all-kids country" and "animals" before giving his enthusiastic assent.

"I've got two other prospects for you, as well," Toby added. "My sisters Oona and Sussi. They're a couple of whippets, and always up for adventure. I'll ask them tonight, but I'm certain they'll be on board."

Indeed they were. The final additions to the team were Roddy Rodin, a rake-thin carpenter's apprentice who was reputedly able to bring anything wooden to life; and Filbert Terrafirm, a lumbering giant of a boy with no visible skills but whose calm disposition and muscle-bound strength made him a clear asset.

Before Juniper quite knew it, two weeks had flown by and she and her group found themselves on the eve of their great departure. Alta had spent the full fortnight in the guards' barracks, going through an intensive course of training, drills, and maneuvers. King Regis had praised her swordsmanship in the highest of terms, approving her for the post of Juniper's royal guard, but Alta seemed determined not to rest until she achieved some superhuman level of skill. As far as Juniper could see, she was far past that point already.

Meanwhile, two wagons had been loaded with every sort of provision imaginable—cookware, tools, bedding and other necessaries, vast stores of every type of food. There were animals, too: five plump nanny goats and a dozen chickens. Paul the gardener-to-be had already proven his worth by bringing in a crate of well-packed seedlings for a host of summer vegetables. Juniper's own carriage had been stuffed to its gilded walls with every belonging she could possibly need to rule a country-in-the-making. Not to mention enough gowns, baubles, and accessories to outfit her for any number of parties.

Late that night, with the rest of the recruits tucked into the guest wing, ready to be up with the sun and on their way, Juniper sat sleepless in her suite, gazing out over the palace grounds. It was all so unknown, the wide world beyond her velvet window drapes. How would she fare? What would she do without the luxuries, without the guidance, without the structure that had hemmed in her whole life? Already she could feel new doors opening in her mind, could feel herself pausing where before she would have rushed on by, questioning where she would have agreed without hesitation.

Unbidden, her mother's face flashed into her mind.

Her mother was smiling.

Princess Juniper's Grand Expedition: List of Settlers

Juniper Torrence: Me ♥

Erick Dufrayne: Chief Adviser

Tippy Larson: Personal Maid

Alta Mavenham: ~~Baker~~ Queen's Guard

Paul Perigor: Gardener/Groundskeeper

Leena Ogilvy: Head Cook

Toby Dell: Animal Supervisor

Oona Dell: *(She thinks more than she speaks—will be interesting to see how she develops as we get to know her better.)*

Sussi Dell: *(She's young but has a sharp eye and smart ideas—I like her already!)*

Roddy Rodin: Builder/Fix-It Guy

Filbert Terrafirm: *(A conundrum—but a fascinating one! Let's see how he unfolds.)*

5

JUNIPER DID NOT PLAN TO FALL ASLEEP. THIS was her last night in the palace—or the last night for a while, as of course this was just a summer country—and she wanted to savor every moment. Also, she was quite simply too excited to settle down.

Yet when the pounding came at the outer door of her suite, Juniper jolted upright at her window seat and found that she'd been dozing for some time. Before she could do more than slap some wakefulness into her cheeks and shake the wrinkles out of her skirts, there was another volley of knocks, and then the door burst open and in swept her father.

The king had obviously not gone to bed either, for he was still wearing his dinner jacket. But his hair was wild, and his eyes were wide and intense.

"Junie," he panted, rushing over, "you're up. Good."

"What's going on?" Juniper asked, still shaking the last sleepy cobwebs from her brain. A dull boom sounded somewhere out in the grounds. "What was that? Papa—why are you here?"

"There's a . . . situation," the king said. "I don't have time to talk much now—I must get back to our defenses. But I need you and your group to leave immediately."

"Defenses? Leave immediately?" Juniper knew she sounded like a talking parakeet, but she couldn't seem to make sense of what was going on.

Her father grabbed her hand and started to pull her toward the door. "All your bags are downstairs and loaded up? There's nothing else you need?"

"Nooo . . ." she said uncertainly. Out her window, angry red light slashed across the black sky, followed by another distant boom. "We're under attack," she realized suddenly.

"Quite." They were in her foyer now, and the king took both her hands in his. "Now listen, my darling. I don't have any time at all, so I can only say this once. There are invaders at the South Gate. They're pushing in hard, but they don't have us surrounded. Not even close. Still, I want you and your crew to leave at once. Take the eastern corridor. Move quickly and get as far from here as you can."

"But—but—if we're being invaded . . ."

"Tosh!" The king straightened, and his gaze was steel. "It's nothing but a raiding party from Monsia. You haven't let all those bogeyman stories get under your skin, have you? When's the last time a Monsian got the better of a Torrean?"

Juniper smiled faintly. Monsia was the perennial blundering bad guy in tavern jokes, or so she'd heard said around the castle. No one in their right mind would perceive them as a true threat. And yet . . . another blast rocked the far wall, and she shuddered.

"Come now, Junebug. These walls have never been breached, not in all the ten centuries since Torr's founding. This is a Monsian tantrum, nothing more. But I *do* want to know that you are well away and safe from any unpleasantness."

Reluctantly, Juniper nodded. Of course her father was right. Being right was basically his *job* as king. And what if this skirmish with Monsia dragged on? She didn't want to miss her chance at a summer kingdom. "You're sure everything will be all right here?"

"I'm positive. Now, one other thing. I've given more thought to your destination. You wanted to journey up to the place I told you about in the Hourglass, yes?"

Juniper's heart leaped into her throat, and a smile crept onto her face.

"Good, I thought so." Her father thrust a sheaf of parchment into her hand. "Do it. The Basin is unknown and out of the way. You'll all be safe there."

"Papa?" This whole night was getting very unnerving.

"I've drawn you a map, and I wrote up some additional instructions for getting through the caves. Your subjects have been woken, and the grooms are saddling the horses. I want you all on the road within the hour. You have gathered some fine recruits for your kingdom, yes? You feel good about your group?"

"Oh yes, truly. We've not quite as many as I'd hoped—ten subjects in all, eleven with me. Not nearly large enough to be a proper country. But going out to Torrence town and recruiting will take ever so long. So we shall go ahead first, get our kingdom good and set up, and then make a return expedition in a few weeks to secure the rest of the team."

The king nodded. "Very well. But it's important that you do not leave the Basin until you hear from me. I fear no ill from our attackers, but I will not have you putting yourself—or your new subjects—at risk if the roads are unstable. I've had my soundest Beacon device packed up for you to bring along. The moment I have routed this nuisance from our land, I will fly you out a messenger. Then you may plan your return trip at will—but you *must* wait until then. Oh, don't look like that! You shall hear from me within a few days; a week at the very most. Now. Do I have your word?"

Juniper swallowed, then nodded.

"Good. So, ten subjects, you say? Then you shall have thirteen in all, for I have three more to add to your party."

"*Three more?* Whoever could you mean?"

"Your cousin Cyril, for one—isn't he a charmer? He's brought a friend home with him from the academy, a noble's son from Longton, who will also be joining you. And there's a girl, too. Some ambassador's daughter."

Juniper wobbled in place. "No, Papa! You cannot allow that infernal boy to come. If Cyril wanted to join, why would he go to you about it instead of me? Anyway, he's far too old. You've seen the notices! I've put an age limit."

The king's voice was firm. "Cyril is going because my adviser wishes to ensure the safety of his child. As I do mine. Now, I won't hear any more about this, my button. Cyril and his friends *will* be going along with your group."

"Oh, Papa!" Her father had no idea what Cyril was capable of. The creep walked a spit-polished path around adults—*a charmer,* indeed!—but in private, his true nature came out. Also, he was *fifteen.* Older than Erick, even!

"They will be excellent additions to the group. You'll see." A low rumble shook the palace floors, with a fresh chorus of yells that sounded a good deal closer than the last. "The boys will also give you some added protection on the road. I'd planned to have a contingent of guards see you safely to the mountains, but Lefarge thinks this will do."

Juniper smiled faintly. That was one small consolation, at least. The last thing her all-kids country needed was to be escorted by a bunch of grown-up soldiers! "We are nearly all adults on this expedition," she said, through a lump in her throat. "Just as responsible as ever could be. And you yourself said Alta Mavenham was the best swordsman of her age you'd seen. We're all smart and strong and well trained." Juniper looked her father straight in the eye. "I've got this, Papa. You can count on me."

The king sighed, leaning in to hug her tightly. "You will stay safe on your journey," he whispered, "and ensure the safety of your charges as well. Promise me that?"

Juniper nodded solemnly, and her father kissed her on the nose. She normally would have hated the gesture, but in this moment, it felt curiously reassuring.

"I will see you again, and soon," he said. "Godspeed."

With that, he was gone, disappearing down the darkened hallway to the distant sound of marching guards.

As she'd been promised, Juniper reached the back courtyard to find the horses saddled and the loaded wagons hitched up for departure. Cyril and his companions were nowhere in sight. Juniper knew she should be happy to have three more recruits, but Cyril was so clearly wrong for this expedition, and any friends of his could be no different. Maybe they wouldn't show up at all and she'd have to leave without them.

She could only hope.

At the front of the procession, Alta was already astride her well-packed stallion, her face turned toward the tall gates. Behind her, Paul and Roddy struggled to lash their packs onto their mounts; Toby pulled his sister Oona up onto the wagon box next to him, while Leena and Sussi had settled in enough at the front of their wagon to be playing at a game of jacks. The mood crackled with excitement. It made the tips of Juniper's toes tingle, completely eclipsing her cousin-related concerns. She broke into a smile as she saw Erick approaching. His hair stuck out in all directions, and she had caught him midyawn, but his eyes were sunrise-bright.

"Everyone is present and accounted for," he said. "Loaded up and triple-checked. I've spread the word to all about our new destination—quiet-like, as His Majesty said. I think this is it!"

Juniper's heart skipped a beat. This *was* it! The courtyard opened directly onto the narrow eastern corridor—a back-palace shortcut used mostly by stable hands and suppliers—which in turn led to a small rutted supply road that looped out from the palace walls. Eventually, Juniper knew, this road met up with the wide white highway that led north from the palace, across the Tricorn Bridge, then past an assortment of towns and villages until it finally reached the base of the Hourglass Mountains.

Not much longer than a day from now, she would be *in her own country.*

But at this thought, Juniper's heart sank with a thud. What about the country she was leaving behind? The cries and battle noise that had echoed so loud an hour ago were silent now, but she wasn't fool enough to think that meant the danger was over. Lying in wait was more likely. As danger tended to do.

"I wish there was something we could do to help out here before we leave," she whispered. "Instead of just running away."

"The king has issued a command," Erick said.

The grounds around them were unnaturally still; even the night birds were sensibly quiet. Then the silence was broken by a sharp, commanding cry. From where she stood, Juniper could see clear over to the barracks as the door was flung open. In a flash of rich purple tunics and gleaming silver, row upon row of soldiers began marching methodically out, heading toward the South Gate. Despite her anxiety, Juniper's heart swelled with pride. A figure on horseback rode alongside the army—a figure a little portly, but not at all gone to fat. A solid, commanding figure wearing the golden crown of Torr.

"His Majesty is a force," said Erick admiringly.

Just like that, Juniper's doubts were laid to rest. Those attackers had no idea who they'd chosen to pick a fight with. "Isn't he, though?" She grinned. "Let's get moving, then. He said within the hour, and that's been and gone again. Plus, this ruckus will cover our getaway."

Erick nodded. "To the carriage, then, Your Highness. Er, Juniper. Off we go to our new country!"

"We'll need to choose a name for it," she said.

"What? You'll not call it Juniper Land?" Erick flashed a grin, and in spite of everything, Juniper had to laugh.

"Maybe I will. I shall have to see the place with my own eyes first to know if it suits." Just then, a clamor erupted behind them. The gate leading from the stables swung open to reveal three youngsters astride finely groomed horses, approaching at a slow walk. Behind them, a groom led another two horses pulling a bulging wagon covered with tightly wrapped oilcloth.

Juniper groaned. "Oh, filch. I'd been hoping they would oversleep and miss departure. Erick, these are some last-minute additions to our group. My father insisted."

"They don't look too happy about this."

Juniper decided not to add that *she* wasn't that happy about it herself. The new recruits were dressed for travel, their horses slung with saddlebags that looked packed to bursting. Cyril was in the lead, the edges of his mouth turned down so sharply that they looked in danger of cutting his chin. Behind him rode a boy who looked like a badly copied sketch of Cyril, complete with perfectly coiffed hairdo and lemon-pucker scowl. A younger girl completed the trio; she mostly looked half asleep.

"I suppose we're all here, then," said Juniper. She waved a

hand toward the newcomers. "Welcome to the expedition! We're just ready to push off."

Cyril caught her eye briefly and didn't quite shrug, but neither did he answer. Stifling a yawn, he walked his horse right past her and Erick's gaping mouths, heading toward the front of the procession. After a moment's hesitation, the other boy and girl followed in Cyril's wake, though they both bobbed their heads and murmured, "Your Highness," half under their breath. As if they weren't quite sure they wanted Cyril to hear.

Here we go again, she thought. Yet surely things would be better this time around. She would be ruling her own country, after all. Cyril couldn't push her around when she was queen.

Could he?

Forcing a smooth and unruffled expression onto her face, Juniper turned to Erick. "Let's head out. Alta's already saddled up at the front, and I'm sure she's getting anxious." She'd have plenty of time to ponder the problem of Cyril. Right now, she wanted to get moving.

Erick nodded and waved his arms over his head to signal Alta. The girl returned the gesture, drew her horse around, and called out to the guards to open the gate to the eastern corridor. Juniper's carriage was about halfway down the caravan, behind the horseback riders but in front of the wagons—three of them now, counting the newcomers' personal junk collection, which brought up the rear. Neither Cyril nor his friends paid their luggage transport any notice whatsoever, so Erick finally called Filbert over to drive the third and final wagon.

Satisfied that all was in order, Juniper moved toward her carriage. To her surprise, a mahogany trunk sat in front of the step. "Erick?" she called. "What is this?"

"Oh—that. A servant dropped it off just before you arrived. I believe His Majesty sent it for you."

Curiosity getting the better of her, Juniper pulled the latch and lifted the lid, then gasped at the sight of the polished wood shape nestled inside, all shiny buttons and gleaming levers and fine colored glass front.

"What is it?" Erick asked.

"It's the Musicker. But what's it doing *here?*"

"Musicker? For making music?"

Juniper nodded. Her tongue felt swollen in her mouth. "I haven't seen this in years. My father's had it in storage for ever so long. What could he be thinking?"

"Perhaps that he loves you very much and wants you to be able to hold dances in your new kingdom?"

"Perhaps." But Juniper had her doubts. Her father's love for her mother was as fervent as it was silent. All her treasures had been shut away in a special vault for safekeeping. To see this here, now, was alarming at best. Suddenly Juniper felt the need to fill the moment with words, anything to drown out the worried buzz of her thoughts. "It's Gaulian made, like our timepieces. They're whizzes up there, Papa always says. He's wanted to have a Gaulian craftsman on staff at the palace since forever, but they hardly ever travel, even the diplomats. Having some at my Nameday party was quite the gem in Papa's crown."

What she didn't say about the Musicker was what made her love it best. The daring contraption had been commissioned by her father as a wedding gift for her mother, who had loved nothing more than to crank it up loud on a late summer's night. In a rush it all came back to her—the sound of laughter and her mother's long cool fingers gripping Juniper's small sweaty ones, pulling her up from the carpet and spinning her round and round in time to its haunting tunes. Suddenly, it seemed perfectly fitting that this gift should be coming with her to her new kingdom, whatever reason had prompted it.

"Let's get it inside, then," Erick said. "The horses are already starting to move out."

Pulling open the carriage door, Juniper peered into the cramped interior. Every bit of open space was stuffed with carefully packed belongings and indispensable items, including a giant trunk of volumes from the royal library, which Erick had dragged down at the last minute and pronounced essential.

"Not much space left in here," Erick said, with a wicked grin. "We'll have to see if there's any room for you at all after I wedge this in."

Juniper fought a most un-princesslike desire to put her tongue out at him. But after a few minutes of grunting effort, he climbed out and swung into the driver's seat on the outside of the carriage. "It's a bit tight, but you'll fit. *Just.*"

Taking one last look up and down the row of goods and horses and people—*her* people, her new country on the move—Juniper climbed up the carriage steps and squeezed inside.

It *was* a tight fit, maneuvering around all the bags and boxes and bundles. One particularly voluminous traveling cloak was fully blocking her way, and Juniper raised a booted foot to shove it aside when, quite suddenly, it came to life and reared up at her.

Juniper fell back with a shriek. The cloak seemed to grow eyes and a face and—and—it was . . . *laughing* at her? Juniper's heart pounded wildly, and she collapsed into her seat.

"Oh, Your Princessness Juniper, you should only see your face!" howled Tippy, unfolding herself from her traveling cloak and breaking into a celebratory wiggle right there in the narrow space.

"Everything all right in here?" Erick asked, ducking his head down from above to peer in the window. "Tippy Larson, what are you doing? Come up on the box."

"With great gusto, Master Erick," chirped the younger girl. She glanced at Juniper. "Er, no bad feelings? I didn't mean to scare you *quite* so much, only . . . the prank went off rather well, didn't it?"

"Oh, yes," said Juniper faintly. She waved Tippy off and pulled the door shut behind her, trying to understand what had just happened. As a princess, one simply did not get *pranked* very often. In fact, with the exception of a certain distant cousin in years past, she hadn't had much of this sort of thing at all. So to say she'd been caught off guard would have been a wild understatement.

But it was more than that. There'd been a moment, a single frozen heartbeat while the animated cloak rose as though to sink jaws into her throat, when Juniper's whole body had rung with a feeling of dire premonition: It looked like fun and games, this expedition. It looked like a group of well-organized youngsters setting off against the blackened sky, ready for a summer of carefree play. Yet even now, with the prank unmasked and Tippy bouncing cheerfully on the outside seat, setting the whole carriage shaking, even now with the dull groan of the carriage wheels creaking into motion and beginning to jostle across the graveled ground—even now, a cold thread wound through Juniper's chest.

She had the sinking feeling that nothing about this expedition would unfold as planned. And that even now, events had been set in motion that could never be undone.

Outside, the clip-clop of horses' hooves started up in earnest. The carriage lurched and picked up speed. They were on their way.

6

THE HOURGLASS MOUNTAINS WERE NO MORE than a long day's journey north, and with their early start, Juniper hoped to make it all the way before nightfall. Their road would veer perilously close to the Monsian border, which made her nervous. But the king hadn't shown any concern over their path, viewing Monsia more with scorn than fear or alarm. He should know, shouldn't he? Monsia was more than twice the size of Torr, its people famous for their greed, their excessive laziness, and their prize-winning heads of cattle. Torr, by contrast, made up for its small size by boasting the fiercest army on the Lower Continent—and the largest, to boot. King Regis's confidence was not idly held.

At first, Juniper kept busy enjoying the scenery, studying her father's map, and making notes in the small, leather-bound journal she'd stuffed into her new waist-pouch. The pouch had been a parting gift from her father. Stitched in butter-soft leather and dyed an eye-popping shade of pink, it had roomy pockets and wrapped her waist snugly, ending in a jeweled clasp. For a newly minted queen-on-the-go, Juniper could want for nothing better.

As the miles passed, however, her mood shifted from relaxation to general restlessness. Why had she packed herself into this stale little cubicle? She was glad for every peaceful hour—no sign of invaders, no road troubles, no foul weather—but before long, the boredom rankled thick as a wool wrap on a midsummer's night. By the time the caravan pulled into a clearing at high noon, Juniper had had enough. There was only so much to write, and frankly, she was listed out. (She'd never thought that could be a possibility, but there it was.) Legs stiff and cramped, she pushed open her carriage door and toppled out.

"How are you holding up?" Erick climbed down from the box seat, swinging his arms in wide circles. Nearby, Tippy doubled over and started somersaulting across the grass, clearly no worse for the long ride.

"Better now that I'm out of that snuffbox! I believe I shall ride outside with you when we set off again," Juniper decided. "You have space up there on the seat, don't you?"

Erick's eyebrows shot up. "Juniper, you can't."

"Can't?"

"Well." Erick stuffed his hands in his pockets, eyes on the ground. "As a matter of fact, your father pulled me aside last night. Gave me a bit of a talking-to."

Juniper felt her cheeks heat up. "He did *what?*"

"Don't take it that way. You're royalty! It's our job to protect you."

"It's *Alta's* job to protect me. She's my guard. You're my

adviser, and that's a different job altogether." Juniper knew she was being snippy, but couldn't seem to stop. Was it *still* going to be like this in her new country? Had she just traded one closely guarded cage for another?

Erick sighed. "Look, once we're into the mountains, it'll be different. But you're the crown princess. With that attack on the palace, on top of everything else . . . The Monsian border is just across the river. Haven't you heard all those stories about spies and ruffians hugger-muggering across the border to look for weakness and opportunity?"

"*Stories*," Juniper scoffed. "Nobody believes that stuff." Relations between Torr and Monsia had been strained for centuries. In recent decades, Monsia had shut down its borders and forbidden any exports or trade with their continental neighbors. They would not even allow external census-takers or mapmakers into the territory to make their reports. But in the end, Monsians weren't anything more than a nation of rude, lazy bullies.

"Still." Quiet but stubborn, that was Erick. "Your father is right to have us play it safe for now. Plus, you know, he *is* the king."

Juniper squinted, suddenly distracted. The sun was in her eyes, but a figure was approaching, and for a second, it was almost like looking into mirrored glass. Then Alta stepped out of the light and settled into her own shape—familiar, and yet . . . Juniper eyed her guard critically. Alta's hair and skin tone were darker than her own, her build more on the sturdy side to Juniper's slender. But for height, for shape of face, even the way they moved . . . it was a very near match. Juniper knew a good opportunity when she saw one.

"Come here," she said, grabbing Alta's hand and tugging the bewildered girl back into the carriage. It was a tight fit around the mounds of luggage, but she managed to explain her idea, quash all protests, and exchange their outer costumes in a matter of minutes. Whispering into Alta's ear, and tugging the hood of her cornflower-blue traveling cloak down further over the other girl's face, she pried open the door, gave a little shove, and sent Alta teetering out of the carriage.

"Listen, Juniper," Erick said, leaning in toward Alta, who recoiled. Juniper clapped her hands and flung herself from the carriage, crowing. She'd scuffed up her hair and pulled Alta's cap down over her forehead, wrapping herself from neck to boot in the other girl's muddy, uncertain-smelling cloak.

She could see the result in Erick's gobsmacked expression.

"You see?" she said. "This is how we can do it. Just like magic."

"See what? That you gave Alta your cloak? All I have to do is look at her face, and I can tell immediately it's not you." He looked flustered, though. She'd got him good.

"Of course," said Juniper, drawing herself up in a very un-Alta-like pose, while the other girl stood fidgeting uncomfortably between them. "But we're not trying to hoodwink *you,* are we? It's only the distant people—bandits or enemy soldiers or the like. Right?" She turned to Alta. "Look, I didn't give you much explanation. Only I'm tired of riding in the carriage, and Erick here made some fool oath to my father that I can't set my face out where I might be seen. Therefore you must . . . er, *would* you mind terribly taking my place in there?"

"Riding in the comfort of a carriage, while Your Highness goes on horseback?" Alta looked aghast.

"Oh, certainly not," Juniper said, thinking quickly. "That is to say, there *is* a measure of comfort to be had in there. Or so it would appear *on the surface*. But in truth it'll be ever so dangerous. What if we get accosted by ruffians? They might try to attack the carriage, and I'd be helplessly massacred if I stayed in there. You, on the other hand—I bet you could fight them off without even coming to a sweat."

Alta thoughtfully stroked the hilt of her sword, which looked drolly out of place paired with the finely woven royal cloak. "Very well," she said at last. "I shall be happy to undertake this task. I would have needed your directions once we reached the base of the Hourglass anyway, which should be before sunset."

"Before sunset *if* we ever get moving again!" said Tippy, suddenly underfoot and weaving circles around them like the world's most annoying girl-sized gnat. "Leena and Toby are back with lunchmeat buns from the village, and everyone wants to keep on traveling as we eat." She paused. "All but Cyril and his cronies, naturally."

"We haven't even stopped a full hour," Erick said. "No one wants a longer break?"

"Not a one!" Tippy lowered her voice. "Or maybe everyone just wants to get as far as possible from you-know-what. Also, I expect they don't want to be camping out under the stars tonight. I wouldn't mind that myself! But if we can get all the way to our new land, so much the better."

"So much the better indeed," said Juniper. She turned to Alta and said with mock seriousness, "Milady, if you would take the carriage, I shall get back to my position at the head of this caravan."

Alta's cheeks turned scarlet, but she swung her skirts around toward the carriage, stumbling a little over the hem as she did so. "Thunderstar," she called over her shoulder. "That's the name of my mount, and he's a double handful."

With a barely suppressed thrill, Juniper sauntered up the row to Alta's horse and spent a few minutes scratching the fine creature's nose. She dug into the inner pocket of her traveling gown and found a single cube of sweetcrystal. Suppressing the thought of her beloved Butternut, she fed Thunderstar the treat, then pulled herself up into the saddle.

The world looked different from this height. Thunderstar was at least two hands taller than Butternut, and obviously the kind of spirited mount her riding master would have called "unsuitable for royalty." His coat gleamed black in the high noon glare and his body under Juniper was a watershed of barely controlled strength. He took the lead and set off at a brisk clip, so that Juniper had to rein in and walk him in circles while the rest of the procession got started. A fine beading of sweat started across her forehead. It occurred to her how simple a thing could sometimes seem from a distance, how apparently easy to manage.

She gripped the reins tighter and willed her arms to be steel. She *was* in control.

At the crossroads, the path broke into a multipronged fork. To the right, three separate roads wound toward eastern Torr and the main cities of Sari and Longton. Still farther to the east was the spooky and mysterious Spyglass Lake, which lay like a thumbprint at the end of the Hourglass range, marking Torr's border with Gaulia to the north. A narrow pass between the mountains and the lake was the only recognized border between the two countries, as the lake fed a network of rivers that flowed straight to the coast.

By contrast, the left-hand road was rough and ill-used. It crossed the Lore River and led to the dread Monsian Highway, which had gone to disrepair since the closing of the border back at the turn of the century. Now the crumbling highway was used mainly by vagrants and desperados venturing out from Monsia in search of mischief or worse. Monsia bordered Torr all along its western and southern flanks, and the fact that this one road was their only link was a clear sign of the two nations' long-standing hostility.

The idea of Monsia launching a real attack on Torr was, as Juniper knew from a lifetime of Political Discourse lectures, historically laughable. Yet today, laughter was the furthest thing from her mind.

Juniper nudged Thunderstar left toward the Monsian Highway, feeling bone-weary from the day's travel. Or at least, that's what she focused on to keep the twinge of fear at bay.

Behind her, Cyril's voice rang out, mocking and pitched loud enough to carry. "Surely we're not turning onto the *Monster*an Highway?" Even without looking back, Juniper could hear worried mutters ripple down the row of riders. It was bad enough they'd had to flee in the dark of night, bad enough they had to take this road at all, without Cyril aggravating things!

Not for the first time, she wished Erick were riding next to her. When she and Thunderstar had taken the lead, Cyril and his fellow nobles, whose names she'd learned were Jessamyn and Root, had formed a sort of barrier blocking back the other riders. She'd compensated by keeping a horse's length ahead of them whenever possible—for all the good that was doing.

"Come on, Cyril. You're not *afraid* to travel the Monsian Highway, are you?" she called over her shoulder, with one hand steadying Thunderstar and the other juggling her father's map.

"Afraid? Not a chance. I only wonder what's going through the mind of everybody's *favorite* princess—directing us up this wickedly perilous road while *she* stays hidden away at the back of the line, in the safety of her gilded carriage."

On the verge of whirling her mount around and getting up in Cyril's face, Juniper froze. She'd been setting a hard pace for the last hours, leading the pack and not exchanging more than a few words with the others. Still . . . her Alta disguise had been intended to fool far-off brigands. Could it really have taken in Cyril himself?

Well, then.

Pulling Alta's leather cap down further over her face and smoothing the map across her lap, Juniper lowered her voice an octave and kept her body turned away. "In any case, Cyril, you need have no fear. We take this road for a league or less. Then we turn off north onto the Hourglass Pike."

Without awaiting a reply, she gave Thunderstar his lead and set off, turning fully away from Cyril and ignoring further rude questions shouted at her back.

As she trotted along, she took another look at her father's map. Studying the chicken-scratch lines for the millionth time, she suddenly wondered *why* the king had drawn his own map. Had he been too much in a hurry to have his scribe do a proper job, with all that was going on? Or could there be some deeper reason?

He'd said that the Basin wasn't on any maps and that no one knew its whereabouts. Was it possible that King Regis wanted to *keep* things that way?

Juniper squirmed in her saddle. Too many questions, and no answers in sight. She distracted herself by picking up speed, noting that her caravan of followers matched her increase. Apparently, no one wanted to spend any extra time on the Monsian Highway.

The incline began gradually, but even so, Juniper's heart skipped a beat when they came through a tunnel of sweetgum trees and saw the long-awaited fork in the road. From here, the way would grow increasingly steep, until they reached the base of the Hourglass Mountains. And then the real fun stuff started.

"Take a right at this bend," Juniper called.

"Isn't it time for a rest?" Jessamyn whined. "Look at that green pasture! We might stop there and have some provisions."

"Princess's orders," Juniper called over shoulder, then ducked her chin and laughed into Alta's cloak.

This new road was narrower than the hard-packed Monsian Highway. The scenery was quickly changing from the lush, well-cultivated farmlands of central Torr, becoming drier, more sparsely populated, and generally run-down. More exciting by far were the Hourglass Mountains, which loomed larger by the moment. By now, though, they had passed the fifth hour after noon. Could they really make their final destination by nightfall?

"Say! You up there!" Jessamyn whined again. "Did you hear me? I am tired, and we're ever so far from all that trouble back at the palace. I *shall* stop under that tree over yonder."

"We're not stopping," Juniper said firmly, lifting her eyes from the map to scan the landscape around her. According to her father's directions, they were to travel just a few leagues more, and would then reach the cave's opening that would take them through the mountains. But how was she to spot one particular gap in this never-ending rocky cliff side?

"Cyril, make that odious girl listen. I have no longer any sense of my lower self," Jessamyn wailed. "My legs are two blocks of dead wood, and my back does ache so!"

In a fit of frustration, Juniper stuffed the map into her waist-pouch and whirled her horse around. "Carry on," she barked at Cyril, who now headed the procession. "Keep the group moving at full speed ahead. You, come with me." She knew she was acting very un-Alta-like, but at this point, she didn't care. Her disguise was nothing more than a lark, and she was sick to pincushions of listening to Jessamyn's whining. Neither Jessamyn nor Cyril showed any sign of recognizing her as she rode past them, though.

Juniper pulled Thunderstar to a stop in front of her carriage and waved at Erick.

"Hold up for a moment," she said, then turned to Jessamyn. "There. Take *his* spot on the bench. It will give your behind a rest, and there are some provisions in the carriage."

Jessamyn squinted at Erick in confusion. "Up there? On the *driver's* seat?"

"If you thought to ride inside the princess's carriage——" Erick started, and Tippy chipped in: "There's no room in there, and that's a fact. It's crammed with bags and boxes and, er, her princess-pants, of course!" She winked audaciously at Juniper, but Jessamyn was too steamed to notice. Indecision crumpled the noble girl's face as she opened and closed her mouth.

"It's your call, Lady Jessamyn," said Juniper curtly. "I shall head back to the front now, but we need to get the carriage moving again one way or another, for all the rest await behind us."

"Oh, very well," said Jessmyn, sliding off her horse and totter-ing toward the carriage on fish-belly legs.

"You will manage these magnificent creatures the rest of the way, Miss Tippy?" Juniper asked.

"Will I ever!" the little girl chirped, bobbing up and down on the seat. "I've been leading them along all by myself for the last hour, haven't I, Erick Dufrayne?"

"She most certainly has. Lady Jessamyn won't have to do a thing but recline at her leisure, shield her face from the sun, and nibble on dainties."

The switch was quickly accomplished, and in a matter of minutes, Juniper and Erick breezed past Cyril and Root to re-claim the front of the train. "Let's pick up the pace, shall we?" she said. "I'm certain it's not too far to the next stage of our journey."

"Next stage?" Erick's voice sounded faint. "The sun is nearly set. How much longer do you intend us to go out here?"

Juniper grinned. "Out here? Not long at all." She paused, then gave in to the thrill of her disclosure. "Oh, all right. The next, and the final, trek we'll need to make—wait now, *don't* disagree just yet, not until I tell you just why we can and *must* make the journey tonight! Well, a cave is what it is, and the entrance can't be too far off, if the map tells true."

"A cave? Inside the Hourglass Mountains?"

"Just so. And not a cave alone, but a whole network of them. They tunnel right through the mountains, and my father said the way is wide as walls. The floor is rough, so we'll have to go slow, but we can make it for sure. Even the wagons. It's a good thing we used the smaller narrow ones, and had the blacksmith outfit them with his sturdiest wheels."

Erick seemed to consider this.

"There's a secret, too, inside the caves. Wait till you see it." She patted her waist-pouch, the parchment inside giving off a faint crinkle. "So, what do you say? Can we push all the way through tonight?"

Erick bit his lip, obviously more than a little uncertain.

"Look," Juniper said, looking sidelong at him across their mounts. "I realize this is all new. But you're my adviser. *My. Adviser.* That means I *want* your advice. So none of this holding back. Got it? Next time I catch you stammering and biting off your words, I'll . . . I'll . . . bop you on the nose."

Erick's face whipped through a rainbow of conflicting emotions. Finally he settled on a slow smile. "All right, then. You're the queen, and I'm your adviser. So what if I . . . that is, how do you want me to respond to you when I . . . you know—*disagree?*"

"Do you?"

"What?"

"Do you disagree? With this plan?"

Erick grinned. "This plan? Not at all. I think it's smashing."

Juniper felt a surge of relief. "I'm glad to hear it. But to answer your question: As my chief adviser, you may have any opinion at all, and you should express it at will. I'm not just saying that because you're agreeing with me right now—I really do want your counsel." She paused. "And I meant it about the bopping."

"I got it," Erick promised. "My nose is precious to me, as it happens."

"Now let's be off, shall we?"

She dug her heels into Thunderstar's side. The horse had been traveling for hours with very few breaks, and she knew they needed to stop and rest soon. But they didn't have much farther to go. The Hourglass Mountains completely filled the near sky, stretching across the continent like a great, impassable wall. But if her father's map was to be believed, they were not nearly as impassable as they seemed.

The way through was there. It was close.

They just had to find it.

7

THE CAVE'S MOUTH LOOKED IMPOSSIBLY small—in fact, if the moon hadn't been so bright and full over this clearing, Juniper might have missed it altogether, overgrown as it was with bluevine and clinging pink-and-red mandevilla.

"This way, everyone!" she called out. "We enter here!"

She galloped ahead of the slow-moving group, with Erick close on her heels. At the entrance she dismounted, gathered up the reins, and pushed through the opening with gusto, tugging Thunderstar in her wake.

"Isn't this something?" Erick's voice behind her was pure awe.

Once inside, Juniper bent to feel along the floor. "Shine your torch over here," she said, wishing her father's scribbled instructions had been just a *little* bit easier to follow.

"I still can't figure out what you're doing."

It was as close as Erick had ever come to complaining, and Juniper grinned. It was mean to keep him in suspense, but she couldn't help it. The moment of revelation would be worth it.

Finding a sharp rock that fit comfortably in her hand, she stood up and patted along the wall. It was surprisingly dry—well, perhaps *not* surprisingly, given what she was about to do—but for long minutes, she found only bare, smooth rock.

"Well?" Erick asked curiously.

"Almost . . . oh! I've got it!" Her questing fingers had finally reached their goal: a deep, wide groove chiseled out of the rock wall, the inside rough and ridged and ever so slightly tacky. Victory! Juniper shifted the rock in her hand, pulled back, and thumped hard in the center of the dip. She missed the first time, and the second strike didn't have nearly enough force behind it, bringing nothing but a dim flash. But the third time—the third time—

Under her striking stone, the groove burst in a flare of hot white light. It was brighter than she'd expected, and Juniper dropped her rock and scrambled backward, bumping into Erick. She could see him clearly now in the brilliant glow, standing with his mouth agape.

"Worth waiting for?" she crowed.

"What in the mighty storms *is it*?"

"That's the secret I was telling you about. My father wrote about it on the map. I've no idea where he learned it, or why we've never put something like this to use in the palace. It's a sort of alchemical powder, and when struck hard enough, the spark ignites the pitch that's left on the wall. And then . . ."

She turned to look at the glowing indentation, which cast enough light that the cave walls around them were clearly visible.

As they watched, a strip on the far side of the groove caught flame and blazed outward, a wide fiery band licking along the wall away from the cave's entrance.

"It's pointing the way?" Erick asked.

"Yes! And it gets even better. The burn span is quite brief—five to eight minutes, no more. See how the bowl is already starting to flicker ever so slightly lower? It lights up, leads the way, then burns itself out. And it can be reused time upon time, so long as it has some hours to replenish. Oh, what's keeping the others?" From just outside, she could hear Cyril's voice raised in a complaint about tight spaces, over the sound of clearing and hacking as the opening was tested before the vehicles' passing. "Do you have those moonstones? We'll drop some along our way in case this burns down before they all make it through."

Erick fumbled in his bag and set one of the stones down by the wall. They had been coated in a luminescent resin, which glowed an eerie green in the wall's flickering light. At that moment, the vines at the opening rustled and Paul burst through, tugging his mare behind him. His eyes were wonder-wide in the flickering ghost light. The other horseback riders quickly followed. Despite the assurances her father had given, Juniper held her breath, then let it out as the first of the wagons cleared the opening with ease. Those vines sure covered a wide-open space! As the chamber filled, the gathering torchlight brightened it further, and the reflection on the moonstones was like a signpost calling them forward.

"We'll lead on down the passage. Just follow the lighting," she called to the others. "Come on, Erick—let's blaze ahead!"

• • •

Getting through the rest of the cave took hours. The curving passage wound upward in wide, lazy loops, but the flare along the wall burned steady and true. It kept them moving at a stiff pace, though. Despite their growing exhaustion, the rest of the group caught up double-quick once they realized how brief the light's span was; nobody wanted to be left in the warren of caves with only torchlight-off-the-moonstones to point the way.

The horses took the journey surprisingly well, clip-clopping meekly behind their equally silent riders. Even Cyril was subdued; more than once, Juniper looked back to see him blinking uneasily in the semidarkness. At every step, Juniper waited for a corner too sharp, a ceiling too low, or walls too narrow for the carriage and wagons to pass, but each time she was relieved to find an adequate, if not entirely comfortable, fit.

"Do you suppose this tunnel's been widened at all?" Roddy mused, running a palm along the smooth passageway wall.

Juniper would have answered him, but just then, the strip of light flickered sharply. She raised her torch for a better look. The flare jumped to another hollow on the wall, which blazed up like a miniature sunrise. The space around them was instantly bathed in a day-bright glow, and Juniper's mouth dropped open. The cavern they'd just entered was enormous. She might have been in the ballroom back at the palace, so high were the ceilings and so far off was each wall from the next.

"Hellooooo!" Juniper shouted, her voice bouncing around the room like a dizzy chipmunk. *Hello-llo-llo-llooooo!*

Behind her, others took up the buzz of call and conversation, tiredness giving way to a sudden excitement at having apparently reached their destination—or some stage of it, anyway.

Erick was still walking straight ahead, and in another moment, Juniper saw what had caught his eye. The bright splay of pitch-light was already starting to burn down, but clear across the cavernous room, one of the walls looked slightly less shadowed. "I think this is the exit," Erick said. "It's full night out there, so it's hard to say for sure, but we've certainly walked for long enough. We could have cross-tunneled six mountains by this time."

"The air current is fresher here," Juniper agreed, waving a hand through the open recess, "and look at all this bluevine covering! Just like the entrance down below. I think you're right—this *is* the way out."

"Well then, what now?"

"We'll stay in here tonight—it's got to be ever so late. And there's no point venturing out to a new territory in the dead dark. I'll make the announcement now, have everyone bed down for the night."

Erick raised an eyebrow, looking pointedly at her rugged, muddy cloak. Juniper looked down. "Oh. I'm still Alta, aren't I? I'd almost forgotten. You'd better spread the word, then." She grinned. "Imagine traipsing through the caves in my silken gowns! That Alta does know how to dress for adventuring."

As Juniper pushed through the group toward the carriage,

her head down, word spread around her that this was journey's end. The wagons were lined up along the walls and weary travelers staggered about, beginning the process of settling down for the night. Lit torches were set up around the camp, and as Juniper reached her carriage, the flames set shadows dancing off the wolverine figurehead on the gilded front panel. Just below it, the familiar Torrence crest—a fist crossed with a short dagger—filled Juniper with mingled pride and homesickness. Approaching Thunderstar, she patted the stallion's quivering flank. He had more than earned this time of rest. They all had. She looked proudly over the straggly band of settlers and felt a sudden rush. *This* was her kingdom now—a traveling kingdom, still, but it was a start.

Then Tippy was next to her, with a currycomb in hand, tugging on Thunderstar's reins and beginning to groom the horse for the night. Juniper nodded and began to move away, then stopped. In her new kingdom, everyone would be allowed to receive their ruler's gratitude, no matter who they were. Her Comportment Master could go dandle in his own ditties. "Thank you, Tippy," she said.

"No problem, Your Princessness," Tippy chirped. "Only you might want to go and nose in over yonder. Erick's getting some pain from the snooty lot."

It was all too obvious who Tippy was referring to, and Juniper hid a smile. Still, there was one thing she had to do first. Spotting Alta's anxious face at the carriage window, Juniper dove up the steps and in three minutes flat had resumed her easily recognizable outfit. Her time as a pretender had been deliciously freeing, but she was glad to feel her familiar cornflower-blue cloak swirling around her skirts.

As Juniper picked her way across the rocky floor to the far side of the cave, a whine cut through the buzz of tired activity. "You want me to do *what*?" She found Erick cowering in front of a horrified-looking Jessamyn.

"*Everyone* is pitching in to help out," he said, trying for firmness but not quite succeeding. "There's over a dozen horses that need feeding and tending, and plenty of other chores besides." He shot a glare at Cyril and Root, who stood nearby looking studiously relaxed.

"Who died and made you ruler?" Cyril said scornfully.

Juniper clenched her hands into fists. "He might not be ruler, but he *is* right. We *all* have to do our part."

Cyril looked her up and down, then yawned into his hand. Without another word, he turned and strode off into a shadowed passageway, his torch flickering in his wake. Root glanced in Juniper's direction, then followed his friend. Jessamyn looked from Erick to Juniper. Then she pulled her fur wrap tighter to her shoulders and swept over to a nearby boulder. "Oh, heavens, I *do* feel faint with weariness! I simply must rest after this frightfully long day. I'm sure you understand." She swanned down onto the stone, leaning back against the wall and shutting her eyes.

Erick's face was purple. He opened his mouth, but no sound came out.

Juniper put a hand on his shoulder. "They're nothing but rotten scofflaws. But, frankly, I'm too tired to worry about them right now. I'll help out with the horses." She thought Erick's eyes would bug out of his head.

"You'll *what?*"

"Do you think I've taken equestrian lessons twice a week for the last ten years without learning how to care for a horse?" She tugged the bag of oats from his hand.

"But you're—you're—the *crown princess!*"

"I know." Juniper sighed. "I think everything's going to be different now that we're on our own. Cyril and that lot will figure it out soon enough. Hopefully. Back at the palace, I had someone to dress and undress me, to powder and perfume me and brush my hair out morning, night, and any other time I desired. They'd even clean my teeth if I let them. It's not going to be like that here." She looked slyly at him. "Unless you've got a hankering for the dental arts?"

Erick laughed. "Well, the horses really *could* use your help. Only . . . and I'm not sure it's my place to say anything, but should you be backing away from the sort of challenge Cyril threw at you?" He looked uncomfortable. "In the stories, a confrontation like that always has to be met head-on, or there are consequences later. Not that I've ever managed to do that myself, mind you."

Juniper's stomach clenched. He was right, of course. But the thought of taking on Cyril and the others, at the end of this day in particular, was too exhausting for words. She turned away and pulled open the bag of oats.

Erick's voice behind her was resigned. "When we're done with the horses, I'll lug some of the bundles out of your carriage. Free up the seat so you can sleep in there tonight. His Majesty would have me drawn and quartered if I let you sleep out on the stone floor."

8

THERE WAS NO SCHEDULED REVEILLE CALL TO wake Juniper the next morning. No maidservant bustling around the room, lighting a fire in the grate and placing fresh-cut flowers on her side table; no tempting scent of breakfast wafting from the far kitchens. Still, against all reason, within the span of a moment Juniper found herself sitting bolt upright on her carriage seat, wide-awake. After the briefest blink of disorientation, it all came back in a rush: The journey! The Hourglass! Her *own country*!

In a trice, she'd thrown off her covers, shaken out her skirts—yesterday's outfit, for it hadn't felt right to don nightclothes there in the carriage—and sprung out into the cave. The recessed opening leading outside was clearly visible now, a diffused wash of sunlight bathing the near walls in a cheery off-yellow glow. A giddy rush rose inside Juniper, and she began darting from bedroll to bedroll, gently tugging at one person and whispering in another's ear, before finally whirling in a circle.

"Wake up, settlers! It's high morning, and we are the proud

inhabitants of a fine new land. Wake up, everyone! It's time to go *exploring*!"

Tippy was the first to react, materializing at Juniper's side like a quivering whirl of energy. The others staggered up one after another, sleepy yawns melting into bright blinking eyes and eager looks.

"Let's go! Let's go!" said Tippy, punctuating each statement with an energetic bounce.

"Maybe some breakfast afore we set off?" murmured Alta in Juniper's ear. "I think there are rolls left over from yesterday's luncheon stop. It's not so very much, but—"

"Oh, yes indeed! And I saw a jug of elderberry cordial wedged in my carriage, though goshawk knows where it came from. That shall do for starters, and we can eat heartily at midday." Juniper squinted at the opening, suddenly unsure how close to midday it might already be, given their late stop the night before. "We must find a spot for the timepiece as soon as we're settled in. I feel quite adrift without it."

Despite the uncertain schedule, the morning meal was zipped through, and Juniper led the way toward the exit. Only as she glanced back over her shoulder at the visibly eager group did she realize that Cyril, Root, and Jessamyn were not among them. That explained the freely joyous mood! Well, let the troublemakers sleep as long as they liked. This would be far more enjoyable without them.

Erick reached the opening first. He turned to Juniper, and a corner of his mouth quirked up. "Your Highness, Princess—no, make that *Queen* Juniper of the Hourglass. Shall we?"

"My high royal adviser Erick Dufrayne," Juniper said. "We *shall!*" She reached out to grab his hand, and together they pushed through the vines and out of the cave.

The first word that came to Juniper's mind when she stepped into the perfumed sunlight of the Basin was . . . *enchanted.* The early-morning sun peeped over the mountaintop opposite, sketching the valley in a charcoal-and-honey glow. They'd emerged on a wide rocky outcropping partway up the inner face of the Basin. From here, they could see the whole valley—no bigger than the palace grounds in all, but how much space did they really need? This was paradise, and it was perfect.

Farther down the slope, the ground was dusty and graveled, studded with boulders and hard-packed red earth. In the distance was the faint roar of a waterfall, the apparent source of a stream that divided the valley crosswise from west to east before it disappeared in a cluster of spindly trees. The land on the far side of the stream was a riot of wild green growth.

"Egad," breathed Erick.

"It's magnificent, isn't it? Absolutely perfect."

"Would you look at that tree?"

On the near side of the stream, perhaps halfway down the valley, a giant dropsy tree spread fat green leaves. "I've never seen a dropsy grow that big!" Juniper exclaimed.

It was obviously no ordinary tree; even from this distance, they could see how it presided over the valley, watchful and sober and almost regal.

"Shove on over, then!" Tippy chirped into Juniper's back. "I'm getting trampled here behind. Er . . . shove over, *please*, Your Very Highest!"

Juniper scooted sideways on the outcropping, making room for the rest of the group to spill out behind her.

"For the wonder!" Alta breathed.

"'Tis truly a place of magic," said Leena with reverence.

Erick was already starting down the rocky cliff side. The trail had clearly seen feet before theirs, but it still took Juniper's full concentration to keep from skidding on the loose, dusty gravel.

"We'll have to leave the carts up in the cave," Erick said.

Juniper hadn't thought of that, but of course he was right. The wagons would never fit this narrow track. "It will take a lot of trips to bring all our provisions down this way, but it doesn't have to be done all at once. Little by little, as we need it, right?"

Ahead of her, Erick stopped moving. He eyeballed the rocky ledge and the base of the ground down below. "There was this one thing I read," he said. "Tallow Dorfman's *Ingenious Devices of Practickal Usage*—he's got all sorts of inventions and ideas in there for making work go more smoothly. There's one that's fiery clever— using a system of ropes and stabilizing boards to lower an object straight down. Pulley or some such? It's just what we need here." Erick grinned. "I think I stuffed the book into one of my bags."

"I bet you did," said Juniper. Every one of Erick's bags was book-lumpy and breakback-heavy. His pulley idea did seem like the perfect solution, though, and she opened her mouth to say so, but Erick was off again, careening toward the valley. The ground was barely a long jump away, but at this point the path split and a second trail led sharply to the right.

"Wait a moment," she said to Erick, who'd already landed below. Then she called back toward the others. "Look over here, all! What do you make of these openings?" She turned onto the narrow, curving trail, which hugged the inner cliff in a wobbly-straight line. After a couple minutes, the rock face opened into a door-shaped gap.

Leena, Roddy, and Sussi were just behind her as she pushed into the little cave. Light spilled in the wide window, illuminating a smooth rocky floor and walls that shimmered faintly in the dim light. A long flat stone at the far edge begged to be covered in bed cushions, and two round boulders could make cozy stools.

"Why, it's an apartment!" exclaimed Sussi. "A tiny little home! May I live here? Oh, may I, Your Highness?"

"There's another one just ahead," called Roddy from outside. "And ever so many more along this trail. There's enough for each of us to have our own, I'd expect!"

"I shall set it up directly," Sussi exclaimed. She dropped the bulky bag she'd been holding and whipped out a fancy cloth embroidered in scarlet and turquoise, which she spread over the nearest stone, flinging a burst of color around the room. A small white vase set atop the cloth, and the room suddenly looked warm and lived-in.

Juniper clapped her hands together. "This is even better than I'd hoped! We shan't need to build houses after all, not unless we want to."

"See these little knobs along the wall?" Sussi crooned, quite in her own world by now. "I shall hang my gown and my traveling cloak right here. And look at these cunning hollows, all up and down the wall! Wee shelves, they are . . ."

Grinning, Juniper stepped back out into the trail. Boys and girls scurried in and out of the openings, laughing and calling, lugging bags and bundles into their new rooms. "Have you claimed your apartment yet?" she asked Erick, dropping down to join him on the ground below.

"There's time," he said, waving a hand. "Look at how many there are. We shan't run out."

"I feel as though we've done a good week's work already, and we've only just put foot to soil!"

Erick nodded and patted the sack slung over his shoulder. "More time for reading is what I say."

Juniper shoved him. "Forget reading! You've had enough musty tomes for a while. Your task this summer is to revel in the glorious out-of-doors. I mean, look at this place!" With that, Juniper took off running, and Erick followed close behind, his book sack thumping on his back.

The next hour was spent in a frenzied rush of exploration, discovery, and delight. The river cut across the middle of the Basin, and they had to go some distance to find a spot shallow enough so they could wade to the other side. In contrast with the southern bank's dry, dust bowl landscape, the north bank was carpeted in lush, green grass. They followed the river to its source, where a gigantic waterfall thundered down into a crystal pool. Turning back around, they could see the river cascading straight across the valley to its far eastern tip, through the copse of young trees they'd seen from the cave—*fruit-bearing* trees, if Juniper wasn't mistaken—until it disappeared into a gurgling tunnel that cut down through the mountain and out of sight.

"This is the mouth of the River Lore!" Juniper exclaimed. "It cuts through my Basin just like it cuts through all of Torr."

"That sounds . . . significant?" Erick offered.

Distantly, Juniper recognized that he was teasing her. Mostly, though, the rush of discovery and exploration had left her feeling breathless and awestruck and very, very queenly.

"The Basin," she murmured. "That name is not nearly impressive enough for this place. I do like the word *basin,* though. It's got a solid ring to it." It also made her think of her father, who had called it by that name.

Erick looked up. "Call it Queen's Basin, then. That's a proper regal name, and you get to keep the bit you like."

"Queen's Basin." Juniper turned the name over in her mind, then smiled. "I like it. No, I *love* it. Queen's Basin it is. How does one name a country, do you suppose?"

Erick smiled. "Done," he said.

Queen's Basin was a larger-than-life gift that got better the more they unwrapped it. By the time the sun was high in the sky, however, Juniper and Erick agreed that by far the best and most magical spot was the giant dropsy tree.

They named it the Great Tree, because sometimes the most obvious name was the best. It loomed near the center of the Basin, on the South Bank but with thick branches extending over the Lore; a careful climber might follow one branch along its length and hop down onto the springy grass of the North Bank. The Great Tree had wide, dark leaves and craggy branches. From the ground, the trunk's base was so wide that Juniper thought every member of Queen's Basin touching hands outstretched still couldn't have spanned it entirely. A giant wheel-shaped stone had been pushed against one side of the trunk, and by scrambling up it, Juniper could reach the lowest branch and swing herself up an arboreal sort of staircase.

"Did someone build up there?" came Erick's voice behind her. The branches creaked under her weight, then his, as they shifted up the three or four levels until . . .

"Oh!" Juniper gasped as she scaled another branch and pulled herself into the heart of the tree. Above her stretched a dense green canopy, the leaves diffusing the sunlight to a pale translucence, so the heart of the tree felt like a magic bubble, wide-open yet perfectly contained, blocked in from the outside world. And the base—

Juniper swung off her branch and landed on a smooth, wood-plank platform. Someone *had* been here before, had sawed and sanded rows of boards, had fastened them to the branches in a solid floor that stretched in a full circle around the Great Tree's trunk. Juniper jumped a little in place, and the floor didn't shift.

"It's sturdy!" Erick remarked, scrambling to his feet behind her. "Who could have made this, do you suppose?"

"Perhaps it was my father," she said, remembering what he'd told her about his trip so many years before. It seemed impossible to think of him engaged in such backbreaking effort, or producing anything quite so solid. It was an odd feeling, to be surprised by someone you thought you knew inside and out.

"Look over here," Erick called.

The tree's trunk continued up over their heads, with narrowing branches and lightening leaves. But Erick was leaning *into* the trunk, which was about as wide around here as a broom closet.

Then Erick . . . disappeared. Juniper ran over and peered at the trunk. To her surprise, it opened into a tiny round room— cozy with silky-smooth walls, hollowed from the trunk in what seemed a natural fashion, navigating around the grooves and bumps of the still-living tree's inner core. The chamber was big enough for three or four bodies to pack in tightly. It was the *perfect* size for one girl to stretch out in comfort.

Juniper fell in love with it on sight.

"This shall be my personal chamber," she pronounced. "And the Great Tree will be our gathering spot. We can throw a little housewarming party tonight." She thought back to that all-kids dance party, the night that had started this whole adventure. Would it be like that here? The mood, the energy, the—

"Tonight?" Erick asked doubtfully.

"Well, yes. Why not?"

"It only seems . . ." Erick hesitated, then reached up to rub his nose. "Well, we haven't even begun to settle in. And yesterday's journey was awfully long."

Juniper considered. "Tomorrow? Oh, very well, I suppose you're right. Three days' time, then. We must set up, and plan, and get everything ready, for starters." She paused. "You didn't happen to bring along any books that deal with country-settling, did you?"

Erick grinned. "Do you really need to ask?"

Down below, Juniper could hear the buzz of conversation growing. By now the others would have finished their own early exploration, and they would be looking for what came next. Also, Juniper's stomach informed her, it had to be well past time for luncheon.

Stroking the wall one final time, Juniper scrambled back out onto the main platform. "We'd best go gather up the others." She felt both giddy and strangely serious, as though her proper life was catching up with her after an enchanted morning away from reality.

The two clambered down what they'd already begun thinking of as the staircase, where the branches were so arranged that you hardly felt you were descending a tree at all. They dropped to the rim of the wheel-stone and from there to the ground.

Back out in the open after being under the Great Tree's dome, Juniper squinted a little. The sun beat down on the valley like a flaming torch. They were high up in the mountains, she knew—ever so high, not far from the peaks—and a sprinkling of snow could be seen on the very tip-tops. Yet here in their crater of a valley it was full-on summer, as hot as any day in Torr. Tilting her hand to block the sun's glare, Juniper saw that the rock face all around the bowl-shaped valley glowed silvery white in the midday rays. It was as though the stone itself amplified the light and stored it and sent it spilling into the canyon like a torrent. How was that possible? It was a true wonder.

Erick took off across the clearing to where the others were dashing wildly about, arms frenzied and garments aflutter. Juniper began to run after him, then changed her mind and slowed her pace. She could see why her father had loved this valley. She herself had been so caught up in its magic this morning that she'd gone whole stretches of time without thinking once of the palace, or the danger facing both her father and Torr. She had a feeling that such carefree lightness could become rather addictive.

It all came back to her now, though. Erick was right; there *was* a lot to be done. And a lot at stake, too. By now, her father's army must have repelled the attackers. He'd promised a messenger, which was likely to arrive in the next day or so. But until she knew for sure that all was well, she had to stay strong and clearheaded. And ready. Queen's Basin was a paradise, yes, but it was still a long way from being a country. Building it had to come first. It's what her father would have done. *Get work done, then have fun*—that was what he'd always taught her. And this was his mountain paradise, wasn't it?

There would be time for freedom and chasing down joy and running wild through the fields. It just wasn't that time yet. Juniper walked slowly and regally toward the clearing, clasped her hands, then stood and waited for her subjects to settle down.

It was time to be queen.

9

BEING QUEEN, IT TURNED OUT, WAS RATHER easier thought than done. After a certain amount of darting and dashing, Erick and Alta managed to corral everyone in the open space near the Great Tree. The group was wild and unruly, and Juniper searched in vain for the queenly poise she'd felt just minutes ago. How did her father manage being responsible for an entire country, with millions of people looking to him for guidance and organization? Here she had just thirteen subjects, and she felt completely outnumbered.

Well, she thought, *maybe I don't quite have even thirteen subjects.*

Across the clearing, Cyril approached with long strides. Jessamyn and Root followed behind him to either side. Cyril's hair was sleek and shiny, his tailored coat crisp and spotless, and his nose lifted so high, Juniper could see clear up his hairy nostrils.

"Well, well, well," he murmured in tones of highest scorn.

"Cyril," she said, voice clipped. "It's good of you to join us."

"Such a quaint little spot you've turned up here," he replied, throwing himself down on a nearby boulder, crossing his arms on his chest with an expression of infinite boredom. *Waiting for me to fail.* The words popped into her mind, and she registered her own limp curls, her skirts crumpled from yesterday's travel. Cyril knew the path her thoughts were taking; she could see it in his face. Juniper shook herself. She was her father's daughter, and nothing—no pride-filled noble, no unruly mob, no mind-boggling mass of tasks to be done—would shake her confidence before she'd even begun.

"Gather round!" she called out, but her thin voice barely left the ground. She scanned her surroundings: Roddy and Filbert arguing about how the boards might have been affixed into the dropsy tree; Sussi wading out into the stream and exclaiming about depth; Toby running three leashed goats around in wide circles; Tippy stalking one kid after another, then popping out from behind them like a manic jack-a-box.

Cyril caught her eye, cocked his chin, and smirked.

Without breaking Cyril's gaze, Juniper brought her thumbs to her mouth, and—delighted to put her mother's years-ago instruction to such a fine practical use—let out a piercing whistle. There were no chandeliers to rattle out here. But the sound electrified the clearing, rocketing through it like a slingshot and quashing the hubbub outright.

"Well, that's better," said Juniper. "Let's all come in close now, shall we?"

Stragglers pushed in to the circle. The hush thickened as everyone settled and turned toward Juniper.

She cleared her throat. "Hello, everybody. I'm so glad you've all made it here safely to our *very own* new kingdom!"

"Juniper Kingdom!" Tippy materialized, all elbows, between two taller kids in the front of the group. "Hip, hip, hooray!"

To Juniper's surprise, the group broke out into a loud cheer and chorused, "JUNIPER KINGDOM!" She glanced over at Erick, who winked and chanted along with them.

She lifted her hands and the group quieted. "I won't say that doesn't have a certain ring," she said. "But my chief adviser and I have put some thought to a proper name for our new country, and the result is . . . Queen's Basin." She let the words sharpen in the air and carve their own space like a shimmering sign above the valley.

Then they were swallowed up in another round of cheering, and Juniper's confidence swelled further. The moment felt rather majestic.

She liked it.

At the back of the group, Cyril's stance was tighter, his smirk replaced by a scowl. Good enough for now.

"Citizens of Queen's Basin!" she yelled, and waited for the buzz to die down. "It's my honor to be here with you and to celebrate our very first day as settlers of our own proper country. Now comes the best part: We get to set things up. We're all on our own here, and there's only us to do all the things that need doing. I guess you can see that's pretty much *everything*. But here's the thing:

Whatever it is we do—we get to decide *how it's done.* This is our country, and we can build it *any way we want to!*"

She had to lift her hands for quiet again.

"But that doesn't mean we're going to stand for anyone loafing about." She met Cyril's gaze head-on. "We're going to work harder than we've ever worked before. We're going to build the very *best* kingdom there ever was. We'll have fun, too, as we go. A little 'welcome to the Basin' party in a few nights, to start with. But once my father's messenger arrives and we get the official word that all is well back home—*then* we're going to have an enormous *royal ball.*"

This time the cheering went on and on, and Juniper could feel the blood rushing to her cheeks. When she refocused on the back of the group, though, all she saw was an empty spot. Cyril, Root, and Jessamyn were gone. She sighed.

"All right, everybody. Let's start by bringing all the belongings down from the cave. The carts will need to stay in there, and the horses won't be able to bring much down that narrow walkway. That means most of the sacks and bundles will have to be carried down by hand—unless, Erick, you want to talk with Roddy about rigging up that pulley contraption?" Erick lit up like a torch and started digging through his book bag. "Alta, will you organize the unloading? See what can be left there for storage and what we need right off?" Alta nodded and moved to one side.

"I think you've all seen the caves along the south cliff. Those will be our dwelling homes, so make sure you've claimed one for yourself. Or one to share, as you like. I'm setting up my base in the Great Tree, so let's take the rest of the day for settling in, then gather again this evening to discuss the morrow. I think we can find some dried meat and fruit to pass around for a luncheon meal, and we'll have ourselves a proper dinner tonight."

Leena raised her hand, an uncertain frown on her face. "Yes?" Juniper asked.

"What will be done for the dinner, Your Highness?"

Juniper waved a hand. "First rule of my new kingdom," she said. "I'm to be called Juniper. It's only"—she shrugged at the startled looks—"easier that way, don't you think? And as to dinner—" She paused. "You've signed up as cook, so the provisioning is to be your domain."

Leena clasped her hands in delight. Clearly, this was the answer she'd been hoping for.

"So instead of general unloading, you should focus on sorting out the food and preparing a simple meal. Alta, you'll make sure the foodstuff is unloaded first and delivered down here, won't you? There's an ideal place for a kitchen. Come along, Leena, and I'll show you."

The crowd quickly dispersed, most of them following Alta back toward the cliff. Leena shuffled awkwardly behind Juniper as they walked the few steps toward the riverbank. "See over here?" Juniper said, seeking to put the other girl at ease. "It's right up alongside the clearing—which shall be our proper dining hall, by and by—and just on the banks of the river."

It wasn't much to look at: a hammered-out spot that had obviously seen plenty of stamping feet. Stones were already gathered in a makeshift fire pit, the ghosts of long-dead charcoal fires faintly visible in its center. Leena stepped into the space and seemed to unfold into a stronger, clearer image of herself. "It'll do famously, Miss Juniper. This is something I can work with. Water right nearby and all."

"Wonderful! I'll leave you to it, then." She made to turn away, but Leena spoke again.

"Up in the Great Tree, you're going to be planning things, projects and buildings and so on?"

"Yes . . ."

"I should like to be first on the list," Leena said, and the light of ownership was in her eyes. "A country runs on its stomach—that's what my ma always likes to say. So I think the kitchens should be seen to first. This fire pit will do to start, but we'll need a good cookstove before too much longer. And an oven by and by. Counter space . . . storage . . ."

"Certainly," said Juniper, grinning and backing away slowly. "That sounds capital. It's all on, er, the list. See you later, then?"

Leena didn't answer. She was bent over the ground, a sharp stick in hand, sketching menus in the dust.

Hours later, Juniper had tried a dozen different sitting positions on the hard wooden floor of the tree house, and was thoroughly fed up with each and every one. Not for the first time, she wished she'd thought to pack a few of the floor cushions from her lounge room back home. "Have we made *any* progress?" she asked hopefully.

Erick looked up from the parchment spread open in front

of him, blotting it carefully where the ink was still damp. "Basic schedule is done, and some of the job rotations. The ground map is nearly complete. We've designated the cooking area, bathing spots, privies, midden heap, and animal paddocks. We have enough sleeping rooms for everybody." He flashed a wide grin. "I'd say we're off to a smashing start."

"Good!" said Juniper, letting herself topple backward and shuffling her arms and legs outward, as though to make an invisible dust angel on the bare floor. "Because if I stay sitting here another minute longer—"

"Begging pardon?" came a voice below them, and Juniper jumped. She and Erick scrambled to the edge and peered over the side. Perched halfway up the branch staircase was Alta. Her hair was even more disheveled than usual, and grime streaked the bridge of her nose. Her general air told of a long afternoon productively spent. Her look, though, was one of puzzlement.

"What's the matter?" asked Juniper. "Come on up and tell us about it."

"I'd rather you come down and see for yourself," said Alta, adding quickly, "There's nothing wrong, mind. Only rather— peculiar."

Needing no further persuasion, Juniper and Erick followed Alta down the tree, across the clearing, and through the graveled expanse to the base of the cliff. They scaled the winding trail and reached the entry cave only slightly out of breath. The inside seemed larger now, lit up by an array of torches placed in recesses along the near walls. One empty wagon was parked on the far side of the room, and a second stood half unloaded to the side, gaping out sacks and boxes and assorted packages. But Alta led the way to the third cart, the one that had come with Cyril's gang. The tarp had been pulled off and several large containers removed, but for the most part, it was still fully loaded.

"What's the problem?" Juniper asked.

Alta hopped nimbly up to the driver's seat, from where she leaned over toward the cart bed. "Those nobles already came and took out everything that was theirs. That's what they said, anyhap—so I thought, what's all this stuff left, then? Well, look at what I found!" She shifted the containers and reached in with both hands. Heaving, she drew out a large sack, tossing it to the ground at Juniper's feet. It landed with a jangling metallic thud, a sound Juniper recognized immediately.

"What?" she whispered.

She peered inside. The bag was full of gold coins, gleaming reddish in the flickering firelight. Locking eyes with Alta, Juniper grabbed the nearest torch and scrambled up into the cart's bed, where she dug into the rest of the bundles. There was a large bag full of carefully packed jewelry, gemstones, and ornate family heirlooms that Juniper had never seen outside the Treasury. One very small, elaborately carved marble coffer held the Argentine Circlet, an ancient crown that had adorned the first kings of Torr, until it grew too old and fragile for everyday wearing and was saved for ceremonial events. Several flat, bulky packages contained well-wrapped oil paintings, some of which Juniper had seen hanging in the Great Hall just last week. One giant trunk was packed with centuries-old historical volumes, and another with cedarwood sawdust, in which nestled an array of fine porcelain figures, delicate sculptures, and ancient clay pots.

They were looking at the cultural heart of Torr.

Alongside those items were other, rougher cases, packed into the mystery cart like eggs in a well-filled nest. Oversized bags of flour, millet, and cornmeal. Bundles of vegetable seeds. Two barrels of dried beans and another of salt pork. Boxes of preserved fruits and several massive jugs of cordial. Bolts of cloth in thick wool and fine cotton weave, and piles of quilts and blankets and cushions.

"None of this has to do with Cyril and his gang?" she asked Alta.

"Definitely not. They made it clear they'd given their bags to a servant to load and expected a servant to deliver them direct to their rooms."

Juniper raised her eyebrows.

"I gave their bags the quick trip down," Alta confessed. "Tipped them right over the ledge into the valley. It's all gone now from below, so I suppose they managed to collect them. In any case, I'm sure they would have said so if anything in here belonged to them."

Deep in thought, Juniper jumped down from the wagon and brushed off her skirts. Valuables aside, the foodstuff largely consisted of things she'd already packed in the first wagons, just . . . a whole lot *more* of it. The rest were items she'd planned to stock up on when they made their trip back in a few weeks. After all, her father was going to send his all-is-well messenger any day now.

Wasn't he?

She opened her mouth to explore her worries further. Then she saw Erick's and Alta's faces—a complicated mix of confusion and alarm and . . . trust?

They thought she had a plan. She was in charge, after all.

Well. She had absolutely no idea what was going on. But one thing she *did* know: She didn't want to look too closely at the reason this wagon had been sent. She had a feeling she may not like what she found.

All she could do right now was take each day as it came. If there was more news to come, they would learn it soon enough.

Erick gave a low whistle. "So nobody knows what's in this cart but us."

"And that's the way it needs to stay," said Juniper. The others looked unsure, so she went on quickly. "All those treasures? The gold? Civilization's not so far off, and that's temptation if ever I saw it. There's a good reason why these things were sent with us. We need to stow everything away safely until it all becomes clear."

By that time, surely, any bad news would have turned to good.

In the end, all the valuables—gold and treasure and historical objects alike—were stashed in a tiny alcove that Tippy found off the main room. For of course the three of them hadn't been alone long before the little girl bounded into their midst, brimming with questions and crackling with mischief. Any number of passages led out of the giant entry cave, but the one they chose had a wide, low access point, and would appear impassable to someone of normal size. In reality, though, it overhung a stone lip; the bags and boxes were turned sideways and lowered easily through the hole, then dragged farther in around a bend. In this dry, dark spot, they would be safe for the foreseeable future.

"Now we certainly have enough food for our stay," said Alta, eyeing the mountains of provisions.

"We should leave these up in here, too," said Juniper. "Though in a more accessible spot, away from the treasure. It'll be our store-room, and we can bring what we need down in batches."

"Leena's all piled up in boxes and bundles as it is," said Tippy, with a wicked gleam in her eye. "I helped her stack some of them myself."

"Tippy!" said Alta, groaning. "Tell me you didn't——"

A distant thud rang from the valley below, followed by a rolling series of clangs and a stream of curses. Tippy shook her head sorrowfully. "Those cook pots! They do stack up *so* tipsy-like . . ."

The interruption brought a welcome laugh, and the four moved quickly to fill the newly christened storeroom with the extra provisions. But as the last of the bags and barrels were stored carefully away and they headed back out into the late-afternoon sunshine, Juniper couldn't help glancing back at the narrow opening to the treasure room. Why had her father—for it could only have been him—packed the cart with all those extras?

What was *really* going on back at the palace?

QUEEN's BASIN

Kitchen and
Dining Area

Housing
Caves

Great Tree

Beauty
Hut

Princess Juniper's Daily Schedule: Queen's Basin

7:00	Rise, Personal Grooming
7:30	Breakfast
8:30	Task Assignments, Answering Questions, General Organization
9:00	Perform Various Odious Tasks (whatever's left un-done from yesterday)
11:00	Roving to Ensure All Is Well / Help Out as Needed
12:30	Luncheon
2:00	Personal Leisure and Quiet Time
4:00	Roving to Ensure All Is Well / Help Out as Needed
5:00	Planning for Tomorrow (and long-term)
7:00	Dinner
8:00	Questions, Assorted Tasks That Need Doing
9:00	Evening Leisure
10:00	Pre-Bed Grooming
10:30	Worry about Papa and the Fate of Torr
11:00	Sleep

10

THE NEWLY MINTED CITIZENS TOOK TO Queen's Basin like water bugs to a pond. They spent the rest of their day unpacking, setting up their personal caves, and generally getting ready for the following day. The slower pace came as a relief after the long, hard trip.

Dinner that night was a festive affair. Paul and Filbert had dragged a bunch of flat boulders into a loose circle by the spot they'd designated as a dining area. Leena had finished with her cave in twenty minutes flat and spent the rest of the day in her brand-new kitchen, embracing her role with a speed and skill that surprised almost everyone. But Juniper had seen that look of ownership and knew it well: the look of someone finding that thing she adores, and taking it, and making it her own. And so as the sun sank behind the canyon walls, the fourteen settlers gathered to enjoy potatoes roasted in the coals, fresh sage griddle cakes topped with sweet butter and honey syrup, and a mix of shredded carrots, celeriac, and radish greens. Sitting on her flat

110

stone, holding her pewter dish and sipping every so often from her mug of mulled cider, Juniper thought this might be the best meal of her life. From the contented munching all around, it seemed the group agreed. Not even Jessamyn raised any complaints, though she and Cyril and Root sat on the circle's outer edge, angled away from the others, exchanging scornful glances from time to time.

Juniper put them completely out of her mind.

Before long, it was full night. Slipping the last bite of salad into her mouth, Juniper set down her plate and looked up. The sky was big and black and studded with bright hot stars, which, from here, so high up in the mountains, looked like clever cutouts in the shadowy curtain of night. Sitting outside in the dark was not something Juniper had done often; that "had no part in a princess's lifestyle," as her Comportment Master was so fond of saying. She wasn't too old to remember, though, how much her mother had loved the night. The Anju were a notoriously secretive tribe, and Queen Alaina had never told her young daughter many specifics about the customs or rituals or traditions of her own youth. She did, however, fill Juniper's head with lore and legend and fascinating tales of everyday life in the wild. Her mother's favorite bedtime stories were set under a blackened moon, with the starry sky draped like a thick, warm shawl across Juniper's sleepy shoulders.

Stars like these, she thought now. It was like slipping into one of those stories, and she could have hung in this moment for a good long time. Instead, she was jarred from her thoughts by a sudden flash. In the sky above the cliff where they had entered the Basin,

111

the white stars suddenly flared red, followed moments later by a low rumble.

"What was *that*?" Juniper asked, and others turned to follow the direction of her gaze.

"A storm?" suggested Oona timidly. She'd come late to dinner, and the sitting stone next to Juniper's had been the only one left free. Erick sat on Juniper's other side, but everyone else seemed to be keeping a slight distance, as though they didn't know quite how to act around someone who was ruler, peer, and fellow settler all at once. Juniper could well understand; she scarcely knew how to act around herself.

Now she gave Oona an encouraging shrug. "It could be. Strange, though, to see the sky turn that color."

"I've heard tell," came Cyril's haughty voice, "that the Monsians of the far west have dark and fearsome weapons, such as would make our swords and cannons no more dangerous than waving tree branches."

"What are you saying, Cyril?" Juniper said. She was not nearly as impressed by this information as Oona appeared to be; the girl was practically swooning in her seat.

Cyril smiled placidly. "I'm not saying anything. Only . . . I've never seen a storm flash *red* before."

His words sent a ripple of unease through the group, as kids turned to each other, muttering and questioning. Juniper herself felt shaken. She scanned the sky for long minutes, but it had resumed its peaceful look. The tendril of fear stayed, though, twining and twisting its way around the circle. Juniper realized that the mood of the group was in her hands. Pushing her own worries into a hard knot deep in her belly, she stood up and cleared her throat, waiting until the brabble stilled and all eyes were upon her.

"Speech!" Tippy called from her seat.

Juniper knew there was nothing she could do about the ominous sky. She had no way to know what was befalling her father or her country back home. All that was in her control was this moment, this place, these subjects. And that, she *could* handle.

"Here we are," she said. Then she squared her shoulders and put her hands on her hips, as she'd seen her father do when he addressed the court. It was a subtle change, but had the effect of pulling in the onlookers' attention, like sucking water through a straw.

She raised her voice: "Let's take a moment for reflection, shall we? Only think how far we've come to get here!" A murmur rose, then died out just as quickly. "Look," she went on, "none of us know what's going on back home. But we do know this: My father, our King Regis, has ruled Torr for the last twenty-nine years, and he's come through plenty of hard times. He's promised that he will send us word when all is safe, and that will certainly be well before our planned return trip in two weeks. Until then? We just need to sit tight. Keep busy. And enjoy our brand-new kingdom!"

The response was louder now, with calls of "Queen Juniper!" and "Queen's Basin!" and "Hurrah!"

She lifted her hands, and the noise stilled. The knot in her stomach hadn't loosened, but she managed to keep her voice steady and strong. "We've done some good settling in today, and that's something to be proud of. Roddy and Erick turned those diagrams of Master Dorfman's into the best pull-and-lift device I've ever seen. We've got a start to our dining area"—she waved a hand at their circle of boulders—"and there's Filbert and Paul to thank for that. And Leena for this great meal—and a good start on the kitchen, to boot. Toby got the horses settled for the night and found a temporary spot for the goats and chickens. That's pretty astonishing for just day one!"

She waited while the cheers and scattered applause died down. "But I don't need to tell you how much more we've got ahead of us. Erick and I were planning all afternoon, and here's what we figure: We need to get proper animal enclosures set up first thing and establish a method for their care. We need to start on the edible gardens. We need to get the kitchen in a good working order."

"And a cooling box, if we might," cut in Leena. "Perhaps an oven, in time."

Juniper nodded. "Remember, this trip is about doing the basics. Setting up our country. Building the framework, if you like. When we head back to Torr, it will be for a week or two as we recruit more settlers and gather additional provisions. So this time, right now, is for kicking things off right. We've all got to do our part—and that means cleaning up as we go, too. Dishes and general tidiness, all of that. We want a place we can be proud of! We'll get our kingdom running smooth as rivers before we head out, so we have something solid to bring our bigger group back to. A *true* summer kingdom all our own!"

There was a disdainful snort from the outer circle, and Juniper's only surprise was that it had taken so long to come.

"You have something to add, Cyril?"

He stretched out his long legs and drawled, "Only my most *respectful* observation: It would take a lunatic to imagine that this ragamuffin group could make any kind of a so-called country work." He paused. "Your Highness."

Cheeks burning, Juniper forced herself to take several slow breaths before she answered. "If that's your opinion, then there's nothing I can do to change it. But how Queen's Basin works depends upon each of us, doesn't it? If you want to be here, you'll have to do your part, like everyone else."

At this, Cyril rose slowly to his feet, seeming to tower over her even from across the circle. "Ah, but I *don't* want to be here. That's the point, isn't it? I wasn't given a choice, and I'm bolloxed if I'll lift a finger alongside these boot scrubbers and dough rollers."

"You may not want to be, but you *are* here!" Juniper snapped. "And you *have* to mind what I say. It's the rules!" Why was it that every confrontation with Cyril left her feeling more like a petty child than an actual ruler?

Cyril strode across the circle to stand in front of her, matching her stance exactly. He loomed over her by nearly a full head. "Oh, *do* I?" he sneered. "And what'll happen if I don't?"

Juniper met his gaze, but didn't trust herself to speak. What could she possibly say that would make any difference?

"I thought so," he said, then turned on his heel and strode off into the darkness. Root and Jessamyn stood, looked uncertainly around the circle, then scurried after him.

"All right, everyone," Juniper said wearily into the silence that followed. "Let's make quick work of this dinner mess and then we can all turn in."

That night, Juniper slept restlessly. She'd settled into her new bedchamber in the hollow of the Great Tree, returning from the disastrous dinner to find that Tippy had made her up a cozy-looking bed.

"Pinched the long seat cushions from the royal carriage, didn't I?" the little girl crowed proudly. She'd also scrounged up a smaller cushion to use as a pillow, and a pile of duvets fluffy enough to rival Juniper's bed back in the palace.

"This is magnificent," Juniper breathed. And then, loving that she could say this now without any fuss: "Thank you, Tippy."

The little girl beamed and turned to go.

"Where will you be sleeping?"

"Out there somewhere?" Tippy said vaguely.

Juniper smiled. "Do you have a bed set up, then?"

Tippy took a deep breath. "Got to be nearby in case you need me in the night. That's what Elly said afore I left. 'Be always nearby her Highness's side, but don't go making a nuisance of yourself,' that's what she said."

Something undercut her words, a nervous energy that Juniper couldn't quite figure out. Then Tippy's shoulders slumped. To Juniper's surprise, she scooted past the chamber's narrow opening, took hold of the knobby trunk with both hands, and started climbing straight up. "This way, then, Your Most Princessful," she called gloomily over her shoulder.

Mystified, Juniper found that the bark had been notched to make an easy-climbing ladder. She followed Tippy up the tree. Immediately above her own room was a second opening—small and round, like the burrow of a very large squirrel. A girl-sized squirrel, possibly. As Tippy disappeared inside, Juniper leaned in after her. The chamber had satiny wood walls with rippled edges. Wildflowers had been wedged and woven into cracks in the walls, and the very air was the woodsy perfume of summer. On one wall was tacked a delicate charcoal sketch of a girl's smiling face. Elly.

"I'd only thought . . ." said Tippy, and Juniper realized the girl was on the verge of tears. "I found this spot, and it just felt so . . . round? Like a nest, it were. But I shall move out directly." She reached over and began pulling down the flowers.

Juniper caught Tippy's arm in surprise. "Why would you move out? This is the most perfect little chamber I've ever seen. No bigger than a button, but if you're comfortable here, then it's yours."

Tippy's whole face opened up. "Truly, Your Royalty? You would give me my own room, in your own tree palace?" And the little girl dove forward, arms outstretched.

The timing was unfortunate. Perched as Juniper was on the rim of the opening, the tackle-hug knocked her backward and the two toppled, like a half-made sandwich, to the smooth wood floor below.

Tippy scrambled to her feet and poured out a stream of

apology, fanning the winded Juniper with her skirts and patting her cheeks with grubby hands.

"I'm quite all right," said Juniper, recovering herself. She stood. "Wait a moment, though—I have something to give you before you climb back up." Leaning into her chamber, she grabbed a thick quilt from her bed and thrust it at the astonished Tippy. "Take this. No, don't you dare hand it back. I've got plenty, and look what a warm night it is! We'll see what else we can get for you tomorrow, but you must use this in the meanwhile. I insist."

Tippy took the cover, shaking her head solemnly. "And after I pushed you clear out of a tree! You are the cat's royal whiskers, milady. I mean that most sincerely."

Juniper grinned. "Thank you, Tippy. And now we'd best head to bed. Shall I toss the quilt up after you? It's awfully bulky."

"No need," Tippy replied. She reached up and tied two corners around her throat so the quilt trailed behind her like a fluffy patterned cloak. Then she stood on tiptoes and kissed Juniper on the cheek. "Night, Your Princessness," she said, with a smile and a curtsey bob. "Hope that don't bother you none. Elly never let me go to bed without my good-night kiss."

Then she scurried up the trunk to her tree hole with the quilt sweeping behind her like a train, leaving Juniper to her snug bed, her warm cheek, and a curious lingering sense of belonging.

Still, once Juniper had changed into her nightclothes and curled up under her covers, sleep felt as far-off as the palace walls. What was her father doing right now? She thought of his final good-bye—was it really just two nights ago?—and the emotion that had

118

swept his face. He'd clearly been wondering if he was right in letting her leave, and Juniper had dashed off as quickly as she could, fearful to the last that he would change his mind and send them to the coast instead—or keep them home altogether. But he'd just hugged her tight and told her to take care and that he'd see her soon. She'd left with barely a backward thought.

Only now, in the dark, did she reach out and pull him close again in her mind, whispering to him all those things you can never tell a parent face-to-face. Even when you only have one of them left.

11

THE NEXT MORNING, JUNIPER ROSE BEFORE dawn. According to her brand-new schedule, she could sleep for several more hours, but her body seemed not to care and popped her wide-awake anyway. She dressed quietly, determined not to wake Tippy so early. She was pleased to have brought some dresses that had no eyehooks or heavy lacing up the back. Her trunks and traveling cases had been towed up the day before, thanks to a smaller pulley system Roddy had set up at the base of the tree. These had been stacked to form a makeshift wall in front of her little room, sectioning off some personal space from the rest of the wide-open platform.

Her toilette was quickly accomplished—clever Tippy must have slipped out late to fill her washbasin—and her teeth cleaned with a good chew of licorice root. She slid her bone-carved comb from its hidden pocket in her sleeve and ran it through her long curls. They probably still looked wispy as a summer field, but given the setting, that felt curiously all right.

Now she had two important things to tend to.

Lifting the lid on her clothing trunk, she slid aside the soft skirts and silky undergarments and hefted out the timepiece. It was nearly half her height, and she wished she'd thought to take it out before the trunks had been hoisted up the tree. But she had no patience for waiting now. Wrapping it tightly in one of her duvets, she tied the pulley rope securely around the bundle and lowered it to the springy ground below. Then she scrambled down to inspect her handiwork. Perfect!

It took some effort to get the timepiece to the spot she'd selected, midway between the cooking area and the soon-to-be dining hall, where the sitting stones were still gathered in a loose circle. There was a flat rock, waist height, and last night Leena had used it to lay out the serving dishes. But this would be better. Juniper heaved the timepiece up onto it, then stuffed some fallen dropsy leaves under the base so it didn't teeter.

The moment it was in place, Juniper felt better. Stronger. More organized. She lifted her outer skirt and polished the glass surface of the timepiece till her own satisfied reflection smiled back at her. She was responsible for the time and scheduling of an entire country, after all. She would need to be extra vigilant and make sure to keep everyone well on track. Reaching into her waist-pouch for her journal, she added an item to her list: *Assign someone to perform a check of the timepiece every second day at high noon.*

Her next task would take a little longer. She collected the bulky satchel containing the device her father called the Beacon, and set off up the cliffs that overlooked Torr. She really should have done this the moment they'd arrived, but she'd wanted to scout a bit and find the perfect spot. Plus, she'd preferred to wait till no one else was around. Her father's most prized form of communication was best kept to herself, or to a trusted few. The crag she'd finally settled on took longer to reach than she'd expected, what with lugging her heavy load up the rocky escarpment. Finally, though, she was there.

Juniper took a moment to collect her breath and stretch her arms, then she set to work. She gathered a mound of stones, stacking them to form a rough cave with the open side facing Torr. In there, she affixed the Beacon. Four separate whisper-thin strands of metal twined loosely around a blown-glass stem. This marvel of Gaulian craftsmanship responded to the buffet of wind with a thin stream of sound—so faint and high-pitched that Juniper could hear it only if she concentrated hard. The messenger would hear the Beacon loud and clear, though.

"A week at the most," her father had said.

All that was left now was to wait.

With her tasks accomplished and the sun barely scratching at the horizon, Juniper took the rest of the time until breakfast exploring her new kingdom more carefully. She walked along the riverbank with her parchment map in hand, stopping to sketch in the details of places she'd rushed by the day before. She discovered an old wooden bridge crossing the river not far downstream from the Great Tree. Could this, too, have been built by her father? Juniper felt a little thrill as she drew it in on the map.

Farther down the North Bank, she came to the fruit orchard.

The trees were young, most barely taller than she was, with skinny trunks and spindly branches. But, oh, they were leafy! And more than that: They were bursting with fruit. With little effort, she identified a handful of apricot trees, two especially fruitful fig trees, and a whole grove of sugar chestnuts. There were bushes, too: mulberries and redcurrants and—her absolute favorite—prickly-leafed carmines. Her mouth watering in anticipation, Juniper tugged up her kirtle and gathered handfuls of the large, pale berries.

By the time she turned to head back, tottering a little with her awkward load, she could hear a hum of conversation coming from the dining area. She smiled as she hurried across the bridge. What would Palace Juniper have thought of an entire morning's unscheduled, unsupervised, largely unproductive adventure? Juniper of Queen's Basin, on the other hand, felt rather proud of her early-morning jaunt.

"Good morning, everybody!" she called as she approached the yawning circle. Cyril and Root were nowhere in sight, and Juniper wasn't sure if she felt irritated or relieved. Equal parts of both, perhaps. Jessamyn *was* there, and visibly fuming.

Juniper poured her carmine berries into a clay pot and plopped it on the low center table stone. "Anybody hungry?"

Leena's eyes lit up and she rushed off toward the kitchen. The others stuttered to life, slowly at first, then with more gusto as the delicious berries began to work their magic.

"So what's that new thingummy over there?" Tippy chirped between mouthfuls.

Juniper beamed. "Oh, that's the timepiece! Surely you've seen

123

some of these up around the palace? They're *such* a wonder, and ever so simple to read! By these lines and markers, you can tell the time nearly to the minute." The fine, silvery sand trickling through the maze of stops and levers behind the glass seemed to mesmerize the watchers. Or maybe they were still just half asleep.

"It's almost like magic, innit?" Tippy said at last.

"Almost," Juniper replied. "But far more useful. This is how we'll know when to come for meals, and when to rise, and all the other elements of our daily schedule." She looked eagerly around the circle, but for some reason, the others didn't seem nearly as thrilled by the concept as she was. They would come to see its value, though, in time.

The silence was broken by Leena's call that the rest of the food was ready. And it was astonishing how much rewarmed griddle cakes and steaming mugs of carob-flavored goat's milk (Toby had been up early at the milking) could do to perk up a mood. As the sun slid hot fingers across their backs, soothing tired muscles in a warm sweep of relaxation, Juniper put down her plate and savored the satisfaction of a meal well eaten before finally turning to call the group back to attention.

"I've got two things to say," she said, thinking how much easier it was to stay in charge without Cyril's bulldog scowl on the fringe of her circle. "First, we shall divide into groups to start on our key tasks. Oh—don't forget to take your dishes with you when you go. There's a washing setup in place by the riverbank—couldn't be easier." She pulled the journal out of her waist-pouch and opened it to the right page. "Now, when I call your name, go on over and make up your groups, all right? So, Toby, you're on animal enclosures and upkeep, with Oona and Tippy. Roddy and Filbert, kitchen construction. You can talk with Leena about what exactly she needs. She'll be there to help you out, too, when she's not cooking."

"I've been thinking about the cold box," Leena cut in. "I think I can figure a way to work it in this spot where the stream runs especially deep . . ." She hesitated. "If Your Highness'll grant me permission?"

Juniper waved a hand. She liked the way Leena felt free to speak up with suggestions. The silent movement of some others around the circle, lacking any visible expression, left her vaguely worried. Were they unhappy with their tasks? Did they feel put-upon or overworked? She wondered how her father dealt with these sorts of issues. Though maybe it didn't matter so much if you were an actual ruler and not just playacting at a summer kingdom.

Leena had gathered up her team and was shuffling them toward the riverbank, so Juniper hastily went on. "Paul and Oona, you'll get the garden started." There was an awkward silence. She looked up. "What? Is there a problem?"

Oona looked like a bug caught under a water tumbler. She was standing next to Tippy, who nudged her hard and stretched up to whisper in her ear.

"Come on, then!" Juniper burst out. "I can't organize things if you won't *talk* to me!"

"It's only," Oona said miserably, her face scarlet, "only that you put me first in the animal group and again now in the gardens. I don't know which one to do."

Juniper could have laughed out loud. That was all? She looked down at her list and saw that, yes, she'd duplicated Oona's name on her job assignments.

"Look," she said, addressing them all, "I'm not some kind of iron-fisted ruler. We've got to pull together to make this country work, to make it our own."

"Aren't we required to do as you say, then?" asked Jessamyn, with a saucy tilt to her chin.

"Well, yes, you are, actually. But I'm not . . ." She paused—should she really say this?—then barreled recklessly on. "I'm not always going to be right. That's a fact. So you should always come to me if you've got questions or aren't sure about something I said. There's got to be leadership; it's like that anywhere. But it's going to take us truly working together for this to be a success. And that's what we're here for, after all!"

After that, the rest of the task assignments went smoothly. Oona went with Paul to the gardens. Sussi volunteered to look into the water situation and set up some boundaries for the official boys' and girls' privies and make a bathing rotation list. Alta grudgingly admitted that she could build a pretty decent oven, given the time and ample supply of that heat-conducting rock that was so abundant in these parts. And nobody was dodging dish duty, which Juniper counted as a particular win.

"The planting team's on the small side, and we want to get the seedlings into the ground as quick as possible," Juniper went on, consulting her notes. "So, Jessamyn, you can join Paul's team." She'd had Cyril, Root, and Jessamyn in their own group, but hunting the noble boys down for work wasn't something she had the stomach for at the moment. Easier to just put Jessamyn on an existing task.

But Jessamyn set her plate down next to her rock and stood up, smoothing her rumpled skirts. "No, I shouldn't think so. I'd planned to take in some sun and finish reading the new *Flower Bard Epic* today. You all can carry on without me, I'm sure."

Juniper felt heat rush to her face. She jumped to her feet and cut Jessamyn right off. "Oh, no you don't! You're part of this team—you've got to be." In desperation, she nearly stomped her foot. "You're on the list! You've *got* to do it!"

"Do I?" Jessamyn asked. "I don't see Cyril or Root working, so why should I? My papa promised me I might do as I pleased this summer, and it pleases me to spend my time in the pursuit of leisure." She raised her chin defiantly. "If you want to know, I should much rather be back at home in my own boudoir, but so long as I have to be here, I certainly will not be digging around in the dirt like some common clod!" Eyes flashing and skirts swinging, Jessamyn shoved her pewter dish aside with her foot and swept off in the direction of the caves.

The painful silence ground on Juniper's nerves like broken glass.

Finally, Tippy spoke up. "What was the second thingum?"

Juniper looked at her blankly.

"Way back at the start of our meal. You said you had *two* things to tell us. What were the second?"

"Ah, yes!" Juniper grabbed eagerly at the change of subject. "About our moving-in party. It's to be a small one, mind—this shan't be our grand ball, not yet—but we'll have a little after-dinner celebration. Two nights from now, I thought. We'll be more settled in by then, and ready to celebrate our brand-new country. We can gather in the Great Tree, get dressed up, and bring out our sweetest of sweetmeats. And I shall introduce you all to the glory that is the Musicker!"

This was met with general enthusiasm, which reassured Juniper somewhat. Still, she couldn't help but notice how more than one head swiveled off to stare in the direction Jessamyn had gone. And at her dirty dish, sitting defiantly on the edge of the circle.

Juniper stewed over the Jessamyn problem all day, and on into the next. While she took her turn digging privy pits, while she lugged stones for the oven, while she squatted by the stream washing her dish at the end of each meal. By the following night, as she and Erick readied the Great Tree for that night's festivities, her mind was a tangle of uncertainty and discomfort.

"What should I have done?" she asked, for probably the tenth time. "I should have been firm with Jessamyn, I know I should have. Cyril and Root, too—they just waft in for meals and don't lift a finger. It's not right, and everyone knows it! I keep opening my mouth to tell them 'no work, no food.' But I can't quite get it out."

How to stand up to Cyril, that was the problem. Long years of adopting a hide-and-avoid strategy were proving very hard to break. Truthfully, he intimidated her far more than she dared confess.

Erick smiled in sympathy.

"It's ever so much harder to be bold on the second step than the first, isn't it? I should have made Jessamyn do the gardens that first day, should have gone to Cyril and that Root's cave with their work tasks and seen to it that they did them. Right from the start."

"And how would you have enforced it?" Erick asked, tacking a colorful twist of ribbon onto the center base of the tree. "It's not like you could drag them bodily to the fields and sit on them until they began working."

"Oh, but think how satisfying that would have felt!" Juniper giggled, then got serious again. "I didn't imagine I should have so hard a time wrestling with these laggards. That's not the way I pictured my grand summer kingdom."

Erick shrugged. "Aren't all the best things worth fighting for, though?"

"I don't suppose I've done much of that yet, have I? Fighting?"

With a grin, Erick quipped, "A house solidly built is its own defense, but a weak foundation invites trouble."

"Why, Erick Dufrayne, how wise you are!" she said, jabbing him in the ribs. "Quotations and everything. I knew I made the right choice for my chief adviser."

Erick's cheeks colored. "Um . . . it's just something I once—"

"Read in a book. I know." Juniper grinned. "You're right, though. That is the important thing, book or not. Now come over here and help me get this Musicker going."

"I've been wondering how that works. Let me guess—it's got a chamber inside with dozens of tiny sackbut players and a harpsichord or two? Ready to play on demand?"

"Aren't you smart," she scoffed. "You'll see for yourself once we get it going."

The long, squat Musicker rested on a low table stand that Roddy had built that morning. A sturdy hand crank jutted out of its side. "Turn that," she instructed, then lifted the polished wood top and peered in at the maze of gleaming gears and knobs and latches and buttons. As Erick churned, the mechanisms ground to life and began to glide along under their own power, moving with a low, friendly purr.

"Don't ask me how it all works, for I couldn't say," she said. "But I do know this. Every bit of this device is set up with music in mind. There's any number of gongs and bells and musicky whiz-bits tucked inside, and when you slide this lever . . . you see?" As she spoke, a gentle stream of sound began to rise from the box. It sounded like harp music—tinny and boxed, for certain, but clear and recognizable nonetheless. She moved the lever to the right and the music sped up, with what sounded like strings weaving in to the rest. Still farther, and some trumpets joined in. Now she felt like lifting her heels and dancing.

"Does it play actual songs?" Erick asked, still turning the crank.

"I don't think so. The way it was explained to Papa is that the musical components are all there, and a certain mechanical intelligence, if you will, throws the sounds together in a variety of pleasing combinations. So you choose your speed and instrumentation, and the device does the rest. I suppose you'd never get the same music twice, if it works as it should." Juniper considered Erick's pumping arm. "Also, it doesn't need to be cranked incessantly. Once it's started up with gusto, it will run for some long minutes. When the energy begins to flag, we take another turn at it."

The music was coming loud and strong now, filling the tree house. Before she could fully settle into it, however, a voice broke into her thoughts.

"Is this the right time, Your . . . Juniper? For the party?" Sussi had cleared the landing, and now stood with the air of a crawfish dropped into the wrong pot.

"Oh, certainly! You're right on time. At least . . . I think you are. The timepiece is out in the dining area, I'm afraid." She grinned. "But that's as may be. We are ready for the party. Only . . . didn't you want to get dressed up?"

Sussi bumped a step forward as Leena came up behind her. The two girls exchanged an awkward glance. Sussi smoothed a thin hand across her crumpled skirts. "I *have* worn my best," she whispered.

Leena lifted her chin in quiet confidence. "We don't have anything better, miss," she said. "These are our finest, and we had to wear them for our travel as well."

Juniper's cheeks flamed. Suddenly, she was sharply conscious of her fresh-curled hair, her powdered cheeks, the crimson watered-silk skirt swishing above her matching calfskin slippers. "Of course," she murmured. "I'm dreadfully sorry."

The girls shifted uncomfortably back toward the staircase. "Maybe we should——" Sussi began.

Juniper dashed over and grabbed each one by a hand. "I've been a dunce," she said, tugging them to the center of the floor. "I don't know what I was thinking. Here." With that, she tugged from her collar a hammered-silver brooch in the shape of a flying bird, clipping it onto Leena's fusty brown dress. Then she undid her creamy silk sash and tied it around Sussi's waist in a giant bow. "A little better?"

The girls grinned.

"Now, you *must* taste these cheese straws, for without a doubt, I have not ever had the like!"

"And the music, miss," said Sussi. "It's——"

"It's some form of deviltry, that's what it is," came a harsh voice, crashing through the room like a rock hammer.

Juniper spun around.

Cyril's head was just breaching the edge of the boards as he pulled himself up to the main landing. A loud muttering behind him said that Root was close on his heels. Of course he was.

"What are *you* doing up here?" Juniper asked, squeezing her hands into fists, pushing back the mild panic that always came with Cyril's arrival.

"We're holding a party, aren't we?" Cyril strode around the platform. "Hmmm, a rather tawdry décor you've started out with. Wax candles—unscented, I see. What are these streamers made from? And the floor throws . . . well!"

That was the last straw. March in here and insult her mother's throw rugs, would he? Reaching deep inside, Juniper scraped together her courage. "They're genuine chamois pelts, if you must know. But what *I'm* really wondering is what *you* are doing here. *We* are having a small party, celebrating a half week's work well done, and I don't remember inviting you. In fact, this is the first time I've seen you all day!" Once she finally took the plunge, standing up to Cyril felt surprisingly *good*. The tree house was pindrop-quiet. Root and Jessamyn stood on either side of Cyril, and Oona was climbing up to the landing, with Toby close behind.

Erick was right. Some things *were* worth fighting for. And this kingdom, *her* kingdom, topped that list.

Juniper turned to the Musicker and pulled the volume bar all the way down. Those moments were all she needed to steady her voice and make it smooth and hard. "Cyril and Root. I have not seen either of you each morning when I hand out work assignments, though you're quick enough to collect your food at meals. And, Jessamyn . . . you still refuse to take part in any tasks, though you well know my disapproval." Oh, they knew, all right! Their smirks were pure malicious glee. "Well. I'll be hobbled if I'm letting you come to our party and sit in our tree house and listen to our music—celebrating our settlement, our *country*—while you refuse to take part in the work needed to make that country run."

She raised her chin and looked Cyril right in the eye. "You can't have it both ways. You're either part of our group—and that means doing your share of the work, too—or else you're not. And if not, then you're not welcome here." She took a deep breath.

"Not for our parties, and not for our meals, either. You work with us, you share our food. Otherwise you can fend for yourselves."

The landing was full now, as the last of the kids had arrived for the evening's event. Heads swiveled between Cyril and Juniper, like spectators at a summer's butterfight.

"So, what's it going to be?" Juniper challenged.

Cyril gave a careless shrug. He stepped forward, as though to move past Juniper toward the platter of crispy cheese sticks. But she sidestepped to stay right in his way.

"*What* is it going to be?"

He stared her full in the face, and she forced herself not to flinch. At last he lowered his eyes, barked out a laugh, and kicked at a bauble that had fallen from the branch above. The delicate object hit the trunk with a dull crack, but Juniper didn't take her eyes from his.

"Come on, everybody," Cyril spat. "We can find better entertainment elsewhere."

He spun on his heel and launched himself over the side of the platform. Root followed and, after a moment's hesitation, Jessamyn did, too. Oona took a half step after Cyril, then quickly turned back to the main group. No one else moved.

Juniper forced a smile. Had she done the right thing, making Cyril choose like that? Well, hunger was bound to bring him back to the group before long.

"That certainly was awkward," she said into the bone-still room. All she wanted right now was to forget that rabble-rouser even existed. "I think we've had quite enough unpleasantness for one evening. You've all worked hard, and we've seen some amazing progress."

She looked around the circle, the positive words buoying her flagging spirits. "So let's put all that aside, shall we? You've earned your time off. We needn't give those party wreckers another thought."

She spun around and pulled the Musicker's volume back up, then slid the lever right to its topmost beat. Stringed music—fast, rhythmic, irresistible—pulsed out of the tiny sound holes. Juniper's feet began tapping of their own accord. "Who loves to dance?" she called out, fluffing her skirts.

Then the drumbeat began, and the night erupted in a swirl of stamping feet and sweaty cheeks and rowdy, uproarious laughter.

Just one evening of peace, that was all she wanted. Tomorrow she'd think it all through carefully, figure out what to do next. Tomorrow she'd worry about the threat to her fledgling kingdom.

It was a threat she knew would keep.

12

IT SOUNDED LIKE PART OF THE MUSIC, AT FIRST: a high-pitched noise undercutting the melodic tones of the Musicker. Tippy was the first to notice something was wrong. Juniper caught her looking anxiously from side to side, and once she turned her own attention from the swishing skirts and stomping feet, Juniper heard it, too. Pushing through the dancing bodies, Juniper flung herself on the Musicker and snapped it off.

All gazes swung in her direction, and for a moment, the silence was a blanket, thick and damp. Then the sound came again. It was a scream, loud and terrified, coming from somewhere outside the tree house and seeming to reverberate everywhere at once.

"That's Jessamyn!" Erick said. He dashed for the staircase, with Alta almost treading on his fingers in her haste to follow.

"You stay up here," Juniper said when Tippy moved to come along, too. She raised her voice. "All of you stay in the tree house—we'll go find out what's going on and be right back. I repeat, nobody leave here until we return!" The little speech cost

136

her precious seconds, and by the time she reached the base of the tree, Alta and Erick had vanished into the darkness ahead. From down here, though, the shrieks were more easily distinguishable, and Juniper had no trouble following in their direction.

She came upon Erick and Alta moments later, by the newly built animal pens, which lay in a deep smother of darkness. The two were bent over a crumpled shape that resolved itself into a quivering Jessamyn.

"She seems unharmed," Erick said, pulling Juniper aside while Alta comforted the frantic girl. "But she's in a true state of panic. We haven't gotten her to tell us anything at all."

They quickly decided that the best thing was to get Jessamyn back to her room. Despite the darkness, the path wasn't hard to find, for the stones that soaked up the sun's heat by day also glowed faintly in the moonlight. The glimmer brightened as they neared the cliff, and by the time they hit hard stone and began their uphill climb, Juniper could make out the others' expressions: Erick's was uncertain; Alta's was resolute; Jessamyn's was blank with shock. She'd stopped wailing, at least, and didn't seem to have any trouble walking.

By the time they reached Jessamyn's cave and had bundled her inside, the girl's supercilious look was back, and she seemed quite herself again. An uncomfortable suspicion rose in Juniper's mind. She sat next to where Jessamyn reclined on her cushioned bed with a hand flung across her brow.

Juniper kept her voice neutral. "Jessamyn, how are you feeling? Can you tell us what happened?"

"Oh, I cannot speak of it!" Jessamyn moaned. She started to

hiccup, and Juniper grabbed her free hand and patted it soothingly. Erick and Alta hovered silently near the entryway.

"You're safe now. And unharmed, I think?"

Hesitantly, Jessamyn nodded.

"Good. But we really do need to know what happened. And if there is any . . . you know, danger still out there. For the rest of us." Jessamyn looked entirely unmoved, so Juniper tried again. "Or to *you,* of course. We want to make sure it doesn't happen again. Whatever it was."

Jessamyn sat up suddenly, eyes wild. Juniper immediately regretted her suspicions; no one could playact a terror this raw. "The truth is . . . I don't know what happened." The girl shuddered, and clasped her arms as though seeking warmth or comfort. "I was in here trying to sleep, not that it was possible with so much racket from your little *party* up there."

Juniper made comforting noises, waiting until Jessamyn went on.

"Well, there was no way I could sleep, so finally I rose and decided to take a short walk around. Get some air."

Juniper noticed that Jessamyn was wearing a fine ruffled gown, tight of bodice and high of collar, and delicate heeled slippers. Had Jessamyn been on her way back to the party, perhaps hoping to join the group and move away from her troublemaking friends?

"As I made my way down the trail, just to take the air, you understand, no other purpose"—her eyes dared Juniper to contradict her—"all of a sudden, I heard . . . I saw . . ." She shuddered violently.

"What?" Juniper pressed, keeping her voice gentle.

But Jessamyn shook her head. "I saw angry orange lights, flashing off and on. I could not see clearly in the darkness, but there were bodies—giant, fearsome figures skulking about, riding upon monstrous, bulky-looking beasts. They made no noise, but crept about with evil intent." She stopped, and after a minute, Juniper saw she wasn't going to say any more.

"Then what?" she asked.

"Then *nothing*. That was all. By this time I was near to the fences, where you found me, and the shapes were shadows, and they began to gather right upon me! I screamed, and I suppose I frightened them away, but I myself knew nothing else until I felt hands shaking me." She tossed Erick and Alta a disdainful nod. "Those two gave me such a fright, I am scarcely recovered."

Juniper frowned at her. "Well, you gave us something of a fright, too! That's really all this is about? You saw bulky shadowed shapes *near the animal pens*? Have you considered that perhaps it was our own goats and horses you saw roaming about, casting warped shadows in the moonlight?"

"Casting shadows upon what, the light beaming forth from their demonic eye sockets?" Jessamyn was fully recovered now, hands balled into fists and leaning in toward Juniper. "I. Know. What I saw! There were evil lights, and forms that were man-shaped, only larger and more vile. You can believe me or not, as you please. But now I wish to be left alone. At least that infernal racket has ceased. You all may go."

Juniper stood up, looking uncertainly at Jessamyn, who lay

back down and turned her face to the wall. "Look," she said. "I didn't mean to doubt you. I'm sure you saw . . . *something* out there."

"Pull the curtain fully over the door on your way out," Jessamyn retorted coldly, and Juniper had no choice but to retreat. She didn't bother drawing the curtain; shock or not, there was only so much attitude she could handle.

"So what do you think of that story?" Alta asked as they trudged back toward the Great Tree. "Do you believe her?"

"I've no idea what to believe," Juniper said wearily.

The next morning, Juniper and Toby, along with a few other early risers, trekked over to inspect the animal enclosures. To one side was the goats' pen, surrounded by a fence made of long, thin tree branches woven with thick knotted rope. Near the back of the enclosure, the goats huddled in a furry mass. Opposite them, the gaggle of chickens squawked around the overturned wagon bed that was now their home. The nearby horses' enclosure had higher bars and a sturdier fence.

Or . . . it *used* to.

Yesterday, the brand-new fence had stood upright; today it bulged grotesquely inward, limp branches teetering in loose soil. The ground inside the horses' enclosure was fully torn up and trampled. Inside, five horses nervously pawed the ground, eyes darting from side to side.

Five horses, where there should have been fourteen.

"What's happened?" Juniper asked. "Where have they gone?"

Toby just shook his head. "I've had a quick scout all around—they're nowhere nearby. The prints lead out from here and get lost on the hard rock trails."

"It's as though the fence was sat on by something really big," said Tippy, "what stretched it out beyond repair. That's just not nice at all."

Toby vaulted the fence, a bag of feed in hand, heading for the remaining horses. Juniper was gratified to realize that Thunderstar was one of those still in the paddock.

"What'll we do without horses?" came Sussi's thin wail from among the group. She stood close to her older sister, with Oona's arm wrapped protectively around her. Still, the younger girl's voice trembled as she spoke. "We're trapped here in the mountains, then, aren't we? With no horses to ride back?"

"We're no such thing," Alta said firmly.

Juniper quickly turned to face the anxious onlookers, whose number had doubled in the last few minutes. "Alta's right. We're going to track these horses and do our best to get them back. But don't forget the wagons up in the cave—we can easily pack everyone into those for our trip back, if needed. There's no cause for alarm."

Erick was squatting a few paces up, near the broken fence. "Look at this," he said.

"Everyone else, stay back," Juniper called. She didn't want to lose the chance—however slim—of finding identifiable tracks. "Give us a few minutes to inspect things."

Alta got busy yelling the watchers out of the way, while Tippy darted here and there with featherlight tread, making a great show of her own pint-sized investigation. All the hoofprints in and around the paddock crisscrossed over one another so that it was hard to pull anything else from the scene.

"This here," said Erick, pointing to a slight rise just above the enclosure, away from the muddle of hoofprints, "is where we found Her Sniffyness." He flushed and quickly corrected himself. "That is, Lady Jessamyn. See how the ground is all trampled by our feet? But down here . . . look."

Juniper leaned in. Much of the ground in this part of the paddock was dry and graveled and showed no clear marks. But right at the enclosure's edge, the ground was softer. Quite separate from the hoofprints, she could clearly see some very distinct, oddly large prints.

"Are those—they are hoofprints, aren't they?"

Erick hesitated. "There was this—"

"Let me guess," said Juniper. "A book you have on the reading of prints?"

"What? How did you know that?" Erick looked so startled that, despite the tension of the moment, Juniper burst out laughing.

"Is there anything you *haven't* read a book on, Erick Dufrayne?"

Erick ducked his head. "I suppose not. This volume is very well regarded, though. Said to include every animal in the near continents."

Juniper frowned. "And these prints?"

"Nothing in there even comes close."

The prints were large—nearly twice the size of the horses'

hooves. The precise shape was hard to make out in the dry, trampled earth. But Erick was right: These could have been made by no ordinary beast. "What do you think, then?"

"Truthfully?" Erick shook his head. "I've not the faintest idea. The shape's like no animal I've ever seen. They seem almost . . . *unreal* somehow."

"Monsters!" cried Tippy with glee. "Horse-thieving monsters! Riding whatever monsters ride. Fire-breathing dracos? Truly this is a glorious day!"

"Hush, you!" snapped Alta, having successfully corralled the onlookers and now pushing in to see for herself. " 'Tis nothing of the sort."

"Of course not," Juniper said, getting ahold of herself. "There's no such thing as monsters. We'll find a reasonable explanation to this once we track them down, you'll see." Still, a small shudder ran down her back.

They set to work scouting far and wide. But as Toby had said, the tracks were quickly lost in the dry, packed-stone trails of the South Bank cliff side, and did not reemerge. Whoever—or *what*ever—had taken the horses had made a clean getaway.

So it was a quiet, skittish group that gathered around the sitting stones for the morning meal. The arrival of Cyril and Root did little to ease the tension, and Juniper looked up in dismay at seeing them. Had they come to join the team or to challenge her further? Well, their jaunty walks, their smug and unruffled expressions made the answer to that pretty clear.

Another thought sprang to her mind. Juniper narrowed her

eyes. "Where were you two last night?" Even as she said the words, though, the unspoken accusation did not ring true. It was all too easy to believe these two were behind the disturbance—with Jessamyn as co-conspirator, even. But those odd prints told a different story. And what could Cyril want with nine horses? Where would he put them?

Juniper didn't believe in monsters; there had to be a logical explanation. But one thing she knew for sure: Those hoofprints had not been made by any creature known in the land of Torr.

Cyril didn't seem to notice her stormy expression. "That's a jolly question," he said, and she was surprised to see a spark of good humor on his face. "For after we were so rudely ejected from the festivities last evening, Root and I set off to do some adventuring of our own. Isn't that right, Root?"

"Right it is," Root agreed, and Juniper wondered idly if she'd ever heard him talk before. He was so good at being Cyril's silent partner that she barely thought of him as his own person.

Cyril waved grandly toward the group. "So much progress has been made in construction and establishment. I propose—"

"Wait!" Juniper cut him off. "I meant what I said last night. Are you here to join in the work today? You're not welcome to our meals otherwise."

Cyril just smiled more broadly. "As I began to say—everyone has been working *so* hard. And Root and I have discovered the most delicious new spot." He turned to face the group. "What would you all think of taking a day of rest and leisure?"

Juniper opened her mouth to disagree. For one thing, Cyril

was totally sidestepping the issue of helping with the work. For another, they hadn't even been here a week! *Get work done, then have fun.* That's the way things should be. A little evening party was one thing, like they'd had last night, but a *whole* day off? And what about searching for the stolen horses? Still, she couldn't miss how the worried faces around her lit up at Cyril's words, how drooping shoulders straightened, a general tension easing out of the air. *I should have noticed how tired everyone was,* she thought. And based on their investigation so far, there didn't seem to be much they could do about the horse thieves.

She stood and raised her voice. "A most excellent *suggestion,*" she said, "and one that I think . . ." She hesitated as all eyes turned toward her, as all paused midword, midbreath—and she took a single moment to marvel at this, the capturing of a group's attention, holding them in the palm of her hand and turning them this way or that according to the need. She saw Cyril's brows draw in, his face darken. He opened his mouth, and she flung her arms wide. "Let us do it! A day of rest and adventure. Have we not earned it? We shall follow Cyril and Root to explore their new spot—and then tomorrow we'll work *twice* as hard as ever. What do you say?"

The chorus of cheers and applause and stomping feet was reward enough, as the group erupted in a gabble of delighted plans and projections.

"It is a swimming hole," Cyril called over the ruckus, and it was clear they heard him, for they nodded and buzzed the louder. But he'd lost his hold. They were fully Juniper's now, and as she turned on her heel, the cool smile she shot him said all that needed saying.

Juniper swept off to locate her bathing gear.

They hiked downriver and crossed at the rickety wooden bridge—passing over one at a time, just to be safe. Filbert looked especially hesitant, and Juniper held her breath as he took his turn. The old boards creaked under his bulk, but the base held firm, with barely a wobble as he stepped gingerly across. In a few minutes, they were all safely on the North Bank.

"So much grass everywhere! This would have made a grand pasture for the horses," Toby said to Sussi as they walked along just ahead of Juniper.

"Can't it still, for those that are left?" Sussi asked.

"Of course." Toby sighed, then perked up. "The goats will love it, too—so thick and green, so much room to run!"

"Look there," Sussi said, pointing. "Wild onions!" Juniper smiled at how alike the siblings looked, walking side by side in the dappled morning light. The rest of the group moved along in twos and threes, with Cyril and Root in the lead, and Oona hanging just behind the noble boys. Jessamyn stamped along somewhere to the rear, fully recovered from the night before but apparently trying to reach her destination without muddying her silk slippers. *Good luck with that,* Juniper thought, while avoiding a look at her own grime-caked sandals.

"Leaping lollapalooza! It's all a-showering over here!" shrieked Tippy, gadding around on the edge of the stream. She was right.

Juniper had wondered how the land north of the river could be so green and lush, in contrast with the South Bank's dry, cracked soil. But now she could see the fine spray billowing up from the river's edge to coat the pasture. The wind here must blow in one direction only.

"Natural wonders," she said. "I can scarcely imagine how much more there is to discover in this wild, unknown land!"

"We should launch a proper scouting expedition," said Alta. "Learn everything about this place and what it has to offer for our country's needs."

"That is an excellent idea!" Juniper exclaimed. "First thing to-morrow, will you head that up? We can make it a regular part of our daily tasks. Take one or two others along."

"I'll go! We shall be on the lookout for those dracos, I swear," Tippy offered, cartwheeling her way across the grass.

Juniper's hand brushed her waist-pouch, where parchment rustled. "Erick and I have been working on a map, but there's ever so much detail still to be sketched in as we figure out the full scope of the Basin. We need to prioritize our tasks and set goals. Then we can run things as efficiently as possible." All of this and swimming days, too, she thought, her heart sinking a little. Was this how a country worked? Truly?

Alta nodded. "First light tomorrow, then. My, but this day is glorious! Do you know what I would be doing if I were back home?"

Juniper shook her head.

"I should be up to my arms in pig's grease, or flour, or coal from shoveling out the great ovens. I can't say that I miss it."

"And I should have been starting out on yet another ghastly groundsweep," Paul said with a shudder, "all the while wishing from my heart that I might spend my entire day out in the green."

"About this time?" Juniper wondered what time it even *was,* and realized with a start that she'd hardly glanced at the timepiece all day. "I should likely be engaged in a vigorous outdoor constitutional, before being packed back to the classroom for another tedious session of geometric equations, or political case studies, or analysis of the treatise of law as it applies to continental invasion across the last six centuries."

She looked sidelong at Alta and Paul, saw the laughter hiding in their eyes, laughter they weren't quite sure should come out. Juniper giggled, and the other two dissolved together, all of them laughing until they gasped, with the sun beating down on their heads, sending out a warmth that was far more than skin deep.

13

FROM THE BRIDGE, THE GROUP SKIRTED THE
newly planted vegetable gardens and cut across the grassy field to
the far side of the valley, heading straight for the crags on the other
side. By the time they reached the base of the cliff, Juniper was
walking alongside Cyril. Root and Oona followed close behind.

"So you stayed out here last night?" Juniper asked. She hadn't
missed how far-off this place was, nor the visibly single set of
tracks they'd seen going and coming—normal-sized feet only, no
strange, erratic hooves. The more she thought about it, the less
possible it seemed for Cyril to have been involved in last night's
horse debacle.

"We set off as soon as we were dismissed," he said with a
sneer, "and only returned this morning."

"That's very generous of you to want to share your discovery
so quickly with the group."

"Why, everything is better shared, is it not?" he said slyly,
and Tippy, popping up on his other side, clapped her hands in

approval. But Juniper frowned. She'd never known Cyril not to have some backhanded motive at work, if she just waited long enough for it to appear.

The cliff they were scaling did not wind gently upward like the one on the South Bank. This was a straight, hard climb. Yet, rugged as it was, there was definitely a rough path leading them up the slope. At some time in the past, this route had seen a good deal of foot travel.

At last they crested a rocky lip and, quite suddenly, the river was before them once again. They must have gotten turned around in their climbing, or the water took some fancy turns, for Juniper had thought they'd left it far behind. But they were now on a ledge that stretched balcony-like over a breathtaking expanse of deepest blue. The rock was carpeted in delicate green moss, and Leena called out to Filbert and Roddy to set down the heavy picnic hampers they had been carrying. The boys did so, then joined the crowd clustering around Cyril as he puffed out his chest and gave the tour.

"Down the way here is a sort of rocky stair," he said. "This vantage point is good for observing, but just below is a shallow chamber of a use for changing garments. And there is a ledge I rather fancy for diving into the pool below."

There was a shocked gasp at the very idea.

"Why not?" he challenged. "That is the deepest part of the pool. The water is clear, and the sun is hot as a fiery draco's den. Who wants to go in?"

"For myself, I came prepared to swim!" cried Root, pulling his tunic over his head and shedding his trousers to reveal a bathing costume beneath. Cyril quickly joined him, while the others stood looking hesitantly around.

Juniper grappled to keep hold of the group. "That is a marvelous idea! I shall retire to change my garments at once. Who is with me?" Several of the other girls followed her into the changing cave, where she took off her long gown and folded it neatly in a pile, tucking her waist-pouch carefully among the skirts. In minutes, she was dressed in her long swimming costume, with its thick drapey fabric and loose bands around each ankle to keep the dress from billowing up. This had always seemed a vaguely ridiculous precaution in the palace's shallow, sedate pools, and she'd wondered how the seamstress had thought up that design.

A memory came to her mind, something her mother had said on one of their late-night adventuring expeditions. On that hot summer night, they'd crept out to the fountain to make mischief under the full moon, with no one to look on but a trio of solemn white doves in the nearby persimmon tree.

"It's tame and well behaved, this water here," her mother had murmured, gripping Juniper around her little waist and twirling her around. "We've got to churn it up if we want any fun at all. But someday—oh, someday I hope you'll get to experience the rush of water that has been left to its own true, wild nature. Water like that is a force all its own. It's a presence you meet on its own terms. It can't help but change you, if you'll let it."

Those thoughts ran through Juniper's mind now, as she paused on the rocky ledge jutting over the crystal water far below. Several kids were gathered in the shallows, edging their way out, while others already splashed in the depths. Despite Cyril's challenge, no one had stepped up to dive into the pool—not even, she couldn't help noticing, Cyril himself.

Well, here she was. Juniper stepped forward and curled her toes over the rim of the sun-baked stone. This was like nothing she'd ever done before. Yet it did not feel odd, or awkward, or even a bit dangerous. It felt right.

Juniper flung her arms wide and stepped off the ledge.

And dropped.

The air rushed past her in a torrent, ballooning inside her suit and flinging her hair wild above her. Then, like an icy thunderclap, the water took her in and the world exploded in a vortex of bubbling, foamy glee. Her teeth chattered, and her muscles strained, and the glory of the plunge seized her like a heartache, like a memory long forgotten. For a single moment, her hands were in her mother's and she was spinning in a wide arc over the fountain, with the dark crescent of the sky beaming approvingly overhead.

Then she kicked up hard and her head broke the surface, and all around her were the cheers and applause of a satisfied audience. Alta had taken her place on the ledge, and Juniper pushed against the water to move out of the way.

"Come on in!" she yelled. "The water's clear as a bell and twice as fine!"

The day was an overwhelming success. Cyril's swimming hole was all that had been promised, and the kids alternated between swimming, eating day-old cheese crackers and long strips of preserved meat and handfuls of sweet-salted apple crisps, and lying about on the superheated rocks, soaking up the midday sun. After a while, Juniper decided to push her exploring further. Quite a number of others had wandered off in various small groups, but she and Erick decided to climb the rocks around the edge of the pool. At the highest point, they sat on some flat stones and gazed out toward the horizon. They couldn't see much beyond the crags and bulk of the surrounding mountains. But the view they did have was breathtaking.

"That's the direction of home," Erick said, pointing. Off in the distance, a greenish-brown line on the horizon, was the warm, familiar soil of Torr.

"It looks so close," Juniper said. "Well, not actually close—but doesn't it seem like we might vault over this rock and touch down there just as easily as doing a forward roll?"

Erick smiled wistfully out at the horizon. "Do you miss it?"

"We'll be back home before long, and then we'll see how much our missing was worth."

Erick started to reply, then narrowed his eyes. "What's that?"

Far down the slope toward Torr's eastern flank, Juniper could just see a dull haze of smoke. "Something's ablaze out there!"

"A house fire?" Erick asked.

Juniper scrambled up on a boulder to see if she could get a better look. She couldn't. There was just the faint cloud massing in the distance, pale but somehow threatening, even from this distance.

"It's awfully big to be a house fire," Juniper said. And the red flashes they'd seen the other night—were those house fires, also?

She kept trying to make excuses, telling herself that all was well back home. Yet every day began and ended the same way: with no word from her father. It was growing increasingly hard to just continue on as they had been.

Juniper squeezed her arms tightly together and followed Erick down the ridge to rejoin the others.

They headed back toward the settlement in the late afternoon. The far-off smoke wasn't visible from their swimming hole, and twice Juniper opened her mouth to tell the others what she and Erick had seen. But each time she stopped. She remembered the fear and anxiety that had followed the first night's disturbance, not to mention last night's strange attack. The kids walking beside her now were hot and sticky and sun-scorched, but they bubbled over with giddy delight. Even though—or maybe *because*—Cyril, Root, and Jessamyn hadn't returned with them, there was a new closeness to the group that hadn't been there that morning. Juniper didn't have the heart to break that up.

Still, her own thoughts were dark and tangled. Her father had sent them here, had commanded them to stay until they heard from him. But were they really supposed to just sit by if Torr was under a proper invasion? Yet what could they hope to do, in any case, their ragtag little group? It was a quandary with no solution that Juniper could see.

"I've a surprise for you all," Leena said, cutting into Juniper's thoughts as they filed down the grassy bank toward the river. "Is everyone hungry?"

There were mutterings of enthusiastic assent, and Leena

danced in response. "My lips are sealed. I shan't breathe a word. But I think you'll be impressed." She took five or six more steps, then twirled again. "I hope you're hungry, and that's all I'm saying." She looked eagerly from one face to the other.

Juniper took pity on her. "Oh, do tell us more?" she suggested.

"Very well, if you *do* keep insisting. It's a plan I've been developing, to make the food preparation easier. I first thought of it on account of how the Hourglass stone holds and carries the heat so well. I had Roddy line it into my stovetop, and before we left this morning, I built up a raging fire. Hemmed it all around with stones and coal and clay, I did, and left a big pot of beans and salt pork on to stew."

"It won't have scorched?" Alta asked.

"That's the beautiful thing—the fire itself will have burned right out, but left all that heat trapped inside. If I've done it right, my stew has been slowly cooking all the day. This will be our best meal yet!" She sniffed the air. "It's almost as though I can smell it right now!"

Juniper did the same, though honestly she couldn't smell a thing.

As they neared the bridge, Leena broke into a run and dashed on ahead, doubtless eager to inspect her special meal. Unfortunately, that was not to be. For just minutes after she'd vanished from sight, a piercing wail rose from the kitchen area.

Juniper and Alta exchanged glances, then broke into a run. They had to slow down when crossing the bridge, still not wanting to burden the structure with more than one body at once. So Juniper was the first to come upon Leena standing, frozen in place, hands over her mouth, gazing at the complete wreckage of the dining hall. The circle was in full disarray, its stones overturned and scattered. A few boulders had even been rolled down the slope and lay half submerged in the river. In the kitchen, the new cooking stove had been smashed to rubble. Ash and coal were strewn everywhere. And over and through and among it all was a wide splatter of hard, undercooked brown beans. The empty pot lay upside down and dented on the far edge of the clearing.

Juniper heard more than one shocked gasp as the rest of the group came upon the scene.

"Who would *do* this?" Leena cried. Then, more softly, "I was really looking forward to that bean stew." She sank to her knees and buried her face in her hands. This was about more than just the dinner, Juniper knew. Something very personal had been invaded, some budding sense of self yanked away when it was only just starting to grow.

As Juniper swept her eyes over the mayhem, a shimmer caught her eye. "No!" she whispered.

All the stones had been overturned. *All* of them—including the flat-topped surface that had lately held the timepiece. Juniper ran to inspect the tangled wreck of glass, sand, and polished wood. It was no use. The precious device had not only been smashed, but apparently trodden on, too; nothing was left but twisted bits of crushed material.

For a moment, Juniper's eyes filled. How would she keep everybody on track, run a proper schedule—how could she manage her country without a timepiece?

Breathing deeply, she fought for composure. What could she do? She would have to work harder, that was all. She'd gotten distracted by the delights of the Basin, slipped into play mode when she should have stayed focused on building the country. But no more. For the sake of her kingdom, of her people, she had to be strong.

Juniper turned and waved her hands to get everyone's attention. The summer holiday feel was gone; now their faces, like her own, were set and hard and all business. "Roddy, Filbert, Alta— can you manage to put the stones back in order? Toby—this mess here? Oona and Tippy, let's see about getting something for dinner." On she went, parceling out jobs so that in a matter of minutes, everyone was busy with a task; and in less than an hour, the tired group gathered around a dinner of dried meat and fruit and potatoes charred in the fire, topped with the onions and fresh sage that Sussi had picked on her way home.

The kids huddled in a tight circle around a hastily prepared campfire, preferring the closeness of other bodies against their own to the more formal structure of the sitting stones. And Juniper thought that, all in all, this was not so very bad an end to this most disastrous of evenings. Far from destroying them, the attack had only served to drive them closer together.

This was tonight.

But tomorrow would be for fighting back.

Queen's Basin Guard Duty: Rotation

Head Guard in Constant Vigilance: Alta

§

Night Patrol: Gloaming to Moonpeak

(day 1) Erick & Tippy

(day 2) Filbert & Oona

Night Patrol: Moonpeak to Dawn

(day 1) Toby & Sussi

(day 2) Paul & Roddy

14

"WE SHALL HAVE TO SET UP A GUARD," ALTA said at breakfast the next morning. The response was a chorus of unhappy groans.

"Yes," Juniper cut in quickly. She and Alta had talked earlier, agreeing that the scouting expedition should be set aside in favor of camp safety.

"What kind of a guard? And who's going to do it?" asked Filbert.

"I've made a schedule," said Alta, but she didn't look as confident as she had a moment before.

"We haven't come here to do *guard* duty," said Paul in alarm.

"Yes, what about all that grand adventure you promised us?" Oona added. "'Summer of a lifetime,' wasn't that on the flyer we all saw?"

A low mutter of agreement followed, and Juniper spoke quickly over it. "We're here to set up our country, that's the most important thing. Adventuring is a lot of things, and certainly there's time for fun. But what do you think, that your country is just going to fall into your laps, fully formed? That you should never have to work for it, never have to put out an effort?"

"Oh, we're putting out effort, all right," muttered Oona, to scattered laughter.

Juniper fought for composure. Cyril wasn't even here this morning, and still she struggled. "Look," she said. "You've seen what we're facing with these attacks. What about the theft of our horses? What about yesterday's destruction? Do you really want to wait and see what happens next? This is *our* kingdom, and we've got to do what it takes to keep it safe."

The silence was not an encouraging one, but it wasn't derisive, either. Juniper pressed her small advantage. "We are citizens of Queen's Basin, but more than that, we are all children of Torr. We might be young, and we *are* only few, but we will *not* be pushed around. Should we take these threats lying down? I say *no!*" She scanned the rapt faces around her. She had their attention now. "This is *our* settlement. Queen's Basin will be what *we* make it—as much or as little as we have it in us to give. And I say we give it *everything*, and make it *epic*. A kingdom for the ages!" Juniper took in a breath. "This is our heritage—and this is our time. And so I say . . . *What will you give your country?*"

In the subsequent roar, the matter was settled.

From there, everyone moved on to warm peppermint tea, fire-roasted eggs, and stewed apricots, but all eyes stayed on Alta as she unfolded her plan: She'd split the night in two segments and assigned each a pair of guards, which alternated every other day. "I've left Leena off the rotation," Alta explained, "for she's got her hands full aplenty with cooking every meal. And Juniper, of course." Cyril, Root, and Jessamyn were also absent from the list, but Juniper doubted that would surprise anyone; in any case, they weren't there to notice. Still, the schedule was a good one, and Juniper told Alta so.

Then something occurred to her. "Have you given any thought to training?" she asked. They were sending these guards out to patrol the grounds . . . and then what? Raise a fiery holler upon any creature sighting? That wasn't good enough. "If we should come upon any beasts, or other unsavory elements, our guards must have some basic fighting skills."

Alta considered this. Juniper knew that the other girl was the only one with any real arms training, and since their arrival in Queen's Basin, Juniper had told her to keep her sword packed away. Now it looked as if the time had come to pull it back out. Several faces around the circle brightened.

"Yes," Alta said at last. "I've set myself the task of patrolling the whole round-about of the Basin all day long, as well as whatever specific guard duties might be needed in Your Highness's care. But your point is an excellent one. We should first hold a thorough training session for all guards." She looked over at Leena. "And anyone else who wants to join in, of course."

"Erick?" Juniper asked. "What do you say?"

Erick startled, dropping the heavy leather volume he was flipping through. This clearly panicked him still further, and he spent a full minute dusting and stroking and generally treating the abused object like a baby dropped on its head. Juniper waited until he composed himself and looked up. "So . . ." he said. "Er, I've had this thought at the back of my mind, and it kept me up all night. I think we should set up a guard duty."

Juniper stared.

Erick looked around at the ring of impassive faces. His eyes fell on the parchment in Alta's hand, and he scanned it quickly. "Oh," he muttered. "You've all been talking about this already?" He waved a hand. "Good—we're on the same page, then. Er . . . so to speak. But I've got more. Here's what I was searching for just now." He opened the book and pointed to a spot.

"*Dagnite?*" Juniper read doubtfully. She glanced at the cover. "This is a compendium of plant life in the Hourglass Mountains. What is that to do with guard duty?"

Erick puffed out his chest. "In *The Legend of Riotous Jayke*, our hero becomes lost in the wilderness and faces down wild beasts galore, but he fortuitously happens upon a grove of dagnite saplings. And that's all he needs to save the day!"

"And what's *Riotous Jayke* got to do with us, then?" Alta asked.

"Simply this: Dagnite is the toughest wood in the kingdom. And there's a treatment you can do—I learned this from another book, Lorde Belcher's *Alchemistry and Its Many Uses*—that will render the wood hard as steel and quite near impossible to burn." He paused. "Guards will need weapons, won't they?"

Alta dropped her schedule and leaned in to read over Erick's shoulder. "Bookish learning at its finest," she said with grudging admiration.

Juniper clapped her hands together. "I approve! Can we get started on that this morning?"

"It still remains to find a dagnite grove," Erick said. "But the description is clear, along with the typical elevations and ground conditions. I'm certain we can find one quite easily—I've got several possible locations in mind already."

"Good, then," said Juniper. "We have a plan. Dagnite expedition leaves first thing, and the guards' training session will be held immediately upon their return."

Over the next few days, the newly established Queen's Basin Guard came together. The dagnite grove was duly found, and Roddy was able to translate Erick's book learning into a practical method for hardening the whittled branches into spears that were both sturdy and flexible. The guards' training began in earnest, and the nightly rotation went off without a hitch. Even Paul pronounced that guard duty wasn't quite so hateful in this new setting. Through all this, there were no more mysterious noises in the night, nor any other visible mischief or mayhem. One guard or another would occasionally tell of hearing clattering noises off toward the edges of the camp, but further investigation never turned anything up.

For their part, the noble kids seemed to grow even less a part of the group over time. They'd once again stopped coming to meals; in fact, since the swimming hole excursion, Juniper had glimpsed them only from a distance. She couldn't help wondering how they were getting by. What did they do all day? What were they finding to eat?

Mostly, though, it was a relief to have them gone.

The world outside Queen's Basin also seemed to have gone quiet. Juniper began rising early every morning and climbing up to the messenger's cave. She wasn't keeping the place a secret, exactly. It was just something she preferred having to herself for the time being. Every day she scanned the skies, but there was never anything to see. She also studied the rolling landscape. There was no smoke, no sign of movement, no strange goings-on at all. On the surface, at least, all was well.

If only she could shake that squirming in her gut that told her this was the *wrong* kind of silence, the kind that means that everything is so wrong that it might well be broken beyond repair.

To keep herself—and the others—from thinking, Juniper made sure every hour of every day was packed from sunup to sunset. They no longer had a timepiece to guide their movements, but true to her resolution, Juniper got things even more zealously organized. The cooking area was rebuilt using green clay, which Alta dug up farther along the riverbank. There was so much of this clay, and it dried so solidly when mixed with red sand from the South Bank, that Roddy quickly made plans for a clay-and-daub method of building walls. Everyone decided to keep their sleeping quarters in the caves—except Juniper and Tippy, of course, who still overnighted in the Great Tree—but Roddy's scheme let them put up a patio roof over the dining hall (they decided on no walls, preferring an open-air feel), and walls and a roof to the kitchen (which Leena said made her feel ever so civilized). Erick also contributed a most inspired plan for a door: tall rush weeds woven

164

into a mat and fastened to the wall, with flexible loops to let it swing open and shut.

"It's a slick design," Roddy said with admiration. "We should make these for our sleeping caves. It's far better than all that hanging cloth everyone's using now."

More days passed, with no word from the palace.

Where *was* that messenger? What could be causing this delay? Was her father all right?

Something had to be done. But hard as she tried, Juniper could think of nothing that would make any kind of difference. And so she waited and watched. And kept busy.

With the essentials taken care of, Juniper turned a critical eye to her subjects, noticing their grubby faces and hands, hems of gowns and trousers alike showing tears and stains. No one seemed at all concerned about this state of affairs.

"Our next task shall be to build a Beauty Chamber," she declared one morning, waving toward the site she had selected. It was downriver a ways, nearly to the orchard, on the South Bank and right up against—and slightly over—the water's edge. The house would end in a narrow bathing room, she explained, with the water lapping under the wall to fill a pool that would stay constantly fresh as it flowed downstream. Into the Beauty Chamber she would move all her gowns and slippers, all the hair ribbons and powders and creams and other trinkets that didn't come near to fitting in her tiny bedchamber-hollow, up in the Great Tree.

"You may all bring your personal beauty supplies," she told the girls. "Anything you don't want to keep in your own chambers, or want to have near to the bathing room."

They celebrated their hard work with a day off, which most everyone spent catching up on sleep and relaxation. Juniper wouldn't let herself stop working, though, not even for a day. She was too restless, too unsettled to slow down. Staying busy kept her from thinking. And there was entirely too much to think about.

The next day, she charged a group to scour the nearby cliffs for smooth, flat stones. "We'll set up a system of pathways leading across our kingdom," she declared. "I've sketched it out on this parchment—and it will take a lot of stones, I know"—she raised a hand over the chorus of groans that arose around the early-morning campfire—"but it will be worth it. Think of being able to walk from the caves to your morning meal without getting a speck of mud or dust on the hem of your gown! Er . . . or trousers, of course." She nodded encouragingly, though the response seemed halfhearted at best. "We shall be able to pull out our best slippers, without need to protect them from the elements. Yes, I think this should be our next task, and all the strongest able bodies shall be assigned to it first."

There was a rustle across the group, and Juniper looked over to see that Oona had her hand raised. "Yes?" Juniper asked.

"Well," the other girl said, scuffing the ground with her toe, "it's only that we've been here coming on ten days or more, and we've gotten ever so much done. But, Miss Juniper, we're all awfully tired." There was a murmur of approval across the group, and Oona pushed on with more energy. "That day off yesterday was welcome, but we've been working without stopping every day from morning till night. Not," she rushed quickly on, "that this is out of the ordinary. We're all the hardest of workers. But we came here for adventure—for work, and to do our share, of course, but also for some fun. We've been thinking it would be nice to have a *proper* day off." She paused, then added, "Like we did that one day with Cyril and the swimming hole."

There was a very loud silence.

Juniper knew she was pushing everyone hard. With so much outside of Queen's Basin that was beyond her influence, how could she not grab hold of what little she *could* control? But they'd *just had* a day off! And there was something sly, almost challenging in the way Oona had said those last words. Juniper had seen how Oona hung on Cyril's every word and gesture—the girl was clearly sweet on him—but this was too much. Still, she could tell from the others' nods and mutters of agreement that she needed to tread lightly.

"There's something to that, I suppose," Juniper said, making an effort to smile. "We've all been working both sides of the knot, and you're overdue for more than just a day's break. But I'm expecting the king's messenger any day now. Any time. Next week is to be our planned supply trip back to Torr." Juniper tamped down her own worry at this train of thought. What if the messenger *didn't* come by then? Were they really to wait here indefinitely, as the king had commanded? She swallowed. "Until then, we absolutely must make as much progress as possible. Get our kingdom ready for our new group of recruits, yes? So, I say we redouble our working efforts now, and then see how things look by the end of the week. What do you all think?"

Oona looked at the ground. Juniper could tell she didn't love the idea, but neither she nor any of the others voiced any protest. There were enough frowns and grumblings, though, that Juniper knew she couldn't leave things like this. She pictured herself back at the palace, dreaming of her own country. It hadn't been about work, not ever.

How had things changed so much since then?

"Well," she said, "there is one other thing. We are still awaiting the messenger, as I said, but perhaps we needn't put *everything* on the sideboard until then. So, let us work doubly hard the rest of the days leading up to next week's supply run, get everything we can into shape. Then—" Oona looked up eagerly, and Tippy grabbed Sussi's hand and squeezed it in anticipation. Juniper herself felt a thrill of excitement. "Then, on the last night before we head out, we *shall* have that promised ball—and it will be the biggest and best party you could imagine. Food and dancing and music to rattle the cliff sides. What do you say?"

This was met with a rousing enthusiasm, and Juniper relaxed as the mood shifted from grousing to giddy. It was a narrow miss. But really, how could you go wrong with a ball?

After the buzz died down, another hand went up. Juniper nodded at Filbert. "It's to do with the food," he said, arms folded across his chest. "Leena did all right at first. But these days it seems like all we've got is bread and dried meats and wild greens made six different ways. Someone needs to take the kitchen in hand and get us some better eats."

Leena leaped to her feet, pumping a fist in the air. "I'd like to see *you* slaving behind a hot fire every day, you—"

Juniper lifted a hand for silence. "You're both right. Leena has been putting in countless hours every day on meals, but she doesn't have the ingredients she needs. I don't know why we're not getting any more eggs, or milk from the goats. I know it can take a while for animals to settle, but—"

"I check them every day," said Toby. "The goats have been given the prime grazing pasture, leaving the horses to get the pickings. But they're still as dry as sticks, every one. And we haven't had six eggs in as many days, across all the hens."

"We must find a way to help them produce. Will you look into that, Toby? Check their diet, their sleeping quarters, make sure they're warm enough. Maybe we can move the enclosure to another spot. We have to get some fresh products into our diet. Surely the fruit trees and berry bushes will bear more soon. And how goes the garden, Paul?"

"The vegetables are planted, but it will be weeks before they grow up. I think—"

But what Paul thought was not then to be known, for a sudden *boom* eclipsed all discussion. The ground under their feet gave a violent shake. It was over in the blink of an eye, but the entire group leaped to their feet in a frenzy. Dashing out of the dining area with the others, Juniper scanned the horizon around them for signs of what was going on. At first, she couldn't see a thing over the high edges of their bowl-like mountain enclosure, nothing but darkening sky . . . and, off in the direction of Torr . . .

"Look!" said Alta.

Just visible over the high mountain's edge rose a column of smoke. Unlike the faint, distant wisps Juniper and Erick had seen from the swimming hole, this cloud was thick and dark and gritty. It looked like it might be just down at the base of the mountains. With it came a distinct smell of burning.

Juniper felt a hand grab her arm and yank her off to the side.

"There!" Erick hissed in her ear. "Look!"

She followed his pointing finger and saw, blurry and indistinct in the gathering gloom, a light-colored speck winging across the smoky sky. Her heart leaped, but she kept her voice low, for Erick alone to hear. "It's the messenger, come from my father!"

Leaving the others to their discussion, she ran toward the cliff's base, with Erick close behind. They made their way up the rocky pathway, ducking out of the group's sight line as quickly as they could and weaving among the rocks until they reached the promontory.

"Yes!" she whispered. The light was fading, but inside the tiny rock cave, she could just make out a pale shape.

"It's a bat?" Erick asked.

"Ghost bat," she agreed. "That's our messenger. My father's

game warden had a fleet of them brought over from the Far Continent, and he breeds them specially. Ghost bats have a highly developed sense of hearing, and they've been trained to listen for the sound this Beacon makes. I know—I can barely hear it myself, but to these creatures, it's loud as a bell. Shall we see what news our winged messenger has for us?" She reached into the cave and unfastened a narrow tube tied around the creature's leg. Breaking off the stopper, she tapped out a tiny sheet of parchment that was closed with her father's familiar seal.

Briefly meeting Erick's eyes, she broke the purple wax blob, unrolled the paper, and began to read.

My Darling Daughter:

As I write this, your party has just left the palace.

You know that our dealings with Monsia have been tenuous in recent decades, and reports of their activities have been increasingly difficult to obtain. Everything I have told you tonight is true: The raiding party at the gate is small, and I am confident we will repel them with ease.

And yet. Something in me is uneasy.

You will forgive me, I hope, for seizing this chance to swiftly send you and your subjects—this representation of the youth of Torr—as far from the fighting as possible. No other living person knows the location of the Basin. It appears on no maps. You will all be safe there for as long as is needed. I have taken the liberty of adding my own cart to yours, supplemented with further provisions, along with some items from the palace coffers and from our cultural stores which begged safekeeping.

I cannot say why I feel this need, and there is no particular event that demands this caution. You have often heard me say that as king I feel some connection with the land I rule, and if that is the case, then perhaps something in the wind or the sky or the call of the birds tells me that everything is not as it should be.

I am likely growing soft in my declining years. The moment I finish this letter, I will write another, dashing off the bright, happy notice that the invaders are put to rout and all is well. I will line both scrolls up on my desk. And I am certain that within a few hours I will return and toss this missive into the fire, while the good news flies to you on quickest of wings.

But for the moment, I will indulge my old man's worry and say: If you are reading *this* letter, time has passed and the worst has happened. I cannot think how, but the palace has been overrun. I implore you, do not do anything rash. Do not send a reply by return messenger, lest it be intercepted. Most importantly, stay where you are! I will find a way to come for you, but <u>by no means</u> must any of you leave the safety of the Basin until then.

Do I have your promise?

All my love,
Your father

15

FOR A LONG TIME, JUNIPER COULD DO nothing but stand, stunned, with the parchment shaking in her hand. Finally, she handed it to Erick. Then she turned and started climbing back down the rocky embankment. The palace had never felt so far away as it did now. She kept to the narrow trail until it split in two, then she scrambled down and, brushing the gravel from her skirts, walked into the large entry cave.

Stopping only to light one of the torches, she pushed into the narrow alcove where they had stashed the treasure. She grabbed the closest bundle and pulled it out: a flat package wrapped in oilskin and bound with twine. Juniper tugged at the ropes until they came loose, revealing the painting within—a fine masterwork in oils, by the revered Torrean painter Marchello, whose work was so highly prized that he had built himself a one-hundred-foot tower, to which he had supplies delivered and up which subjects might, upon invitation, be raised in a special basket to have their exorbitantly priced portraits painted. For the royal family, he had taken the unheard-of step of descending from his tower and setting up in a south wing turret room for a two-month stretch while he produced a whole series of exquisite paintings.

Juniper well remembered sitting for this one, though she had been only five years old at the time. The sitting had felt endlessly long (three full days, with irregular breaks for eating, sleeping, and the occasional stretch) but had also been one of the best times of her life. She had sat on the ornate couch-throne, sandwiched between her parents, and for those three days, nothing existed but their little family. They couldn't shift from the position Marchello was so painstakingly capturing on canvas—she perched on her father's knee, her mother elegantly to the side, with one arm twined around Juniper's small waist, head tilted, a half smile on her lips—but every moment was filled with rollicking banter, silliness, and sly good humor. For those enchanted hours, her parents were transformed into giggly teenagers, telling jokes Juniper just barely understood, singing bawdy songs, finding ridiculous patterns in the wall hangings opposite them, the king telling wild stories from his youth. Juniper had been almost disappointed when Marchello had released them and they'd been free to go back to their everyday lives. For a moment now, in her firelit cave, she was transported back to that time when everything around her had felt safe and enclosed, sheltered by the two people she loved most in the world.

Now she was here, alone, up a high mountain and responsible not only for herself but for a host of other kids—subjects, *her* subjects, her *people*—and now her father, the only parent she had left, was in danger, and there was absolutely nothing she could do about it. It was almost too much to bear. The painted image swam in front of her blurry eyes.

Then she felt a warm pressure on her shoulders, and she remembered. She wasn't alone. Not completely. She tilted her head to the side and found Erick's shoulder, just for one moment—that was all she could allow herself. But it was enough.

She took a deep breath, straightened, and gathered up the cloth and twine. She tied the bundle tightly back together, hiding those laughing faces from all the danger and uncertainty that was to come, tucking them away safely in their alcove where, she hoped, they would survive whatever lay ahead.

Only minutes later, things already weren't going Juniper's way.

"What do you mean, we can't tell them?" said Erick. "Everyone here has family and friends back home. We can't keep this news back. This isn't like that little smoke cloud we saw the other day. This is *big*."

"Don't you see?" Juniper said, exasperated. "That's *why* we can't tell them. Think about it for a minute. Say we do that—gather everyone together, break the news. 'The palace has fallen!' Or wait—'We *think* the palace has fallen; we don't know for sure, but it looks that way.' What happens next?"

Erick was silent.

"That's right," Juniper continued as though he had answered. "Chaos. Everyone starts crying, and yelling, and worrying—and most of all? *Leaving.* Running off back to Torr in a panic, when that's exactly what we're not supposed to do. We're supposed to *stay here.* That's what my father told us—what *the king charged us* to do."

Erick was shaking his head.

"I'm the queen," she insisted, "and it's my responsibility to protect my subjects from things that are too hard for them to take. We *can't* act—can't do a thing—until we know exactly what's going on back home. And that's information we just don't have yet. You see, don't you? Why we can't say anything?"

Erick shrugged. "It's the principle of the thing, it seems to me."

"Sometimes telling the whole truth makes things worse, not better. That's how it is to be a ruler. Sometimes you've got to make tough choices."

"Like how you told everyone I was only thirteen before we left?" he asked quietly. "You've always got some good reason, Juniper. But in the end, the truth's the truth."

Juniper steamed. She *had* to keep this letter quiet. Look at how worked up everyone was already about the new smoke sighting! How would they react if they heard the palace was in danger? She wished Erick could see this and be more of a support. She put her hands on her hips. "Anyway, I'm in charge here. I get to decide what's best for my people, and that includes you." She paused, then whispered, "You know I'm right about this."

"You're not right," he said at last. "But you *are* the queen, and I'm going to do what you say. We'll need to get everyone together right away and tell them about delaying the trip. They're all expecting to head home next week. This changes things."

Juniper slumped. "I know it does. I guess we'll do that first thing tomorrow. They're not going to be happy, are they?"

There was no need to answer that question. They turned in silence and started out of the cave.

"There's something else," Erick said after a minute. "I forgot about it with everything else going on, but I meant to tell you. It's about Cyril."

Juniper's feet almost slid out from under her as she hit a patch of gravel. She caught herself against the rock face and moved more carefully on the downward path toward the settlement. "What about him?"

"Come this way," said Erick grimly, "and I'll show you."

Cyril and Root had claimed for their quarters a big, two-room cave at the far end of the row. Many of the caves Juniper and Erick passed on their way had something draped over the openings—a thick cloak or a stretch of gauzy cloth—though several now had woven doors fixed into place.

Finally they arrived at the last cave, which was hung with a heavy, indigo velvet drape. Erick pushed aside the hanging and stepped inside. A window opening let in the daylight, and Juniper blinked at what she saw: some scattered sheets of muddy parchment. Two or three pairs of wadded-up undergarments. The half-rotted core of an apple and the gnawed bones from some dinner feast.

That was all.

There were no bedrolls, no packs, nothing to show that anybody had lived or even set foot in here for days, maybe longer.

"What's going on?" Juniper asked, striding over to kick at the pile of smelly clothes. "Cyril and Root aren't living here, that's clear. But they haven't said anything about moving their whole camp somewhere else. Where did they go—and when?"

"I've got no idea. I only found out this morning when I came by and happened to look inside."

"There's something poxy going on here. I hoped that banning them from meals unless they helped out would bring them back around to the group. Instead, it's done just the opposite. And all this sneaking around? It's like they're pretending to still live here, the way they've left their door-drape hanging in place." Juniper sighed. "I'm going to have to confront them again, aren't I?"

"They don't come to meals, but they're not the type to go hungry. So they're getting food from somewhere. Jessamyn, too. They show their faces here and there—"

"Dropping in to cause trouble," Juniper interjected.

"—but they steadfastly refuse to work. Maybe some of the time they're off lollygagging. But you know Cyril as well as I do. Unless he's changed greatly since going off to school, he's not just going to slurg around all day. I'd bet jumping beans to the sun that he's got a plan. And it can't be a good one."

"I've had enough of those two." Juniper was surprised to hear her father's own steel in her voice. "This has got to stop. Track them down, Erick, and have them come to breakfast tomorrow morning. We might as well get all the announcements and confrontations over at once."

• • •

As it turned out, Juniper's announcements the next morning quickly sparked confrontations of their own.

"You want us to do *what?*" said Filbert incredulously.

No sooner had Juniper finished her carefully prepared speech than she knew she'd badly miscalculated. They'd be postponing their supply trip back to Torr, she'd said, but she gave no reason for the change in plans. *Then* she'd explained that the grand ball she'd announced the day before would also have to wait. This was a last-minute decision she'd made just before sitting down—and she knew it was the right one. Breakfast that morning was chicory scramble and a mash of wild grain patties with just a flavoring of pork grease. They weren't running out of food yet, but if they really were stuck here for a while longer, they didn't have food to squander on a big celebration.

"I want this to be a proper kingdom, with jobs and work— don't you see?" she said desperately. "Not just fun in the sun all the livelong day. What's the point in that?"

"We *do* work hard—every single day!" Oona protested. "*And* we stay up half the night on this fool's errand of a guard duty, to boot. You promised us this party. We've all been looking forward to it since day one, and we deserve it! We've been working that double-hard you called for. We've earned ourselves a break."

"I'm not saying we won't have the ball," Juniper said, searching in vain for the inner steel she'd so recently felt. "Just . . . not right now." She had seen her father give plenty of unpopular pronouncements, and right now she sounded nothing like him. Inside, she felt even worse: all weak and trembly, properly mash-for-a-backbone. Yet she couldn't back down. How could they throw a wild party, sing and dance it up, or even take another day off to swim and frolic about in the sun, when Torr was suffering who knew what atrocities? The smoke cloud had dissipated overnight and seemed to have taken with it all the others' fears and concerns. Which she was glad for—but it sure didn't make her job now any easier!

She looked across the circle to where Cyril and Root sat, legs splayed, arms crossed, looking smug and satisfied. Cyril had a fine growth of stubble across his face. *Just another way of showing off,* she thought uncharitably. It had been a mistake to make him come this morning. What was it she'd wanted to confront him about again? She was having a hard time remembering. Cyril caught her eye and reached up to stroke his almost-whiskers and shake his head patron-izingly. Show-off.

"We just don't have time to gad about right now," Juniper said, cringing even as the words left her mouth. "We need to keep work-ing as hard as we have been for the next week or two, until we can get everything finished that needs doing. Figure out how to supple-ment our food supply. Make sure the buildings are secure. *Then* we can think about taking some time off." By then, they should have word from the palace. *Then* she could relax. She clapped her hands together. "So, let's get on about our jobs. You all have tasks in progress, I think, but come and find me if you finish and need something new, or if you've other ideas to share."

She started digging through her waist-pouch and rustling her parchment as loudly as she could, hoping that might drown out the unmistakable sound of unhappy grumbling as the settlers began to get up and start going about their day.

"What say you, Root?" Cyril drawled. "Fancy a swim on this fine hot morning?"

Juniper closed her eyes. She had to stop chickening out. She had called them here determined to hit the problem head-on. Now Cyril was doing everything short of openly challenging her.

So this would be it, then.

Catching Erick's eye, she registered his faint nod. She stood.

"This has got to stop," Juniper said, meeting Cyril's gaze. Erick came to stand next to her, arms straight by his side, hands balled into fists. It occurred to Juniper that Erick seemed to have grown in the few weeks since they'd left Torr. She wasn't sure if it was all height or if something inside him was changing, too, if he'd found some renewed strength and solidity in this mountain air. Hopefully together they would be a match for Cyril's rotten genius.

"What *exactly* are you referring to?" Most of the others had left already, but even now Cyril didn't bother getting up from his rock. Root stayed, too, though he looked uncertainly from Cyril to Juniper as though not entirely sure which to follow. Jessamyn was draped over a nearby stone, tracking the exchange with hawk eyes.

"This is our country, Cyril. It belongs to all of us. And from the very start, you've done nothing but try to pull us apart. You've got to stop."

"I never asked to be part of your *country*," he replied scornfully.

"Remember? Nor did Root, nor Jessamyn. You might not have a timepiece any longer, but you've had no trouble tying everyone down to the same backbreaking schedule they had back home. Last I heard, we'd been booted out of your group anyway. So it should be clear by now that we see absolutely no reason to bow to your laws." He paused. "Or whatever it is you call them."

Juniper stiffened and glanced at Erick. He shrugged ever so slightly. It always came back the same thing: What *could* they do?

"Look," Juniper said, gentling her voice as though addressing a skittish stallion. "I know we have our differences, and if I'm honest, I didn't especially want you to come on this trip, either. But you're here now, and we've got to find a way to make it work. It's just no good having two separate settlements, and you pulling off against the main group all the time."

Cyril raised his chin and cocked an eyebrow. "What's in it for us, then?" he challenged. "We've got all we need on our own. We're pretty much self-sufficient, as I see it. Maybe we'll start our *own* country. Why not?"

"You won't."

"Oh, won't I?" Cyril slowly rose, stretched his arms over his head, and looked from one side of the clearing to the other. "Who's going to stop me?"

Before Juniper could figure out an answer, he turned and strode out of the dining area, with Root and Jessamyn close behind.

Juniper took three quick steps out to follow him, heat burning in her cheeks, but Erick grabbed her arm. "Wait," he whispered. "Don't say something you'll regret. We'll figure this out."

So Juniper stood there, trembling with rage, and watched the trio move away as though they hadn't a care in the world. They reached the wooden bridge, where Roddy and Filbert had hammer and nails out, beginning the work of putting up a handrail. Cyril paused, looked back at Juniper, then returned his gaze to the two boys. Pitching his voice loud, Cyril said, "I was sorry to hear about you lot losing out on your party at this end-of-week. I thought I'd throw one myself instead. Make up for certain . . . *lacks*." He threw a smirk in Juniper's direction, then raised his voice so it carried all around the clearing. "Spread the word! Just follow the trail up past the swimming hole—you won't be able to miss it. See you all there tonight at first moonrise. Oh . . . and come hungry."

Juniper's shoulders slumped. Cyril had caught her out yet again.

16

"WE CAN'T *NOT* GO," ERICK SAID, FOR THE third time. "How would it look?"

"I don't care how it looks," Juniper replied stubbornly. "I'm not setting foot in his rogue settlement or going to his fool party."

"You went to his swimming thing," said Alta. She, Tippy, and Erick were the only ones who'd hung back with Juniper. They all sat on the newly carved wooden bench in the Great Tree, gazing at the silent Musicker while raucous laughter echoed through the clearing from the opposite slope.

"That was different," said Juniper. "It wasn't a direct challenge like this is."

"I still think it'd be worse for you not to go at all. Doesn't that mean he's won?"

"He hasn't won," said Juniper firmly. "I mean, what is there even to win? Right?" There was an uncomfortable silence. Juniper looked from face to face, her heart sinking as none of them met her eyes. *"Right?"*

"He wants all of this, Your Princessness," said Tippy finally, her voice thin and watery, voicing the fears Juniper hadn't been willing to admit even to herself. "He wants your people and your place and everything." She paused. "He wants to be king."

Tippy was right, of course. And that was a challenge Juniper couldn't let go.

"Let's head on up," Juniper said.

"I'll stay here," said Alta. "Someone needs to keep guard." She didn't have to remind them what had happened the last time the whole camp had emptied for one of Cyril's outings.

Within a few minutes, the three of them were off, clambering down the tree and crossing the bridge and stomping the now well-tracked path past the vegetable fields toward the flickering dazzle of lights in the near distance.

They had no trouble finding Cyril's gathering. The moon was a slim half crescent overhead, but the little encampment blazed with light. Laughter and merriment rang out, bouncing around the nearby peaks. Juniper climbed slowly, head held high, trying to compose herself. What kind of face should she present when she arrived? Should she slide casually into the group, take her seat among the others, avoid making a statement? Or should she march in and take charge, find some small but important thing to correct, some way to show her authority?

As it turned out, the decision was taken out of her hands. The moment she rounded the last embankment and set foot in the clearing, with Erick and Tippy close on her heels, all the noise abruptly sputtered and died.

Juniper studied the gathering. The kids sat loosely around a blazing fire, tall torches planted in the earth around the wider circle. A low rough log was being used as a table, with a tantalizing collection of roasted meat and nuts and other delicacies strewn across it. The clearing was mostly flat, but rose slightly on the far side, and on this elevated spot—just underneath a torch so the firelight played off his handsome face—stood Cyril.

Arms crossed over his chest, feet astride, Cyril flicked his gaze in her direction. "Well, well," he drawled, "look who decided to show up!"

Juniper stiffened. She'd expected something like this, of course, but here on Cyril's own territory, facing down his arrogant self-confidence, she felt even more shaken than usual.

"Do sit down," Cyril went on, waving at a makeshift bench. It was completely full, but at his words the kids scooted apart like scuttlebugs under light. Tippy made a quick dive for the seat, followed more hesitantly by Erick.

Juniper stood her ground, mirroring Cyril's stance and cocking her chin at a challenging angle. "What do you want, Cyril?" she spat. "Why did you *really* throw this party? Let's get right down to it."

"Ah!" cried Cyril, rubbing his hands together. "Hitting the bulwark head-on. I approve."

Juniper couldn't help noticing the pleased titter that followed his words. She didn't know if it was the food, the place, or the magnetism of Cyril's personality, but the loyalty of the crowd was shifting. She well remembered her father's warnings of the fickle nature of a group, and how quickly it could turn. She had to win them back, and fast.

"Talk, Cyril," she said curtly. "Whatever tricks you might pull, or parties you throw, Queen's Basin is still my responsibility. It was given me directly by our ruler, King Regis."

"Ah yes, your *father*," Cyril said scornfully, and Juniper drew in a breath. Was Cyril challenging not only her authority, but her father's, too?

Before she could figure out how to respond to this, Cyril raised his hands in a calming gesture. "King Regis is a good man," he said mildly. "And he's been a good king. But King Regis is not here, and he's not the ruler of *this* kingdom. What we have in front of us is"—he shot a look at Juniper, then turned to face the others, as though excluding her from the conversation—"let's be honest— a very young girl . . . a princess, yes, but does that *really* qualify someone to rule?"

"What are you saying?" Juniper said, stunned.

"I'm *saying*," said Cyril, his eyes never shifting from his rapt audience, "that you are the princess-heir of Torr, yes. But you are also a girl who just had her thirteenth Nameday. I'm saying that you are weak and soft, and have your head full of dresses and balls and little busy-work building projects. I am saying that you know nothing about building a country. This kingdom can have a better ruler—*should* have a better ruler."

"And that better ruler is *you*?" Juniper was still racing to keep up. Cyril's direct attack had caught her completely off guard.

Now he tilted his head in such fake modesty that Juniper

would have laughed if she hadn't been so horrified. "I don't know if I should say *better,* but I am here. I am willing. I am qualified——" He raised a hand at a murmur from the group. "Yes, many of you are undoubtedly aware that my father, Rupert Lefarge, is King Regis's chief adviser. But if you know your history, you might also recall that he is a direct cousin of the king's. And if history had turned out differently, it has been said that my father might well be the one now sitting on the throne of Torr."

"That is a *lie!*" Juniper yelled. She was no longer tongue-tied; Cyril had gone too far. "Your father might be the king's distant cousin, but he does *not* have a claim to the throne. You are nothing but a pompous numbskull!"

Cyril shifted now, meeting her gaze head-on.

"Am I?" he said slowly, thoughtfully. Then he waved a hand. "But enough of Torr. That is not relevant at the moment." He paused, looked skyward, and stroked his infernal stubbled chin. "You know, in the old days, rivals to a throne might go to battle or call for a duel. I don't suppose that would suit in this case, even if it were still done. No, I propose something very different. I suggest that we let our *subjects* decide who should rule this kingdom. Each one can make his or her choice, and let the majority's decision rest."

"*What?*" Juniper had heard of countries employing this method of selecting a ruler——off-continent, of course, for all the civilized lands were staunchly monarchist——but the custom had always struck her as vaguely barbaric. How could one ever settle into one's role as ruler while having to worry incessantly about public choice?

"There is no decision to be made!" she protested, but when

she reached for steel in her voice, all she felt was crumbling straw. Worse, a quick glance around showed a circle of intent faces—kids who had followed Cyril to his party, eaten his food, danced to his music. Their gazes were now locked on him, considering, nodding, weighing up the idea and, if their expressions were any indication, seeing it as a good one. Only a very few met her eyes when she looked in their direction.

With a sinking heart, Juniper understood. If Cyril asked the group to choose its ruler right now, the decision would not go in her favor. She also understood that he had made her a challenge that she could not ignore.

The moment was a runaway horse, and she *had* to bring it under control.

But how?

"One week," Juniper burst out, raising her voice so all could hear. "I'll recognize your challenge, Cyril, not because it has any merit or because I have any respect for you personally—I most certainly do *not*—but because a wise ruler listens to the people. And I can see that people need to make up their minds about this. So let's settle the decision seven days from now."

Cyril opened his mouth, but Juniper barreled right over him, eyes fixed on her subjects, who now gave her their full attention. "We'll gather at first light in seven days and hold a ballot. At that time, you will be asked to choose who will rule this kingdom: Cyril Lefarge or Juniper Torrence. This is an important decision, and I expect you'll take time to consider all of the factors." She kept her voice strong and steady. She would not plead, or cajole, or whimper. "Consider all of the factors, and make a wise and balanced choice. And now, I will leave you to enjoy the rest of your feast."

She swept a glance around the group, glad that Cyril didn't add anything to her pronouncement. She turned and started out of the circle, then called back over her shoulder, "And I expect to see everyone tomorrow morning at the usual time for work. We still have a kingdom to build and a settlement to maintain. Until then!"

Heart pounding, Juniper marched out of the firelight and headed down the slope. The sudden darkness made it difficult to see around her, and she had to move slowly to keep from stumbling. Footsteps crunched behind her, and she turned to see Erick, flickering torch in hand, hurrying to catch up.

"Well, that was something," Juniper said with a sigh.

"He's a blackguard of the worst sort," Erick muttered. He raised his torch and moved in front of Juniper to light the way. "He's got no right to challenge your rule. And everyone following along like that!"

"I guess I should have expected it, based on how things have been going. I didn't, though. I never thought he'd be that brazen." She'd set herself up for it, in a way—that's what she didn't want to say out loud. Decreeing less fun and more work, without telling the others the reason why. But what else could she do? She *couldn't* tell them the truth, not until she knew more about what was going on. It was for their own good.

"I still don't understand what he's going for, though," said

Erick. "Why does he want Queen's Basin so badly? I mean, no offense, but we're nothing up here. We're playacting is all."

Juniper fought the urge to contradict him. Of course, Erick was right.

"He's a just powermonger. He's always been like that, always has to be the head of everything." Deep down, though, Juniper wondered. Was that it? Cyril waving his fist at the sky, wanting to be king of anything at all? Or was there something else going on— something bigger, that went deeper than any of them could see?

Either way, Juniper had a lot of thinking to do.

It was going to be a long night.

17

THE NIGHT WAS LONG, BUT THE FOLLOWING day was longer. Having grown up in the palace, Juniper was well used to feeling on display. Yet never before had she felt so soundly judged, as though everyone she passed was weighing her every word, step, and action for later analysis and discussion. Even worse was to know that they *were* actually doing that; it wasn't all in her head. More than once, she rounded a corner to find two or three kids conferring together in earnest whispers, only to have them jerk apart upon seeing her and begin industriously working, lips shut tight, gazes skittering away.

The meaning couldn't be clearer.

"I don't know how much longer I can do this," she said that night, lying sprawled out in the tree house next to Alta and Tippy. They had dragged all the sitting-cushions that usually lined the edge of the floor and piled them into one giant cake in the center of the room, with Juniper's coverlet topping the whole thing like fuzzy frosting. There was just enough room for the three of them to stretch out on the sumptuously pillowed heap, though Tippy kept rolling herself into a ball and launching down the slope and across the floor.

"You're doing fine," Alta told Juniper consolingly.

"It's right buggy how everyone's carrying on," Tippy cut in. "It's not like anything's changed about you since yesterweek. Who could stand to have that coxcomb Cyril be king of us, anyway?"

"I wish everyone else thought as you do," Juniper muttered.

"I could find out what they think," said Tippy, bopping upright. "I'm very good at weaseling."

Juniper smiled. It was getting increasingly hard to keep the sprightly girl occupied. The days when Juniper had sat reclining in her chair while one maid secured her stockings and the other fastened emerald pins into her hair couldn't have seemed further away.

"Sure," she said. "That sounds like an excellent use of your time. Wait—not right *now*!"

But it was too late. Tippy was halfway down the tree ladder, yelling joyously, "Bye-o, then! I'll be back around in a bit."

"The moon's already out! What could that girl be thinking?"

"Ah, she'll be all right," said Alta. "She's got a head on her, that one. And Toby's one of the guards out tonight, and he's as alert as they come. Though there's been absolutely nothing to spot since we started."

Juniper scowled. She hadn't forgotten the odd-hoofed attackers, but Alta was right—there'd been not a sign of them since the destruction of the dining area. No evidence of mischief at all, actually, unless they counted the nonproducing animals, and certainly that wasn't related. Juniper had started to wonder if those "attacks" might have been misconstrued: Maybe the horses had just gotten loose and run off into the mountains. Maybe a pack of ordinary, bean-loving animals had torn up the dining area. It was possible.

"I wonder if we should abolish the guard," she mused.

"What?" Alta asked. "That is to say, no disrespect intended, Your Highness. I did say it's been quiet—but that's as likely to be *because* of the guard as anything. And it's not so very long since we had all the problems to begin with."

"That's true enough." Juniper sat up and wrapped her arms around her knees. "But I can't help feeling that this night duty is a growing wedge between me and my subjects. Do you really think it's worth it?"

"I do," said Alta earnestly. "And, pardon my saying so, but isn't that the job of a leader? To do the unpopular thing, to think first of the greater good, even when that's the last thing anyone else wants?"

"Oh, you're right. But it's not going to win me any popularity contests, that's for sure. And let's be honest . . . that's what this is coming down to."

At breakfast the next morning, Juniper twitched uncomfortably through the usual complaints from those who had been up the night before on guard duty. Oona and Filbert argued most strongly, and Toby seemed to be biting his lip to keep quiet. Even Sussi drooped unhappily in her seat. But Juniper had made the decision to stick with the guard, and she wasn't backing down now. What she *was* doing was solidly regretting Cyril's return to meals. Now that he was courting the role of ruler, he was back to being part of the settlement, while still making it clear that he and his cohorts could do anything they liked with their time. And with her queenship in question, there wasn't a thing Juniper could do about it. Cyril was reveling in the discontent, she could see—drawing it out with seemingly innocent questions and leading comments.

Juniper frowned. She needed to get things back on track.

But she'd waited a moment too long.

"Tonight, we can gather at my camp." Cyril broke smoothly into the conversation. "My man Root here has trapped a chamois and will start up the roasting pit in midafternoon. By the time Juniper has finished grinding a hard day's work out of you, *I* shall be ready to reward you with a fine feast."

Jessamyn clapped her hands and twirled around in her fresh, unwrinkled skirt, which was only to be expected. But the rest of the group seemed equally delighted, which was a far bigger concern.

And so the day went. The work carried on efficiently as usual, but through all long, hot hours, the talk was of nothing but fresh roasted meat.

"Don't they see that he's bribing them?" Juniper cried in frustration to Erick later that night. "Why did he have to make his feast a statement? Root could have been providing us with meat this whole time, if he's that fine a hunter. Instead, he keeps his skills all buttoned up, and now Cyril's flashing them like a feather in his own cap."

There was plenty more where that came from. Cyril organized a rock-climbing expedition, squeezing it neatly in place of a path-paving session Juniper had planned for midweek. He pulled out a large bag of candied sweetnuts—which he'd obviously been hoarding this whole time—and handed out giant handfuls with an air of casual generosity. Juniper longingly recalled herself as she was back in the palace, dreaming of a carefree existence, of a place where she would have nothing more pressing to do than kick up her heels under the midnight moon.

How had she thought *that* was what launching her own kingdom would bring her?

But then she would catch herself on the verge of throwing a party or an activity of her own, and she'd bite her lip in frustration. She couldn't do it, *wouldn't* do it. Not only because the thought of being Cyril's copycat gave her the tummy chills. But also because it wasn't *right*. They weren't here to play—well, they were, but not every day. That wasn't what ruling and running a country was all about; she'd seen that plenty from her father. They had things to do, important things. Any day now, they might get another message from the palace, with an update on the conditions in Torr. Surely by now things were improving! When that happened, she wanted to know Queen's Basin was in order and ready for anything.

At last, only one day remained until the ballot casting. Juniper had already set plans in motion for her own celebration, a modest week's-end gathering to be held in the Great Tree. Of course, everyone was off at Cyril's swimming hole today, and she hoped that they would be willing to help prepare everything for the feast tomorrow. This was the way to rest: work hard, then reward yourself with something really enjoyable. Not keep throwing aside responsibilities every day of the week. What kind of country would you end up with *then*?

Juniper hadn't bothered to go along to the swimming hole. She grudgingly attended the dinner parties Cyril threw—she wasn't one to turn down good food, and Root had serious campfire skills—but the day trips were far too uncomfortable.

Of course, she no sooner found herself alone in the camp than she wanted to be as far away from the empty settlement as possible.

How had everything gotten so crooked all of a sudden?

In frustration, she decided to clear her head with a vigorous climb. She went a different way than normal, trekking to the far end of the row of caves and attacking the steep incline above them, heading for a craggy peak that looked directly out over Torr. The climb was nearly vertical, but she kept challenging herself to scale one more rock face, then another, until the camp winked below her like a bluebeetle farm and the clouds were close enough to pet. Her arms ached and her legs wobbled like jelly, but she grabbed the last outcropping and hauled herself up—right to the top of the world.

And, oh, it *was* that!

The plateau was no wider around than twenty paces, knobby and steep like the crooked chimney stack on the top of a witch's cottage. But what really took Juniper's breath was the view. From here, she could see down the mountain, with its scattered trees and forbidding slopes. For a second, she thought she saw tiny moving shapes on a far peak, but when she looked again, there was just the thick, gloomy forest lining the whole near mountain.

But there below was Torr, rolled out before her like an intricately woven carpet, the sight of it squeezing something tight in her throat, opening a core of longing she knew was there but kept well buried. She could see where the Lore River bubbled out of the rocky heart of the Hourglass and started its winding journey down through Torr. She could see the barren fields that edged the base of the mountains, and beyond them the more cultivated fields that denoted the start of civilization.

Except . . . wait. Something wasn't right.

Where there should have been fields of heavy, golden stalks of wheat—where there *had* been, just weeks ago—Juniper now saw just a dark, ashy swath. Could it really be? Yes. Even now, a thin column of smoke rose from the nearest field. She was too far away to see any detail in the nearest village, but she could swear that it, too, looked smoky, and dark, and ruined.

What had she thought all that smoke was coming from, after all? Still, seeing this solid proof of the devastation was something else altogether.

Juniper's legs wobbled, and she collapsed onto the hard stone, feeling the air swim around her. It was all true. Everything her father had feared. The palace *had* fallen. Impossible as it might seem, Monsia—that despicable, sniveling, weak-minded nation—had somehow amassed an army and come in to invade Torr. They had fulfilled the ultimate threat of the Monsian Highway, had blazed into Torr and gone storming south, bringing their deadly force all the way to the palace.

And then what? She'd had no more word from her father; how was he holding up? Her breath caught in her throat. Was he even still alive?

She had to . . . she had to . . .

She had to *do nothing*. Those were her father's orders. Stay put. Watch and wait. While her country fell to the enemy.

"They're all about you," said Tippy later that night, up in the Great Tree.

Juniper looked up. "What?" Her mind was leagues away, her worry about her father tying her up in knots, trying to figure out what she could do, what she could say, and who she could possibly say it to.

"All the others," said Tippy, clasping her hands behind her tousled head with a satisfied grin. "I did my roundabouts, to see what I could learn. They all like Cyril's food and his activities. But they don't like *him* much. You're their leader, and they feel safe with you. Well, most of them do, anyway."

"Cyril should be our master of activities," said Alta with a chuckle. "It's like he's made for that role."

Juniper couldn't even bring herself to smile. She was glad to hear Tippy's news, but her mind was too foggy right now to settle on it.

"All right, then," said Alta, obviously sensing Juniper's mood. "Let's get ourselves off to bed. A big day tomorrow, with a feast to prepare and a party to throw."

"And a ballot to WIN!" trumpeted Tippy.

"Hush, you goose, or you'll throw the evil boot on the whole affair," Alta said, but there was a smile in her voice as she ducked down the ladder. "I for one am happy to retire to my good warm bed and let tomorrow bring its news by and by."

"Good night," Juniper called distractedly. She had to think. She had to plan.

What on earth was she going to do?

She spent hours that night pacing across the plank floor of the Great Tree, nearly torn in two by worry—fear for her father and Torr, and concern about the coming ballot. Finally she gave way to her restless frustration, grabbed hold of one of the branches over the main floor, and started to climb. The Great Tree was wider than it was tall, so there wasn't terribly far to go, but the branches were wide and fat, and soon Juniper found herself at the tip-top of the old trunk. There the branches came together in a pointy sort of crown, and Juniper slung her feet down on either side of the fork. She laid her cheek against the bark, which at that height was smooth as silk.

On this dark, moonless night, she couldn't see the details of her little kingdom, but in her mind's eye, it was as clear as any Marchello masterpiece: from the paved walkways to the animal pens to the clay-and-daub roof of their dining area, to the stream that sliced the kingdom neatly in half, and on over to the lush grasslands and the early vegetable gardens and the orchards of the far end. Up the craggy slopes she could just see the red-coal glow of Cyril's campfire—several red glows, actually. What was Cyril up to, in his secret hideaway? Juniper pushed the troublemaker out of her mind and focused on her kingdom.

All of this was hers, entrusted to her by her father. But the sight didn't fill her chest with the kind of hot-springs fizz that it used to. All she could think of was the devastated countryside of Torr and how she'd had one task, just *one* simple task: establish a country, rule it, keep its people safe until she heard from her father. Instead, here she was, feeling like a horse latched to a carriage that was far bigger and heavier than it had ever expected.

Cyril! She'd bet that if *he* were to rule this kingdom for a week or so, he'd realize that it wasn't all fun and games. Maybe she should let him have it, just to show him a thing or two.

But even as her hands tightened on the trunk, she knew she would never do that. She'd seen the way Cyril's gaze slid carelessly past those he spoke to, swinging always back around to his own personal space. She'd seen him push aside needed duties and tasks for the sake of momentary pleasure. She'd seen him skim the best things—food and other comforts and conveniences—without a moment's care for the provision of others.

She thought of how her father had toiled every day of his life, establishing laws and bylaws, hearing complaints, resolving disputes of all ranges and types. His primary concern was always to meet the needs of every subject in his kingdom to the best of his ability.

That was how a ruler should act.

Cyril didn't deserve this kingdom. He *couldn't* win the ballot tomorrow—he just couldn't.

Official Ballot Rules for Queen's [Role Pending] Basin

1. Each subject shall receive two stones: one white and one gray.

2. At the time appointed, each subject must drop ONE (1) stone within the ballot basket.

3. Any GRAY stone means a vote for CYRIL LEFARGE.

4. Any WHITE stone means a vote for JUNIPER TORRENCE.

5. May the BEST claimant win!

18

THE NEXT DAY DAWNED DULL AND OVERCAST,
with such a smoke-gray sky that Juniper could think of nothing
but the dead fields stretching down from the Hourglass through
the spine of Torr. She was up before the sun—even though she
felt like she'd closed her eyes only minutes before, which may well
have been true. Tension coiled in her belly like a hunter's trap.
There was nothing she could do about Torr, for now. But what she
could do, what she *had* to do, was fend off Cyril's challenge.

She had to win this ballot.

Yet in actual, practical fact, what could she really do? Building a country out of nothing was no easy task, and she knew that
in going about what needed to be done, she'd had to knock heads
with more than one of her subjects. The truth? There was nothing she *could* do to make the vote go her way.

On the other hand, Cyril had no way to do that, either.

All she had to do, then—all she *could* do—was to continue
as she had, to be herself, to show her strength and the qualities of

leadership she'd been taught her whole life. And hope that Tippy was right and that everyone saw Cyril for what he was—a scheming, opportunistic party lion.

She herself had risen early to help Leena make a truly spectacular breakfast. For the first time in a while, the hens had laid heaps of eggs, and there was enough to make a large cinnamon and sweetroot soufflé. Even the goats had been on task, with Toby delivering nearly a full bucket of their warm, frothy milk. Leena had whipped it up with the last of the carob powder for a steaming hot drink.

Over the silent, satisfied faces of her breakfasting subjects, Juniper caught Cyril's eye and slowly stood up. They had agreed that they would each give a speech, and he had insisted that she go first, in what he painted as a gallant gesture. But she was pretty sure he just wanted to hear her angles before plying his own.

"So," she began, "here we are. It's been a good few weeks, hasn't it?" Encouraged by the milk-happy smiles and the murmurs of encouragement, Juniper continued, "It's hard to believe that we came to this empty, unsettled valley—just us, no proper adults—having no other help, with only the things we could bring along. And look around you. Look at what *we've* done. All of us together!"

She waited a moment, while the kids craned their necks from side to side. The roof over their heads was sturdy and the posts supportive. The food smelled delicious, and just out of sight, the river could be heard skipping over the stones. The day was still overcast, but a tremulous bird began a lighthearted serenade on a nearby tree. Juniper smiled. She looked at Erick, and he nodded his support.

"I set out to build this kingdom because I wanted a place where each one of us could matter, where we could all find our own bit of glow. We don't need anyone outside to tell us what to do—we can make our own way, build our own country, live the way *we* choose." She took a deep breath. Some things just had to be said. "I know I'm pretty young, and I've still got a lot to learn as ruler. But I think you'll agree that I've had the chance to learn from the best. And what's more important, I care about this place. I care about you. And if you'll allow me to—if you'll choose me to continue on as your queen—then I promise to lead you on to even bigger and better things."

Before she'd fully finished, the group burst out in enthusiastic applause. Filbert stamped his big feet in rhythm on his stone, and Oona gave her a rare smile. There were even a few whistles and cheers. Juniper sank into her most regal curtsey and returned to her seat.

When she looked up, Cyril had taken her place in the center of the group. His hands were thrust into his pockets; his gaze was on the ground. He oozed gravitas and depth and mature responsibility—pretty much the opposite of his actual personality, Juniper thought wryly. He looked up, held her eye with a thoughtful nod that was clearly for the sake of the onlookers. Then he spun to address the group.

"You've heard from our lady princess," he said, his voice ringing across the open room, "and I have just a small something to add." He held up a hand. "Small, but very important. Before this, though, I'd say that Juniper has done well at getting this place set up. What needed doing first, what seemed most important, assigning tasks—perhaps not the best choices in all cases, but . . ." He paused, gave the barest shrug, and Juniper bristled at the condescension in his voice. "But it hasn't been awful, either. Still, there's one thing that matters most when it comes to ruling a nation, one thing that's beyond dispute, which every subject *has* to be sure of in their leader: integrity, truthfulness, honesty."

What on earth was Cyril getting at? The kids cast sidelong looks at each other, obviously wondering the same thing. Juniper sat up a little straighter.

"The fact is, while Juniper has been working hard—and working *you* hard—there is also a darker side to the picture. Believe me, there is a lot you don't know. A lot you have not been told." Cyril raised a hand to quell the chattering that had started at his words. "Hear me out. This is important. Have you ever wondered about this harebrained scheme, how it came about to begin with? From one day to the next—*poof!*—a brand-new country has been established, and a group of settlers—children, no less—dispatched to colonize a bit of the far wild north. Almost as though . . ." He looked shiftily from side to side. "Almost as though someone wanted you *out of the way* for some reason."

"What are you getting at?" Alta called out.

"I am getting at *this*. Your so-called *queen* has been keeping you very busy over the last few weeks. But the truth is, during that time, she has been *concealing information from you*. And I am here to bring everything out into the open."

Juniper drew in a breath, because suddenly she knew exactly what Cyril was going to say. She had no idea how, but he *knew*.

"Here is the truth: Torr has been invaded."

"We know that already," said Paul, from his place on the far edge of the group. "That happened the night we left—it's why we hotfooted it out under cover of darkness."

"Do you, though? What exactly were you told?" Cyril's voice was hard. "Was it the simple child's tale of a 'raiding party' that you were given, the story of a petty attacker easily repelled and quickly dispatched? Or . . . shall I tell you what's really happened?" He scanned the crowd, who now gave him their full attention, eyes wide and staring.

Grim and gloating, Cyril went on. "Here's what has actually taken place. A vast Monsian army has descended upon Torr. The palace has been overrun. The king has been taken hostage. And Juniper—this fizgig of a girl who calls herself your queen—*has known about this all along.* All this time, she has been hiding the truth. Lying to you. Playing queen-in-her-castle while your country burns."

The group erupted. Everyone was on their feet, crowding around him, wailing in despair or demanding more information. Juniper took a step back. Things were spinning out of control fast.

Cyril lifted his hands. He stayed perfectly still, waiting until the others quieted. None of the kids returned to their seats, but at least the yelling stopped. A few sniffles echoed through the clearing.

"This is a grave accusation, I know," he said, his voice low and deadly. "If nothing else in this world is constant, a man should be able to trust his ruler. So let's turn the tables now and ask our lady-of-the-moment to tell us a little more. *Why* did you choose to deceive us all, Juniper? Why did you hide the *real* truth about this expedition, choosing to pass it off as a summer adventure, then keep everyone occupied with busywork while this darker plan was at work all along? And why are you *even now* actively forbidding your subjects from returning to Torr?"

Cyril spun around and pointed a finger straight at her. "Juniper Torrence, *what else are you hiding?*"

On cue, every eye turned to Juniper. She swallowed hard. "That's not how it happened," she said, but her voice barely rose above the burble of the river. Too much was happening too quickly, and she was having a hard time figuring out how to skim out the truth from Cyril's careful misinformation. Outside, the bird resumed its chirping; Juniper hated its lighthearted song with all her might.

She squeezed her hands into fists. She had to regain the upper hand. "It was *not* like that. I had no advance notice of the raiding party, and that had no connection to the plans for this settlement. I found out about the attack when you did—that's why we had to leave early, in the night. And that's why my father expressly commanded us to await his word before returning home."

"But you *did* have more information about the Monsian invasion," said Cyril, eyes wide and innocent. "The *real* attack. Did you not learn this information and choose to keep it hidden?"

"I did have a letter last week telling me more about the attack," Juniper admitted. "But that was—" The crowd began muttering, and her head spun. She had to make them understand.

However, she didn't get the chance. A voice rose from the back of the crowd: "Cyril for king!" Then another: "Down with Juniper. I choose Cyril!"

Vaguely, Juniper registered that it was Root, in what had to be a calculated move, for he was standing behind everyone else, crouched slightly and muffling his voice between cupped hands. At the other end of the group, Jessamyn echoed the cry. But the crowd was beyond noticing such details. The emotion of the moment was ripe for harvest, and Cyril was out with his scythe at the ready.

"Now, now," he called out tolerantly, "I share your feelings, but we must do this properly. You all have your ballot stones: white for Juniper and gray for myself. Simply make your choice for ruler and place your stone in the basket yonder. No need to push—there's room for all. Make your decision now, what type of ruler you *really* want, and place your stone in the basket."

"Wait," Juniper called, but she knew it was no use. And what could she say? What reply did she have to give? Nothing, that was what.

She had lost her kingdom.

19

DETERMINING THE FINAL OUTCOME DID NOT take long. After everyone had dropped their stones, Juniper retired to the far side of the room, where Erick and Alta hurried over to stand defiantly by her. No one else would even meet her eye.

As had been arranged, Leena approached the basket and, in full view of the onlookers, began drawing out the stones. She put the white ones to her left and the gray to her right. Juniper kept her eyes on the ground. She didn't need to see the proof of her loss, but there it was all the same.

"Here are the official ballot results," Leena called out. "Stones for Cyril: eleven. Stones for Juniper: three."

Juniper's eyes burned. It was obvious who her two supporters were; they stood by her right now. But had *no one* else truly seen her worth as ruler? Were they just swayed by the passion of the moment, or did the discontent run deeper? The whole group looked slightly stunned by the outcome. Tippy slumped on her stone, knees hugged tight against her chest, face buried in her lap.

Even Tippy?

As seemed to be happening more and more often since she'd begun this expedition, Juniper's thoughts flew to her mother, wondering what she would have made of this situation. Her mother's nomadic upbringing had ill prepared her for the sedate life of a ruler of Torr. She'd adapted, but still had never lost a certain wildness, a looseness of manner that didn't quite fit her palace persona. Deep down, Juniper had always wondered if that Anju blood affected her own life in any way. She'd always loved the untamed side of herself, despite how rarely it could be let out. Only here, in this wild mountain landscape, had she been able to explore that untapped nature, getting a taste of a life free of the palace's strict confines and her own royal expectations.

And now, she'd learned that her nonroyal self might be her truest one after all. She could not rule. She could not even keep this motley crew of subjects content and on her side. This time of self-discovery had just managed to expose her utter failure at the role she had been groomed for her whole life.

"All hail King Cyril of the Hourglass!" came the cry.

Juniper bowed her head in defeat.

After that, things moved quickly. Before Juniper could say even a word, Cyril proclaimed, "I acknowledge your trust in me, good subjects! I assure you that I will not disappoint. And my first task as ruler is to rid our ranks of this traitor. And her cohorts."

"What are you talking about?" Juniper spat.

Her protests were swallowed up as she, Alta, and Erick were surrounded by Root, Filbert, and Roddy, each hefting the guards' very own dagnite spears. Cyril himself shifted his cloak to show a fine, gleaming sword holstered around his waist. Where had *that* come from?

"Come this way, Miss Juniper," said Root.

Juniper exchanged a glance with Erick. So this was where their plan to arm and train the guards had brought them! Then Juniper caught the look in Alta's eye. Since guard duty had begun, she'd taken to wearing her own sword belt again, and now her hand quivered on the hilt. She was coiled tight and ready to spring.

"Stop," Juniper told her quickly. "It's not worth it. Let's wait and see what happens—we'll talk our way out of this, you'll see. First we need to find out what's going on."

"He's obviously been planning this for a while," Erick muttered.

Cyril led the way back toward the caves, with Jessamyn and Oona trailing him like eager bunnies. Root and Filbert marched the captives along the narrow path all the way to Cyril and Root's old chambers. The heavy cloak still covered the door, but Cyril yanked it down, tossing it to Jessamyn. She caught it with both hands and immediately dumped it on Oona.

Juniper's heart sank. A woven door now filled the opening, anchored firmly into the rock wall. Cyril swung it open easily, but it was obviously sturdy and well made.

The cave had been converted to a prison.

Erick ran his fingers along the door's surface as he was

shoved through the opening. Cyril smirked. "Recognize that material, do you? Dagnite, it is. I've had my eyes and ears open over the past couple of weeks. Maybe you thought I was gone slugabed while you all built roadways and roofs and other such nonsense?" He snorted. "Only try and get yourself out through this door. Of course," he added hastily, "we'll have the outside under guard at all times." He tapped Root's spear, and the point gleamed in the dull light. "Hardest wood in the kingdom, don't you know? Could do a pretty bit of damage if it hit the wrong spot."

With that, Cyril pushed Alta in—reaching first to separate her from her sword—and pulled the door shut behind him. He jammed the latch into place, wound it tight with a lock of some sort, and turned to go. Root and Filbert settled heavily on the ground outside the door.

"Wait!" Juniper called out through the door. "What happens now? You can't just leave us here!"

"You," Cyril hissed, barely turning in place, "do *not* get to tell me what I can or cannot do. You and your friends are *entirely* at my mercy. And the sooner you learn that, the better."

With that, he was gone, and Juniper sank back against the nearest wall, unable to meet either Alta's or Erick's eyes. She still felt like she was missing some bigger part of the picture, like there was more at stake here than even she properly knew. But one thing she did know for sure: She had been caught flat-footed and outwitted.

Cyril had taken her on, and he'd won.

• • •

The rest of the day passed slowly. Alta spent the hours pacing the room, half muttering complicated plans and airing impossible goals. Erick spent his time studying the walls from top to bottom and analyzing the bars on the window and door, only to finally turn, shaking his head.

"There's *no* way out," he said, and Juniper could hear his teeth grinding in frustration. "We're stuck in here until that cockalorum says otherwise."

Juniper had figured as much. She herself had spent the whole day sitting motionless. She had no energy, felt no need to get up and move around, had no interest in helping Erick explore their surroundings or Alta brainstorm plans for escape. What was the use? She'd tried her very best, and her best hadn't been good enough. Years ago, she'd lost her mother and hadn't been able to do a thing about it. Now her homeland was invaded, her father's safety unknown, war was declared—and she, Crown Princess Juniper of Torr, former ruler of Queen's Basin, couldn't even keep control of her tiny Hourglass kingdom. What kind of failure did that make her? The worst kind, that was what.

Queen's Basin, indeed!

She sat a little lower and pulled her arms up over her head. All she wanted was to sink into the ground and disappear.

Gradually she realized that the room had gone quiet. She lifted her head and looked around. Alta had stopped pacing and slumped against the far wall, eyes closed, a hand resting on her hip where her sword normally sat. Erick had stretched his cloak out on the ground and was sprawled across it. Outside the window, purple shadows gathered as the last of the sun disappeared over the far rim of the Basin. Distantly, Juniper felt their loss of morale. It seemed like something she should care about, should even try to do something about. But what could she hope to do?

She turned back to the wall and pulled her hood over her head.

Hours later, she opened her eyes and saw that a tray containing three plates of bread and cold meat and boiled carrots had been pushed through the door. She hadn't even heard it open. Neither Erick nor Alta had shifted positions, so she figured they hadn't, either.

The cell was perfectly silent, except for a light snore coming from Alta's side of the room. And then a sound in the distance caught her ear—faint, barely audible at first, but growing in volume until it was unmistakable: the sound of music.

Juniper scrambled to her feet. The far-off notes tugged at something inside her, whispered with an unearthly tongue, spoke things to her soul that words could never say. It was the Musicker. A faint glim flickered in the leaves of the Great Tree, which was just visible out of the corner of her window. Tears filled Juniper's eyes.

"Erick," she whispered, and saw him sit up and turn her way, blinking awake. "I was wrong, wasn't I?"

He didn't answer, and she pushed on into the silence. "Not telling everybody what was going on back in Torr. We're a team—all of us here. I can't do everything on my own, and it wasn't fair to keep that from people. Important information that would matter to them. You told me I should tell the others, and I didn't listen to you. I did the wrong thing there, didn't I?"

She waited out the silence, finally turning to see him sitting up and looking at her with a gentle half smile. "Yeah," he said at last. "You busted that one up a bit."

Her shoulders slumped. She'd had this chance, and she'd blown it. She had *failed*. Failed her country, failed her people.

Or . . . had she?

What had she wanted, after all? To launch out on her own, to build something that would last. To find out what she was truly made of. To listen for that distant music that made her soul dance, and to follow wherever it led.

She'd been wrong. For sure.

But did that mean she was finished?

The music outside grew louder, and she heard a scuffle as one of the guards stood and walked over to the other: Jessamyn and Paul were out there now. There were never less than two at a time to guard the "traitors." She couldn't help feeling a grudging admiration that Cyril had gotten Jessamyn to do some actual work for a change.

A distant shout bellowed across the clearing, and Juniper recognized Cyril's voice. The music stopped. The light in the tree went out.

But inside Juniper, the spark stayed.

What *was* she made of? She'd lost control of her country. But was that the only goal she had set out to accomplish? And more important . . .

Was her story *really* over?

Juniper felt her heartbeat quicken. The battle for Queen's Basin was *not* over. Not at all. This fight had just begun.

The rest of the night passed in a flash. Juniper felt the bones of a plan starting to come together in her mind, but there was still a lot of meat missing. Dawn was breaking over the far horizon when she heard a faint hiss. Moving soundlessly to the barred window, she first didn't see anything. Then a blur of movement flashed outside. Juniper leaned in closer. Even this near at hand, the figure was barely visible: small, dark-swathed, with a muddy-looking face and a pert nose.

"Tippy!" Juniper whispered.

Tippy held a finger to her grubby lips. She moved her face to the bars, and Juniper leaned in till the little girl's mouth was almost at her ears. "I can't stay but a moment. Root is sawing logs, and Oona granted me a minute to give my respects, but she won't stand with me if I get caught." Her voice wobbled a little. "I didn't want Your Princessness to think I deserted you, like. After you done so much for me and given me a proper place in your kingdom and all."

Juniper blinked, joy enfolding her like a warm hug. She reached out to squeeze Tippy's hand through the bars and heard the girl's smile wrinkle across her face.

"Good," Tippy said. "I didn't think you did, but I wanted you to know it sure. I'm on your side. Only . . . well, I could see which way that blinking ballot was set to go. And I thought I might do more good if I looked like I was on that blaggard's side, then got busy finding ways to cause him trouble." She paused. "You heard the music, yeah?"

Juniper felt tears filling her eyes. She squeezed Tippy's hand harder and then reached up to turn the girl's head, putting her own lips up to the small ear. "Thank you for that, Tippy! A million times, thank you. But listen, I have something I'd like you to do." Tippy's head bobbed in place. "Do you think you could get up to Cyril's camp? Where he's been staying all this time? I'm putting together a plan to get us out of here. But if we're to have an advantage over that impostor, we need to know what he's really up to. Can you get to his stuff, dig around a bit, see what you can find, and report back to me?"

"I'll do that for you, Your Royalty, yes, I will! I'm ever so sneaky."

"And, Tippy?" Juniper said, her breath hitching in her throat. "Don't forget your good-night kiss."

Grinning even wider, Tippy leaned in to the bars, and Juniper placed a soft kiss right in the center of her cheek.

"Mistress Ladyship Juniper of Everything," Tippy said, with breathless adoration, "you are the most righteous queen ever to live. I am surely your loyal servant for life! Now, off I go to spy upon the *real* traitors."

Before Juniper could answer, the cold little hand slipped out of her own. Tippy disappeared like the night into the breaking day.

Princess Juniper's Daily Schedule: While Incarcerated

Early Morning: Grooming, Calisthenics & Strength Training

Rest of the Day: Worry. Plan. Prepare.

20

"COME TO ORDER, EVERYONE!" CYRIL'S VOICE echoed around the dining area, managing to sound both bored and bossy all at once. Juniper, Erick, and Alta had heavy ropes wrapped around their ankles, each fastened from one to the other. Their hands had been tied behind their backs by an overly diligent Root before leaving the cave, and Juniper's arms felt cramped and uncomfortable. Despite this, she kept her head high and her face expressionless. She would not cower for Cyril.

Stepping into the dining area, Juniper was shocked to see how much it had changed in just the day they'd been locked away. Scraps of food and discarded personal items lay strewn across the space, and stacks of dirty dishes teetered off to each side. Apparently Cyril was keeping his promise of not working anybody "too hard." Juniper turned up her nose at the smell of spoiling food. At the far end of the room—from which all the trash and dirty dishes had been shoved away, Juniper noticed—was a new item of furniture, which could only be called . . . a throne. The base of a tree trunk had been hollowed out at the center, sanded silky, and rubbed with some sort of shiny oxide. In this majestic seat Cyril now reclined, looking down his nose at his three captives.

On the center table were strewn the signs of a great breakfast feast. Evidently the hens and goats were continuing to produce, for Juniper had not seen such an abundance in all the time they'd been in Queen's Basin. Nor, she thought with a lurch to her stomach, had she seen such waste. The leftovers scattered about upon the plates would have been enough to feed everyone another full meal.

"I have summoned you here out of a simple courtesy," Cyril said, drawing her attention back his way. "So that you might be aware of what is to be the plan going forward."

Around them, the other kids lounged on their sitting stones, bellies bulging visibly. Apparently food coma was another control method Cyril used on his subjects. Juniper tried to catch one eye after another, but finally had to give up: Cyril had them completely gorgonized. The three captives were flanked by Root, Roddy, and Filbert, all hefting their dagnite spears. Juniper didn't plan to escape, but it was clear that she couldn't have anyway.

"As you might imagine, it takes a good deal of effort and manpower to maintain the three of you in your current setting," Cyril went on.

Juniper's head snapped up, but Alta got the words out first. "*Maintain* us? Keep us locked up, you mean!"

In a flash, Root's spear tip was aimed at Alta's cheek. She froze.

"Do not make me force you to stay quiet with gagging cloths," Cyril said, sighing. "It would be so tedious. As I began to say, I have

223

been pleased to accommodate the three of you in my own quarters, but the need for two nightly guards to ensure your good behavior *does* take a big toll."

Juniper pressed her lips together. It was hard to believe, but most of the kids seemed to take Cyril at his word. *What about these ropes?* she wanted to yell at them. *What about those spears ready to jab us if we step out of line?* But she forced herself to stay quiet, and listen, and await her moment.

"There is also another matter. My subjects were given a promise. They were told they might return to Torr after a fortnight, to visit their families, to gather additional supplies, and to recruit new fellow settlers. They were told, in short, that they might go home. And while I think we all see the merits of this little place"—he waved a hand dismissively—"it most certainly is not *home*."

You never wanted to be here to begin with, Juniper argued in her mind. *Of course you want to run away now.*

"And so I have decided that, while I acknowledge my rulership of this little land, and while I will continue as its de facto king, I plan to launch our official return as soon as possible. Tomorrow, we set out for Torr!"

Juniper felt faint. She saw in her mind those charred fields and distant fires; Cyril wanted to bring everyone back to *that?* They had no idea what they would be getting into.

"Cyril," she said, keeping her voice smooth and level, "will you allow me to speak?"

Cyril met her gaze, obviously weighing his options. He couldn't keep up his good-guy appearance if he didn't let her talk, when she'd asked so politely. Yet he was clearly not happy at being pushed into it. He grudgingly bobbed his head.

Juniper chose her words carefully. "Have you given any thought to King Regis's command that we remain here in the mountains until we receive his word that it is safe to venture out? This was what he charged us with before we left Torr, and he wrote the same and more in the letter that he sent to me via messenger little more than a week ago."

"Ah, yes," Cyril drawled. "Your *secret* letter. That all-important missive you did not see fit to share with any of us."

Juniper groaned under her breath. It had been a mistake to bring up the letter Cyril had used to sway her subjects against her. She tried again. "Look, the letter is of no importance. What *is* important is this: We all know Torr is under attack. The roads are not safe. If you take everyone out there now, you put them at enormous risk. The party could be set upon by Monsians—attacked, taken hostage, or even killed outright."

It was so obvious! Was he deliberately choosing not to see the risks?

Cyril folded his arms across his chest. "All I am hearing from you is speculation. You have no idea what the conditions are like out there. And this king you refer to—" At some dismayed looks from the group, he added quickly, "*Our* own king of Torr, well, have we not heard that he himself has been taken captive? How, then, shall he send any further correspondence at all? Yet this girl—his daughter, the heir to the throne—wants to sit here hidden away, wants to look to her own needs and completely ignore *her* family, *your* families, and all those who are suffering out there."

Juniper wanted to cry. He made such a good argument she could almost believe it herself. But it wasn't like that. *Should* they venture back to Torr, ignore the king's command, and see if they might help? Maybe there *was* something they could do. Juniper's brain hurt. She needed to think.

Cyril stood up and opened his mouth.

"Wait," Juniper said. There was no beating Cyril in a direct attack, that was obvious. But this she knew: She *couldn't* let her subjects venture out pell-mell into a battlefield, with no plan and no idea what was before them, pushed forward by an arrogant, power-hungry leader with no sense of basic hygiene.

She needed to win back Queen's Basin.

And the first thing she needed in order to do that was a little more time.

"Wait," she said again. "Cyril, I wanted to compliment you on your new throne. It's very nicely made."

Caught off guard, Cyril looked down. His cheeks pinked, and he broke into a reluctant smile. "It did come out rather well. Paul and Sussi had to work through the night, but it was well worth it."

Neither were here this morning, Juniper noticed, as she glanced around the messy dining area. Cyril sure had an odd sense of priorities in his work strategy.

"It's only," she continued, pitching her voice to stay low and winning, "that after all that work, it seems a shame to abandon it so quickly."

Cyril's smile fell off his face.

Juniper flapped her hands uselessly in their bindings. "No, look. I'm not saying I agree with your plan to leave." She could feel a line of sweat gathering at the back of her neck. "I still think it's dangerous and would put everyone at unnecessary risk. But you're the ruler now, and that's a decision you get to make. All I'm saying——" She looked again at the fancy curlicues, the way the wood gleamed in the morning light, how Cyril's hand reached out unconsciously to stroke the polished armrest. She was right about this, she knew it. "Well, it just seems a shame for you to leave the Basin without first having a proper coronation."

There were a few moments of perfect silence. Then an excited buzz started up behind her. Juniper kept her eyes on Cyril's face. He showed no change of expression.

"Go on," he said finally.

"I have certain items here in my possession," she went on, her voice steady. "Treasures of Torr. One of these is the Argentine Circlet. You've heard of it?" He had; she could see the change in his face immediately.

"You have the Circlet with you, here?" he whispered.

Juniper felt something inside her crack as she watched the greed smear across Cyril's face like duck grease. But she closed her mind against it and threw in the last hook.

"I have it in a safe place. But it will not do me any good if I am captive, will it?"

Cyril's eyes grew sharp and suspicious. "Why would you offer to hand it over to me? What's in this for you?"

"Simply this," she said. "I came here for a grand summer adventure. That's really all I had in mind. And after all this time we spent setting up our kingdom and laying the groundwork, we were not even able to pull off one truly spectacular party. Now you want to take everyone away. You'll be cutting my adventure short, but also? We'll never get a chance like this again." Juniper shuffled forward. The bonds tightened against her ankles, but she closed the space between her and Cyril. She almost had him; she could feel it.

"Give us one week," she said, low and urgent. "Let us out of our cell. We will organize, with you in mind, the grandest party that ever has been thrown. It will be a celebration to rival all others. The Coronation Ball. Once that is over, one week from this day, you may resume your plans to take us wherever you wish." She paused, and swallowed. "What do you say?"

"One week?" Cyril mused. His eyes went glassy as he gazed off into the distance. His fingers tapped across the armrests. Then he turned back to face her, eyes hardening. "Very well. You'll get your time. But make good use of it, for at the week's end, I *will* have your promised crown."

Juniper felt Erick's shoulder bump her gently from behind. She'd done it.

They had seven days to plan their escape.

"I will have your promised crown," Cyril went on, and Juniper froze. "And one thing more. At this week's end, I will be crowned in this throne, by your own hands. And you will bend the knee and acknowledge me as your king."

21

THE NEXT MORNING, THE DOOR TO THE CELL
swung open with the sun. Juniper had been up and waiting for
hours, and now leaped out like a goat released from its pen.

Root stepped behind her to block the opening. "Hold up
there," he said to the others.

Juniper turned around. "What now? We're to plan a feast.
You heard Cyril." She bit her lip to keep from adding several
other unpleasant embellishments to his stupid name.

But Root shook his head. "Your Royal Highness—er,
Juniper, that is—*you're* the one who is to plan the event. These
groaks have to stay here. Cyril's orders." Was it her imagination,
or did he sound faintly apologetic? It shocked Juniper to realize
that she hadn't ever really considered Root apart from Cyril. He
always seemed such an extension of the other boy's dastardly
plans, but for the first time, it occurred to her that there could
be a separate mind and will behind that beef-witted face.

Still, this wasn't the time for musing. She had a plan to execute, and Erick and Alta were an important part of it.

"They have to come," she said, folding her arms across her chest. "I can't plan a ball on my own. It's meant to be grand, and that's more than any one person can do. Even me," she deadpanned, catching his eye.

Something flickered across Root's face, but it was gone as quickly as it had come. He shook his head firmly and pulled her by the arm. "Sorry. I've got my orders."

Juniper was powerless to keep from being tugged out of the way. The door was shut behind her, leaving the other two standing alone in the cell. Filbert swung the lock into place. Juniper craned her neck to see Erick standing at the window, hands on the bars. His look was guarded, but he was mouthing something to her. Root gave another tug and her head snapped around. What had Erick been trying to say? She stumbled on a rock and nearly toppled over. Her breath came in a sharp burst.

Tippy. That was it.

Cyril might split them up, but Juniper could still carry on her plan—using their silent-footed spy to link up the two sides of this new rebellion.

The plan was still on.

Juniper spent the first day watching and planning. The end goal was clear: overthrow Cyril's rule, save Queen's Basin, reclaim her throne. *How* she would accomplish all that was quite another matter. All she could think of at this point was to scout for weakness and look for any way she might delay Cyril's plans.

At first, Root stuck to Juniper like a burr, following her from one end of the Basin to the other. While determined to shake him off as soon as possible, Juniper also decided to take advantage of the extra labor while she had it. The first thing she turned her mind to was giving the camp a much-needed deep cleaning. How had so much muck accumulated in *two days*? Hitching her skirts and rolling up her sleeves, Juniper set to work collecting dirty dishes and stacking them high in Root's arms as he followed dutifully behind her like the world's first walking dish cabinet. It took her the better part of the day: ferrying skirtfuls of spoiled food scraps to the midden heap on the edge of the vegetable gardens; laying the fresh-scrubbed dishes out on the grass to sun-dry; dusting off the string-bough broom and giving the whole dining area a sound thrashing. By late afternoon, her shoulders ached and her skirt gave off a rank, spoiled odor. But Queen's Basin looked like itself again. From the quick furtive glances she caught in passing, she thought a few others might be appreciating the change, too.

As for Cyril, he had made a big show of demanding that she deliver the Argentine Circlet to him in advance, but Juniper held firm. She would hand over the treasure at the ball and not a moment before.

"I doubt you even have the thing," Cyril scoffed, but Juniper just swung around and went back to work. The greedy gleam in his eye was as strong as ever, and he wasn't willing to antagonize her and risk losing that coveted crown. Plus, he had to know the Torrence motto: *My word is all.* Whatever scorn he had for the ruling family, they were well known to speak promises that were ironclad.

Which was certainly true, Juniper told herself with satisfaction, as she scribbled off the end of a piece of parchment with a flourish. She hadn't told Cyril—or Root—a single falsehood. She had every intention of carrying off the planned Coronation Ball.

Only with a few fresh twists of her own.

"Here," she said, stuffing her charcoal stylus back into her waist-pouch and handing Root the finished list. "Take this to Leena. It's got the menu of items to be prepared for the dinner feast."

"Let's go, then," Root said.

"Why don't you take it?"

"I've got my orders," Root said stubbornly. "You're not to leave my sight."

Juniper sighed. "Look, I'm going to ask Cyril tonight at dinner—is there really any use in you following me around like a palfrey? Not that I don't like your company, mind. But what exactly is he worried about? He can't think I will escape, since leaving here is not my goal. And my friends—my *only* friends, apparently— are under full guard." She infused a careful throb into her voice, though she stopped short of dabbing at her eyes. That would have been too much for even Root to swallow. "Wouldn't it be simpler for you to do what you need to without having to watch me all day long? Far more efficient, too."

Root looked uncertain.

"Look at the state of me. I'm in sore need of a spell in the

Beauty Chamber. You can wait for me out here, or you can deliver this list to Leena. As you wish. Or go yourself to tell Cyril about my plan. I bet you'll find that he thinks it a good one."

It only took another minute or two of persuasion to send Root reluctantly on his way, saying he would go first to clear things with Cyril. Juniper had no worry on that count. What she had noticed about her nemesis was this: Cyril was a boy of action. He believed in what he could touch and see. He was smart, but he thought in a straight line; he made a plan and executed it. If she was lucky, this sideways maneuver of hers would slip right under his nose.

Meanwhile, she had important things to tend to. She *did* need to change her clothes, of course. But first, the next stage of her plan.

Juniper let the Beauty Chamber's door swing shut behind her and cast her eyes across the room. Gowns and shawls and cloaks and petticoats hung in neat, careful rows all along one wall, while shelves groaned with slippers and dainty pointed shoes in the latest fashion. Another table was busy with hair ribbons and jeweled pins, with beeswax creams and crystal bottles of flowery elixir.

Then a thought occurred to her. This was a tiny fraction of the items that filled her suite back at the palace—but that's all there was in the room. Everything in here was *hers*. Where were Leena's beauty supplies and gowns, or Sussi's, or Alta's, or any of the others?

As soon as she'd thought the question, Juniper knew the answer, and she was ashamed for not realizing it earlier. Of course the other girls had no fancy gowns, no jewels or face powders. Why should they? When would hardworking Alta ever need to curl her hair and rouge her cheeks for a ball?

Juniper looked down at her stiff, gravy-splattered skirt, at the newly unraveling hem, the clusters of mushed green peas adorning it like rotten gems. What if this were the only dress she owned? Her eyes scanned the room's bounty again.

These shall no longer be my items alone, Juniper promised herself. *They are now the property of Queen's Basin, and anyone may freely make use of them.* And in this light, the wide-open room packed with gowns and trinkets and potions took on a color and brightness they'd never had before. She couldn't wait to tell the others.

Which brought her back to the matter at hand. Undressing quickly, she wadded her soiled skirts into a ball and stuffed them in the laundry corner before pulling an identical dress off the wall. She was glad that she'd brought doubles of her favorites.

She was craning her arms over her head to fasten the last eyehook when she heard a scuffle at the window, then a hard thump. She spun around. "Tippy? Is that you?"

The little girl erupted from a heap of ball gowns. "Oh, Your Princessness! I am all agog to see you. And without those horrid ropes on your alabaster arms!" Tippy flung herself across the room and wrapped Juniper in a bony hug. Juniper squeezed her right back.

Simple acceptance, she mused. What a joy it was.

She untangled herself from Tippy's arms and dropped onto the floor next to her. "We need to hurry," she said. "I don't know how long Root will stay away, and someone else might wander in at any time. What have you learned?"

"I've learned that Mister Cyril is a pig," Tippy said scornfully. She pulled off her clogs and started to rub her dirty feet, as if to emphasize all the effort she'd put into scouting over the past few days. "His camp's a sorry mess. Rotten food all over, big piles of stinky eggs dumped willy-nilly and a sour milky smell everywhere. Ugh! It took all my effort to stay and finish my investigating, let me tell you."

That description didn't surprise Juniper at all, given the quick havoc Cyril had made of the rest of the Basin. But she made encouraging noises, and Tippy went on.

"There wasn't much else, I am sorry to say. But I did find *something*. I'm not sure how important it be, unless you go by its hiding spot: right at the bottom of one very smelly bag of smallclothes." Tippy turned up her nose and let her eyes go loopy, illustrating the depths of devotion that had kept her to this particular search.

"You are positively the best," Juniper whispered heartily. "Do tell me more!"

Tippy nodded, then reached into her bodice and pulled out a stack of parchment pages. She thrust them at Juniper. "Cyril ain't half bad with a pencil. I don't know what any of this means, but I thought you might."

Juniper leafed through the pages. "They're maps," she mused. "But it doesn't look like . . . Wait! These aren't maps of Torr—they're maps of *Monsia*. And these . . . figures, numbers, movements . . . these are troop lists. This is a chronicle of the Monsian army!"

"Monsian?" Tippy echoed.

Juniper's hands felt suddenly cold. What did this mean? She thought back to when Cyril had confronted her. He'd known an awful lot about what was going on with the invasion—but *how* had he gotten that information? She and Erick were the only ones who'd read the letter from her father, and clearly Erick had not betrayed her. Not only that: Cyril seemed to know even *more* than she did. His words rang in her mind: *The king has been taken hostage.* Was Cyril just blowing smoke? Or did he somehow know what had happened to her father in the attack? And here he was hiding maps of Torr's sworn enemy. The enemy that was even now putting their country to the sword.

Could Cyril be working in secret for her father, in some capacity she had not been told about? Juniper shuffled through the papers again. But . . . this army! This was no skittering, tentative Monsian invasion. No. This was a giant force, easily as big as Torr's own ranks. Bigger, maybe. And from the list of exercises and movements, they were strong and fierce and well trained.

Torrence Castle was impregnable—it always had been. Dozens of armies over the centuries had thrown themselves at the gates, only to be defeated and turned around within days—even hours. And her father had been fully confident of this outcome when they last spoke.

So what had changed in those few hours between Juniper's departure and the king's desperate realization that the battle was lost? The castle couldn't be breached from the outside . . .

But what about an attack from within?

Her father could not have had access to this information of

Cyril's. Otherwise, the king would not have so quickly dismissed the raiding party at the palace gates as weak and small and useless. There was only one answer, and suddenly it was frighteningly clear.

Who else was well connected enough, who had sufficient knowledge of Torr's secrets, who else could motivate Cyril to such lengths in his betrayal? *If history had turned out differently . . . my father might well be the one now sitting on the throne of Torr,* Cyril had said.

Well. Juniper had found the true traitor. Cyril's father had joined forces with the Monsians to bring down Torr.

And Cyril was working with him.

No wonder Cyril was trying to lead the settlers back to the palace! In so doing, he would deliver not only this ragtag group, but also the crown princess of Torr—right into Monsia's waiting hands. She knew what a prize she would be to the enemy. Her father had wanted to guard against this possibility; that was why he had sent her to hide in this secret spot until the trouble blew over. Only he hadn't accounted for the traitor in their midst. Nor for his daughter so quickly losing her kingdom.

As the last pieces of the puzzle fell into place, Juniper felt her resolve harden within her. She was not one to give up on a plan once she set her mind to it. She would not be cowed. Circumstances were wildly set against her, but she was far from beaten.

Juniper needed to stop stalling and planning.

It was time to crush Cyril into the ground.

Princess Juniper's Plan for How to Crush Your Enemy

Step 1:   Secure Your Allies

Step 2:   Determine Your Fortifications

Step 3:   Plan for Any and All Eventualities

Step 4:   Launch Your Attack

Step 5:   Overwhelm. Adapt. Overcome.

22

"WELL, DON'T YOU LOOK A SIGHT," SAID ROOT with some appreciation as Juniper flounced out of the dressing room. She'd spent over an hour in there and could easily have spent twice as long, but she wasn't sure how long Root would wait, and she didn't want to arouse his suspicion. Now she was glad she hadn't lingered, for the pile of cracked hazelnut shells at his feet showed that he'd been there awhile.

"I look like a princess," said Juniper, with a toss of her head. She'd spent long minutes choosing just the right look, including a last-minute outfit change: Over a spotless cream muslin dress, Tippy had helped her into a long flounced overdress of an eye-popping peacock blue—one of her favorites, which laced up the back and tied in a massive, jaunty bow. Juniper's hair had been plaited and twisted into an elaborate updo that towered over her head, except for two long curtains of hair that swept down both sides of her face, fastening securely behind her ears. She had to admit that the new look was a *little* hard to see around. But if it served its purpose, it would be worth it.

Based on Root's reaction, it was off to a good start.

He shifted from foot to foot. "I talked to Cyril, just as you said."

"And?"

"He said I ought to remain with you as he'd first ordered. He wasn't too happy with me for asking." Root scowled.

Interesting. Juniper kept her expression carefully neutral. "Well, I don't see *him* trekking around after me all day long. But I suppose I'm glad for your help. Party planning isn't easy work, you know." She clapped her hands together brightly. "Now. Shall we get to work?"

Step one in Juniper's master plan consumed much of the next two days. Her new outfit made it hard for her to dig in to the real dirty work, but her example on the first day had made an impression. While many of the kids were obviously enjoying Cyril's no-rules rule and could be seen wading up and down the river, gorging themselves on berries and lounging about from sunup to sundown, others began to quietly pick up after themselves or to launch several needed maintenance projects without any prompting at all. Aside from Erick, Alta, and Tippy, whose loyalties were unquestioned, over the course of the next day, Juniper discovered by signs and whispers that both Leena and Paul could be counted on to support her when the time came. That put six out of fourteen—nearly half the group—on her side, if Juniper counted herself, which she most certainly did. It was a good start, but not nearly enough. Even the majority, should she get it, would not be enough. She needed to get the *whole* group on her side, or as close to that as possible. And she needed to do so without raising suspicions, which meant she couldn't openly *ask* anyone for support. She had to wait until they decided for themselves, until they came to her.

"See if you can bring any of them up past Cyril's camp," Juniper told Tippy surreptitiously that evening.

"His camp?" Tippy echoed, then shoved in a mouthful of beans and leaned away from Juniper as Cyril looked at them suspiciously.

Juniper kept her gaze focused away from Tippy but, in the next moment, knocked her dish over, spilling the bean stew onto the ground. Cyril's attention was elsewhere, but she knew they had to be careful. She leaned toward the mess and whispered quickly to Tippy, "It *is* lucky that our chickens have begun laying again so generously, isn't it? After being so long unfertile. And the goats, too. It's almost as though . . . some kind of blockage was removed, wouldn't you say?"

Tippy's eyebrows shot up, then knit together in puzzlement. Juniper stared her down, and could see the moment when the realization broke. She looked at her dish, then toward the animal pens in the distance. The hens and goats had begun producing the moment Cyril came into power. Was he some sort of animal speaker, able to magically increase the beasts' productivity?

Hardly.

Juniper knew Tippy's thoughts were following her own track: remembering the state of Cyril's camp, with rotten eggs and sour milk strewn from one end to another. He was a pig, of course. But more than that: It was almost as though . . . he had so much produce available that it couldn't all be used before it spoiled.

And if Cyril had been sneaking in to cause trouble by stealing their milk and eggs, it wasn't a big leap to guess that he'd also been behind the other attacks on the camp. She had no idea how he'd done it or what he'd hoped to accomplish. Wreak havoc, sow confusion, undermine her authority? It hardly mattered now.

Cyril was every bit the villain.

They just had to find a way to let everyone know it.

Tippy swallowed and turned her eyes back to her dinner. "Okay," she mouthed. "I'll try."

Juniper nodded. Tippy wouldn't be able to get many of them up there—though Cyril had claimed the Great Tree as his own headquarters now, he watched everything that went on in the Basin—but every little bit would help.

She knew Cyril wasn't going to give up his new kingdom without a fight. And time was quickly passing.

"How are things out in the camp?" Erick asked her that night, once Root had locked the cell door and Filbert had settled his bulk solidly in front of it. Cyril had recently done away with the curtain, which let in a cool night breeze through the woven door, but made it harder to have any private conversations. Which was, of course, the point.

Juniper carefully removed her blue overdress and hung it from a rocky crag in the wall. After an unexpected tussle with the weeds along the main walkway today, she'd given up on keeping her cream underdress, well, *cream*-colored. But there was still hope for the kirtle. "It goes as well as can be," she said, sighing. "How go *you* in here?"

242

"We are fine," said Alta. "Only running half mad with boredom. Not a book in sight, don't you know?" She grinned at Erick, as though rehashing a familiar joke.

"It has been hard," Erick admitted, in perfect seriousness. "I learned to read when I was approaching my third Nameday. I don't suppose I've gone a full day since then without some book or another near to hand. Even when I had the spotted ague two summers ago, I kept my favorite tomes hidden under the covers in my sickbed. I was too weak to read, but their presence was a comfort." He sighed.

"So, how *have* you been keeping busy?" Juniper asked.

"I have been teaching Erick some sword skills. It would seem that boredom brings out all sorts of hidden talents."

"Sword skills?" Juniper lowered her voice. "But with what weapons?"

"Weapons of air," retorted Alta. "But no less useful for all that. Much of fighting is in the stance and positioning, as you'll know."

"It's rather like dancing," said Erick. "I never could set my mind to fighting back home. But stuck in here as we are, and with the image of Cyril always close to mind . . . well, it does put a new shine on dull metal."

Juniper grinned. "I am glad to hear you're looking to build new skills, and I'm sure those will come in handy before long. Meanwhile, I've got another for you. Alta, will you sit here before me?"

With that, she slid her comb out of her sleeve and began to sweep Alta's hair back from her head.

"Have a care," Alta yelped. "That thing's sharp!"

Juniper grinned. "It's whittled of real polished bone, that's why. Now, Erick, pay careful attention."

Erick's eyebrows rose and he took a step back, but Juniper grabbed his arm and yanked him closer.

"You want me to groom Alta's hair?" he stammered.

"She's not a horse, you dunderhead. I'm going to teach you a few tricks of the trade. Something to keep you busy during your long hours of captivity. It's ever so useful to know how to fix a lady's hair, wouldn't you say?"

Alta looked almost as green-faced as Erick did, and Juniper laughed softly. "Cheer up, you two. It is all part of the plan." She cast a glance through the pool of moonlight, at the figure of Filbert, who was loudly stutter-snoring at the door. "Now, after the hair is fully combed out straight and smooth, you start by dividing it into three even sections . . ."

Over the next few days, Juniper was satisfied to see the planned celebration shaping up smashingly. Sussi and Toby had been re-cruited as Leena's full-time kitchen helpers. It frustrated Juniper to no end how Alta's talents were wasted in lockup; aside from the help she would have been in overthrowing Cyril's rule, she could make a mean pear-hazelnut pie. Still, Toby had come armed with his grandmother's recipe for sweet quince stew, and Sussi proved excellent at chopping, rolling, and stirring.

The younger girl sidled up to Juniper during a rare moment when Root had disappeared to answer nature's call, grabbing Juni-per's work-tussled hands in both her hers. "I'm ever so sorry about the ballot," she said furtively. "I was wrong, and I——" She looked both ways and leaned in, pushing the rest of the words out in a rush. "If I should ever get the chance to change my stone, I'd do so in a heartbeat. That Cyril's a weasel, and no mistake."

With that, Sussi turned back to her work, leaning next to Leena as the three pored over the final menu. Juniper felt her smile nearly splitting her face. She could have hugged the two girls next to her right now. She looked around for Root, but he was still away. Toby, though, was looking at them thoughtfully. Juniper's heart froze. Surely he could tell what they were thinking—what they'd just been talking about. Easily, *so easily,* the whole thing could unravel.

Toby stepped closer.

"We'll all do what we can to sway things in your favor, Your Highness," Toby said, and Juniper thought she would pass out with relief.

"I'm ever so grateful for your support," she whispered. "But we can't talk of this right now. I've got a plan. I shall keep you informed as things unfold."

Root ambled back up, returning to his seat to begin work on a new bag of hazelnuts. But they were beyond reproach: just four humble subjects, hard at work in the kitchens.

"Be very, very careful in anything you say," Juniper said under her breath. "The last thing we want to do is arouse suspicions at this time. The stones have ears." She raised her eyebrows significantly as she kicked a hazelnut shell out of the way.

"Only two days until the ball," said Toby. He raised his voice. "And I've thought of a way we might infuse some cream with fresh lemongrass. My gran was much for the herbal essence, you see." He grinned, and Leena's whole face lit up.

"I do love the sound of that!" Juniper exclaimed. Then, "If we have time, that is. There is still the Great Confection to be planned."

"That's just it," said Toby. "I thought a layer of your excellent sponge"—he nodded to Leena—"topped all over with this cream—"

"Would we have enough cream?" Juniper interrupted. "You do realize how *large* this Confection has to be, don't you?" Behind her, Root shifted and strolled in their direction. She moderated her tone. "Cyril's orders—it shall be the cake to hang all cakes. Roddy is building a wheeled cart for it, and on the very tip-top will rest the Circlet."

"The all-important Coronation Confection," said Sussi, with a conspiratorial wink.

Juniper returned her grin, but kept her voice steady. "Try for the lemongrass cream, or whatever most pleases your palate. I've given all the specifications that are important to me. The rest I leave in your capable hands."

So her loyal subjects now counted eight. Even as Juniper rejoiced, she knew that this was likely all she would get. Root and Jessamyn were unquestionably Cyril's. She'd not seen Oona leave his side in days; the girl was obviously nursing an epic crush. And Filbert and Roddy so thoroughly embraced their guard duty that it seemed clear where their loyalties lay. Still, Juniper's plan was in motion; she would have to make do as best she could.

At least the food was solidly under way, and the Beauty Chamber had been reorganized so that all the gowns were tidy and in order. In keeping with her resolution, Juniper asked Tippy to be sure all the girls would gather in the Beauty Chamber before the big event. Baths were strongly recommended to all the night before, and nobody but Root seemed to find this idea offensive. Juniper pinched her nose mockingly in his direction, and he aimed a playful kick at her shins. The next she saw, he was heading toward the pool, drying cloth in hand, and Juniper dashed off for a few minutes' conference with Toby about important cake-related matters.

And with that, the preparations came to a close. There was just one last thing to be done, and on the night before the coronation, Juniper tackled this with gusto. Standing up with her half-empty dinner bowl in hand, she marched over to stand in front of Cyril. "There's something we haven't talked about," she said.

Cyril looked up and arched an eyebrow.

"It's about Erick and Alta. It's not fair that you're still keeping them locked up."

"They'll be let out when we all leave, the day after tomorrow. Following my coronation."

Juniper's eyes widened. "You're not going to let them come to the ball? You can't be serious!"

Cyril crushed the cracker he was holding in his fist. "I am *always* serious," he hissed. "And don't you forget it. I wouldn't even be letting *you* attend this event if you weren't such an important part of the . . . coronation process. Now go back and sit down."

"They *have* to be there!" Juniper said, stomping her foot. "It's not right, and you know it."

"Sit!" Cyril roared, and the conversation around them stuttered and froze. Looking uncomfortably from side to side, Cyril spun on his heel and strode off into the darkness.

Juniper's mouth turned down, and she put a hand to her chest. She wobbled a little and sat down. In Cyril's seat. She turned her attention back to her food, and only once everyone's attention was back on their own meals did she allow herself a slow, private smile.

23

THE MORNING OF THE CORONATION DAWNED
sunny and bright, and Juniper took it as a sign of clear trails and a
smooth road ahead. Of course, if it had been overcast, she would
have taken it as a sign that the gloomy days of Cyril's realm were
nearing an end. Even rain would have felt like a shower of bless-
ings.

Anything might go wrong; anything at all. But she would be
ready for it. She would take what the universe threw her way and
mold it into everything she needed it to be.

The morning hours blew by in a flutter of final touches and
last-minute preparation. Sussi was the first girl to peer in the entrance of the Beauty Chamber, awkwardly smoothing her mud-
stained skirts.

"Come in," Juniper exclaimed, tugging her inside.

"I never thought I should set foot inside your chamber . . ."

"Why, this isn't *my* chamber!" She scanned the racks of
gowns and pots and bundles. "Well, the items in here are mine, I

suppose—or they were. But I have pledged and made it so: Every item in here is the property of Queen's Basin and fully available to anyone who wishes to use it." Her eye caught on a favorite lace bonnet. "Er, as long as everyone takes good care of everything, that is. Now, what do you want to wear?"

Sussi was struck speechless, but Leena and Oona, who had come in for the end of Juniper's speech, had no such qualms.

"I do love a deep forest green," said Oona, fingering a high-waisted dress of a rich brocade silk.

"That will look *astonishing* with your coloring and your eyes," Juniper exclaimed. "Only the back is a dervish to lace up. Turn around, and I shall help you with it."

The girls thawed quickly, as the room erupted in a whirl of silks and scarves and paints and powders. Even Jessamyn made an appearance—not surprising, perhaps, given her love of dressing up. While she mostly kept off to her own corner, she was quite happy to make use of Juniper's powders and creams. All in all, the mood was as light and frothy as before any grand ball. Juniper advised, assisted, and finally took her turn being fixed up in the elaborate hairstyle she had worn every day for the past week. She was frankly sick of the cumbersome, overly ornamental updo. But so help her, if she made it through this day, she would never braid her hair again. She buttoned the peacock kirtle, smoothed its bulky pockets flat against her hips, and fluffed out the giant bow. She took in a deep breath and steadied her nerves. Around her, the other girls gathered in a flowery bouquet of partygoing anticipation.

Tonight, now, it would all begin to happen.

Tonight she would learn if she truly had what it took to be a queen, to take back her own kingdom.

She was ready.

Cyril was the last to arrive for the dinner feast—except for Alta and Erick, of course, who had been left in their cell with a double padlock on the door in place of their guards. The rest were gathered in a giddy mass, each looking like a cleaner, shinier version of themselves: faces aglow, hair sleek and smooth and styled, the girls adorned in gowns and accessories aplenty from Juniper's stash in the Beauty Chamber. Even the boys had turned up in clean, pressed garments. Slippered feet and heeled boots tapped the immaculate floor in anticipation of the first strains of music. Smiles were everywhere.

Moving slowly and affectedly—not even glancing at his supposed subjects, Juniper noticed—Cyril strode up the stone walkway into the dining area. While his people didn't catch his notice, the surroundings did, and he turned his head to every side in obvious appreciation at what he saw.

And well he might!

At Juniper's request, he had stayed away from the dining area all day while final preparations were made. The posts and roof lintels had been draped and wound with strings of fresh bluevine, and threaded through with wildflowers. The cornices had been fitted with softly glowing candles made with Sussi's own perfumed wax. As the sun set, the whole dining area would begin to glow, growing in brightness from the luminescent berries that were twined in among the floral hangings.

The low serving table in the center of the room was heaped with delicacies of all types: pies and breads, puddings and lightly spiced greens, and a giant pot of steaming fish soup. There was enough for all the settlers to stuff themselves ten times over, and Juniper felt a pang for how many careful meals this one feast could have supported.

They'd had to dip well into the reserves for this. How much farther would their food stores stretch now?

But she had set out to impress Cyril, and she'd succeeded. He strode up and down the food table, smiling and nodding. He reached the end, dropped onto his throne, and called out, "So where's my crown?"

Juniper steadied her breathing. "Patience, Cyril. All things in their time."

"Patience, *my lord*," he corrected.

"You're not my lord yet, *Cyril*," she said sweetly. "In any case, first we shall feast. Then we shall clear and set up for the party proper, then finally, we shall bring out the Coronation Confection."

"The what?"

"Surely you are familiar with this tradition?" It was an antiquated custom dating back to the days of Oufrey the Extravagant, when a giant throne-sized cake was used to deliver the crown to its new ruler. Hearing about it one day in the midst of a dull, obscure political history lecture, Juniper had latched on to the interesting tidbit, loving how it entwined food with royal responsibility.

In this case, it would be especially purposeful.

Dinner was a roaring success. Luncheon had been exceedingly spare, and the elaborately dressed partygoers fell upon the table with gumption, eating their way through sundown and into the first shadows of night. When the pace of consumption began to slow, Juniper nodded to Tippy, who jumped up and edged out of the circle.

"Where is she going?" Cyril called. "Root!"

"She simply goes to set up the Musicker," said Juniper smoothly, "for the dance portion of our evening activity. Which we shall have to undertake here in the dining area, since the Great Tree has been put to other purposes. Root may accompany her up the Tree if he chooses." She took a deep breath. "I myself shall go along with Toby and Leena, to prepare the Confection."

Cyril's eyes narrowed. "No, I don't think so. Root, go with Juniper. Stick to her like treacle. I do want someone to go watch that little tyke, though. Jessamyn?"

But Tippy was already long gone; Juniper alone saw her elf-lock curls disappearing in the long grass, running past the Great Tree—and then doubling back in the opposite direction.

The music began to play not long after, and Juniper sighed in relief. She stood in the kitchen, inspecting the Confection. It was magnificent, four times as tall and three as wide as their largest cook pot, towering with fragrant cream and fancy cut fruits. It had been assembled directly in its place on the specially designed cart, being far too big to have been moved otherwise. The cart was a clumsy contraption, rolling about two hands off the ground on roughly sanded wheels. But it would do. Sussi had braided the pull rope with thick velvet ribbons, which lent an additional festive touch.

"Very well," said Juniper. "It is looking good. I shall leave you to the final delivery when the time is right."

"We shall await your signal," said Leena with a nod.

"It looks precarious," said Root uncertainly. "Perhaps I should stay and help pull it in."

Catching Leena's eye, Juniper said, "I hardly think that necessary. Didn't Cyril command you to shadow my every step?"

Root snorted. "That Cyril takes on far too many airs. It's like he thinks himself a real king."

At any other time, Juniper would have rejoiced at this possible shift in Root's loyalties. But too much rode on this delivery. She needed to get him away from here. Fast.

Before she could formulate a strategy, Leena cut in. "You think I'm going to let you anywhere near my cake? It's bad enough I have to slave away for that prig, without having his grubby henchman's hands all over my creation." She folded her arms and narrowed her eyes.

Root's eyes flashed with momentary hurt, then he shrugged and spun around. "I don't know what I was thinking in making that offer," he snapped. "Let's go, Juniper. Cyril's waiting."

Juniper couldn't get out of there quickly enough.

As she scrambled up the slope toward the dining room, she heard the scuffling of feet from the opposite direction. She quickly broke into loud song to accompany the Musicker, which had launched into a rollicking tune.

. . .

The Confection materialized out of the darkness, edging into the circle of candlelight like a cream-frosted sun. A gasp went around the room. Cyril sat up rod-straight, a giant smile splitting his face. Juniper knew what had *his* attention: At the very top of the cake was Leena's crowning creation—a pillow of painstakingly stitched orchid petals, stuffed with wild greens. On the pillow rested the Argentine Circlet, which played off the candlelight in bewitching shimmers.

Juniper scooted forward, out of Root's reach. All eyes were on the cake as it was wheeled slowly across the uneven ground toward Cyril's throne. Toby moved slowly with the effort of dragging the cart, as though the Confection were very heavy indeed. Juniper slid in front of him and inched forward, matching the cart's pace step for step.

Cyril sat back on his throne, greed and anticipation fighting for control of his features.

Toby brought the cart to a halt.

Juniper turned, stretched up, and, reaching carefully so as not to get any cream on her peacock blues, lifted the orchid-petal cushion in both hands. Holding the circlet like this brought back so many memories—her mother's slim hands raising it for her to see; her father setting it on her head during her eleventh Nameday ceremony; the dull pang she had felt seeing it in the cave for the first time upon their arrival.

She needed to focus.

It all came down to these next few moments.

Stretching out her hands, palms up, with the pillow and circlet balanced flat atop them, Juniper inclined her head and hunched her shoulders.

She did not relax her knees.

"We have gathered here today," she said reverently, "to witness a coronation."

And then she paused, and in that pause, the night came apart. The Musicker abruptly stopped, and in the silence, a wind rushed through the room, puffing out every candle and leaving just the faint glim of the luminescent berries amongst the hangings.

And then—

The Confection exploded.

In the near-dark room it was like a faintly glowing volcanic eruption, as cream and fruit caromed everywhere, and a giant, blanket-covered shape erupted from the froth. This shape soon threw off its covering and became two bodies, yelling at top volume. One was Erick. The other was a girl dressed in a peacock-blue kirtle. Her elaborately braided hairstyle was piled high upon her head and draped down across half her face, courtesy of Erick's new hairstyling skills.

Juniper caught Alta's eye and smiled. "Well done," she whispered.

Ducking into the deeper darkness outside the dining area, Juniper grabbed at her own hairdo, pulling out a handful of pins and shaking it loose and wild. From the pocket of her dress she pulled out a leather cap, which she jammed on her head and pulled down over her eyes. She tugged off her blue overdress, folded it, and stuffed it under a bush, setting the Argentine circlet carefully on top.

Then she moved stealthily back toward the hubbub.

In the center of the crowd, Cyril yelled for light. Jessamyn was letting out shrill animal yips from the far edge of the room. Root and Filbert were struggling to light their torches while standing on either side of Cyril with spears aimed uncertainly outward. The other kids stumbled around in confusion, yelling and calling out questions. Tippy perched on the Confection cart, stuffing herself with chunks of cake that had survived the calamity.

"Psst!" Juniper called, and cocked her head.

Tippy did a double take, then opened her eyes wide. "Well done," she said. "You're the spitting image. But where is . . ."

A few of the candles were relit by now, and struggling groups of kids could be seen, dotted with splashes of creamy lemongrass-infused topping. Cyril was waving his arms and yelling at his guards. His own sword was out and at the ready. This small group converged on Erick and on Alta, who lowered her chin and backed away from the light of a nearby torch. The precaution wasn't needed, though. In the dim half-light, Juniper could hardly believe that she wasn't looking at herself in a reflecting glass.

But she had no time for reflection.

"Stand down!" Cyril bellowed at the crowd. "The princess is surrounded. Her little coup has failed. *Stand down,* everyone!"

Satisfied with his conquest, Cyril took a step back while Roddy, Filbert, and Root advanced on Erick and Alta. He didn't relax his sword, though.

"Now, now, Princess," Cyril crooned. "What do you and your little book boy hope to do against my three fighters? I don't want to hurt you, but trust me, I will if you make me."

Erick moved in front of Alta as one of the sconces flared bright. In the flickering light, Alta seemed to be cowering. But Juniper could see her knees flexing and her body crouching into an attack pose. Erick stood as straight as a sapling, only a faint shake in his hands betraying his nerves at having to use his all-new fighting skills.

"Go!" Cyril bellowed. "Subdue them—do whatever it takes!"

Root, Roddy, and Filbert charged.

"Now!" said Alta.

She shot out from behind Erick and kicked at Roddy's legs. Roddy fell hard, and she grabbed his spear, swinging the flat end hard into Filbert's back and toppling him. Erick seemed paralyzed for a moment, then shook himself and pulled a pointy stick out from his sleeve. He jumped toward Root, waving the stick in a way that was probably meant to look menacing.

"Attack!" Cyril yelled, taking another step back.

Root paused. He looked at Cyril, then at Alta, who was fighting Roddy like some kind of a dervish, not slowed one whit by the lack of her sword. Abruptly, Root turned his spear sideways. "Here," he said, and tossed it at Erick. Then Root spun around and dove on top of Filbert, who had just struggled to his feet. Root pinned the other boy to the ground while Alta and Roddy grappled on.

The rest of the kids stayed rooted to their spots, watching the fight with wide-open mouths. Juniper passed quietly among them.

She slipped behind Cyril, who stood with red face and clenched fists. She hooked her arm around his neck, pressing something cold and sharp right above his collarbone. She felt him freeze, then swallow.

"Drop your sword," she whispered.

"J-Juniper?" he said incredulously. "But—but you— You're over—" He tried craning his neck, apparently trying to reconcile the sound of her voice in his ear with the sight of her lithe form thoroughly routing Roddy's best fighting moves.

"Now!" she demanded.

Cyril dropped his sword with a clatter, his body rigid.

"Citizens of Queen's Basin!" Juniper called, her voice so strong and fierce that all activity ceased immediately. She kicked Cyril's sword out into the bushes, then walked him forward until she stood directly under a lighted sconce. There she shook her head hard until Alta's cap slid off her head, and her own long hair tumbled down over her shoulders.

At the same time, Alta yanked a ribbon out of her bodice and whipped it around her forehead, demolishing the updo and bringing her own features to light. "Infernal lady hairstyles," Alta muttered.

A collective gasp went around the room, and Juniper took in a deep breath. This was it—this was the moment of truth. In her best plans, she would be standing here knowing that the whole group was behind her. Knowing she'd recaptured the loyalty of her people in advance, that they were all on her side.

Instead . . . where did she stand? She couldn't hesitate or wait to find out. She had to take the plunge.

"Citizens of Queen's Basin," she called again. "You have lived under Cyril's rule. You have seen his leadership in action." She took a deep breath. "Tell me that this is what you truly want, and I will let him go right now. I will willingly go back to my imprisonment."

The room was deathly silent.

"Tell me that you enjoy having no responsibilities whatsoever, no rules, nothing to do all day long." She swallowed. "No country to be proud of."

"Cyril's a pig!" Tippy shouted, shaking one creamy fist in the air. "A mess-making pig!"

"He's never once lifted a finger, not since the day we got here and certainly not when he was our 'king,'" added Leena.

"I've heard tell that Cyril was the one behind the attacks on the camp," Toby broke in. "Is that really so? All this time, he's been sneaking to the goats and chickens, stealing food right out from under us?"

All eyes turned questioningly to Juniper. "It's true," she said, tightening her grip on Cyril's neck, lest he should try to get away. "And there's something else you should know as you make your decision. Our Tippy has paid a visit to Cyril's camp and has discovered this: Cyril has not only turned against my rule. He has betrayed his own country. *Our* country. Cyril is working hand in hand with the Monsian army, who are even now invading Torr."

Cyril opened his mouth to protest, but Juniper snapped, "Don't bother denying it. If I'm right, you're *proud* of that alliance, aren't you? You think you're actually on the *right* side!"

She saw his cheeks flame and guessed that his pride was fighting his reason. He glanced around the circle, perhaps seeing himself outnumbered. His lip curled up. "Very well, you've found me out. But there's another thing you're right about—we *are* on the winning side. This puny so-called country is *nothing,* and when my father is sitting on the throne of Torr, as he likely is already, you'll see then who is the one giving the orders."

"I think we've heard enough from you," said Juniper shortly.

"Queen Juniper!" someone yelled, and soon the whole group was chanting. "Hooray for our queen! Hooray for Queen Juniper of the Hourglass!" Juniper looked from one side of the room to the other, at the crowd of settlers chanting her name. Even Jessamyn, looking red-faced and subdued, gave a halfhearted cheer, her fingers straying to smooth her fine silk skirts. And Root's voice boomed over them, loudest of all.

Erick and Alta each stepped forward and grabbed Cyril's arms. Juniper said loudly, to be heard over the shouting: "Cyril Lefarge, *you* are the traitor here. And you are finished."

With that, she loosed her hold on him, pulling back the sharp object she'd had at his neck—her own bone-carved comb. With a grin, she lifted the comb up and ran it through her hair, happy to be rid of that intolerable updo.

And of Cyril, too.

Then she slid the comb back into her sleeve, until the next time she'd need it. As Alta tied Cyril's hands behind his back, Juniper looked around the room, firelight reflecting off the still, drawn faces. "I've had a lot of time to think during the last few days, and

261

there's something I want to say. No, wait a moment, Alta. I want you to hear this, too. And Cyril.

"Look, some of the things Cyril first called me out for were true. I *am* a new ruler, and it's certain that I'll make mistakes along the way. *Have* made mistakes—like not telling you what was going on back home. I wanted to protect you, but I've learned that the truth isn't ever something you should protect others from. Truth is what we set our rule by, and that is what I pledge to you from this moment onward." She paused and grinned. "Oh, one more thing: Erick is actually fourteen. He's older than me, and I'm okay with that. Age is important in some ways, but . . . not so much in others. I don't know why I thought that was such a big deal when we started out."

She took a deep breath. "We began as a rough-and-tumble team. You hardly knew me, and I didn't know you at all. Over the last weeks, though . . . all that's changed. I've come to see each of you not just as the job you fill, maid and cook and builder and guard. But I've gotten to really know you. For instance, Leena, you're an incredible cook, but you're a leader, too. You run this kitchen like an army general! Roddy—if we can dream it, you can build it, but you've as much of an eye for beauty as function, and that's saying something. Erick's read more books than the rest of us put together, and for all his book sense he's got heaps of common sense, too. Tippy is the life of every party, and where would any of us be without her? Alta is the bravest person alive, and we owe the security of our camp to her entirely. Filbert's got the strength of an ox. Paul could bring a stone to bud with no effort at all, *and* he's absolutely monsterful on the dance floor. Sussi is never without a kind word and brightens every day with her smile. Toby has the gentlest hands I've ever seen, and you can see proof of that by how the animals follow him all around their pens. Oona knows her own mind, and once she decides on a plan, that's her course. Root—well, I've come to revise my opinion of you; there's a lot more there than I gave you credit for, and I respect the way you can set your own path against strong odds. Jessamyn . . ." She caught the other girl's eye and smiled. "Well, you have simply fabulous taste in dresses."

The group was quiet. Juniper swallowed. "The lot of you, you're the best subjects I could ever have asked for. Though we all came together a bit haphazardly, I think we've got the makings of a truly fine country. But for that to happen, we need to stick together. And we need to do what we set out to do."

She looked around the gathered crowd. "We need to be a team. So I must know: Who is behind me as the rightful ruler of Queen's Basin . . . and who wants to side with Cyril?"

There was a moment of silence, then Oona stepped out from the crowd, eyes wide but chin lifted. "I'm with Cyril. Forgive me, Miss Juniper. I admire all you've done here, but Cyril has my vote, and I'm not changing it." She slid over to stand by Cyril, placing a hand protectively in his.

"Oona!" cried Sussi, leaping to her feet. But Toby shushed his little sister and wrapped her in his arms.

Juniper waited, but when Oona's expression didn't change, she said quietly, "Very well. Erick, please escort Oona as well. Anybody else?"

To Juniper's vast relief, there wasn't. "Go on, then," she said. "Let's get these two relocated." Suddenly she felt exhausted.

Then Tippy's shrill voice piped up. "What a time, ye people, what a time! But if I was you all, I'd set my sights on demolishing what's left of this here cake. For it's some true masterpiece, and I am personally avowed to eat every last crumb and morsel I can fit!"

Epilogue

Cyril was dispatched with no further fanfare, and something in the group relaxed at his departure. The loss of Oona caused a little more unease. But Juniper was not really surprised at the girl's choice: She'd never seen Cyril speak so much as a word in Oona's direction, but the girl had been besotted with him from the start. Though Toby tried to get her to see reason, Oona had crossed her arms in silent defiance, leaving them no choice but to lock her up as well.

The moment Erick and Alta came back from their unpleasant mission, Juniper called everyone together. After seeing the last of the candles relit, she stood in the splash of light and looked out upon her subjects. They sat in their usual circle—tired, scruffy, but with mouths full of cake and faces alight with restored balance.

Something in Juniper warmed as she looked around the familiar group. She wasn't hiding in the shadows this time, afraid to be seen, like she'd been at the fateful palace dance party that had started this whole adventure. She was one of them now, sitting right up in the midst of the circle. And there they all were: Erick, sitting near a pile of leather-bound books and somehow managing to read three at once; Alta, reunited with her sword and lovingly polishing it with a soft cloth; Tippy, buzzing from seat to seat, clearly about some devious plan or another; Leena, lounging with arms crossed as she watched the satisfied faces enjoying her food; Root and Jessamyn, sitting as far apart as possible, as though to distance themselves completely from their last few weeks' association; and Roddy and Sussi and Paul and Filbert and Toby, each talking and laughing and smiling.

Her people. Her subjects.

And . . . also, in some new and precious way, her friends.

She'd done it. She'd saved her kingdom. There was so much still to do—but in this one thing, in this first step, she'd succeeded. Before she went any further, though, there was something she had to say.

She came to her feet, and the hum of noise quieted. "I do owe you all an apology," she began. Juniper studied each of their faces in turn. How could her Comportment Master have been so wrong? There was nothing weak about apologizing—on the contrary, Juniper felt the words filling her with hot new strength. "I was wrong not to tell you about the letter from my father, to keep from you the details of the invasion of Torr. And I know I worked you far too hard." She smiled ruefully. "I had a lot of time to think when I was in Cyril's little dungeon, and one thing I kept coming back to was the importance of having balance."

"Ah, Your Highness," said Leena, "we don't hold that against you none."

"We certainly don't," cut in Toby. "You do get all strict and ruler-like, but you mean well, and your heart's in the right place. Cyril said and did the right things, what we thought we wanted. But deep down, he was serving his own ends. That's the difference between you two. That's why we're all for you, miss." And, as he had back in the stables on that day so long ago, he put both thumbs up and flashed her a big, bright smile. And Juniper knew that everything would be all right.

"We've come through a lot, citizens of Queen's Basin," she said, hooking her arms behind her back. "And I fear that what's behind us is just the smallest bit of what's still to come. Cyril has wreaked havoc on our camp since the moment we arrived, but despite this, we've come through stronger than ever—and look at what we've accomplished!"

"Is it everything you'd hoped for?" Alta asked.

"What?" Juniper said, surprised.

"When you set out to build your own kingdom, you said you wanted somewhere everyone could be who they were, find their own place and all. Have you found that here?"

Unexpectedly, Juniper's eyes filled with tears. "I found it, and far more besides," she said passionately. "I set out to make a summer kingdom, and instead I found myself a family."

"As did I," said Paul quietly from the back.

"And me," added Erick.

"Me too! Me too!" chirped Tippy. "Not to take the place of Elly, like, but alongside her, you know?"

Then Leena stood, her purple skirts pooling around her.

"We're out of elderberry punch, so I'm just going to hold up my empty goblet, for I've something that's gone too long without saying. Here's to Juniper, ruler of Queen's Basin and the best queen we could ever want. I'm proud to be your subject."

The group erupted in cheers and stomping feet and clinking goblets.

There was a sound to her left, and Juniper turned to catch Root's eye. "I've got something to say also," he muttered, scuffing at the ground with his boot. "I want to express my abject apologies for my part in all the trouble. It's true, all that you said earlier. I swear on my life that I'd no idea Cyril was working with the Monsians— but I did know he was set on disrupting the settlement and taking everyone back to Torr. To get *you* there, Princess Juniper."

Juniper shook her head. "I should have guessed he was behind it all—right from that first stunt with Jessamyn and the horses. It was so obvious."

"Wait, what happened with the horses?" Root looked from side to side, eyes widening in puzzlement as Alta and Erick described the destruction of the fences, the odd shapes Jessamyn had seen, and the theft of their mounts.

When they finished, Root shook his head vigorously. "Cyril and I caused a lot of mischief. Jessamyn, too," he added quickly, over the girl's scowl. "Stealing the food and wrecking the dining area and all. But this thing with the horses—we didn't do it. That night we were setting up our camp and preparing for the next day. I have no idea what you saw that night, Jessie, but it wasn't us."

Juniper stilled. It made sense, of course. If Cyril had taken the horses, they would have been recovered by now. But in that case . . . this meant they had another enemy—one which had been kept away by the guards, presumably.

A shudder passed through her.

Who were these unknown attackers? Was it wild beasts, as they'd first thought—or could it be something even worse? She thought back to a few of her lookout sessions, when she thought she'd seen movement or odd lights in the distance. Could there really have been something—or someone—else out there?

Could there still be?

Juniper stood up and waved her hands. She would give this puzzle the attention it needed, but she couldn't do that just yet. "Quiet down, everyone," she called out. "This is disturbing news, but it doesn't change anything. Most important, it doesn't change what we need to do next. Cyril was wrong about so many things, but I've come to realize that in one thing he was right: We cannot sit here while our country is under attack. If the palace has fallen, if my father is truly held hostage"—she could hear her voice trembling, but pushed on—"and the rest of the country invaded, then we may be the only free subjects left in all of Torr. Cyril has done much to undermine our nation. But he has unknowingly also left us with a significant advantage."

She raised the sheaf of parchments Tippy had recovered. "I've spent a great deal of time analyzing these lists, and they give much information about Monsia's position and about their future plans. Cyril would have marched us all right into the hands of the enemy, which I could never support. But I've begun to wonder if there may not be *something* we can do in defense of our country. If we truly might be the only hope for the land of Torr, what responsibility do we hold to our nation?"

In each face, she could see a vivid reflection of the fear churning in her own gut. She made her voice as hard and strong as she could. "We are a small group, and of a certainty we cannot hit Monsia head-on. But if there is anything we Torreans are known for, it is that we do not easily give in. We may be few, but we are fierce. We may be outnumbered, but we do not ever accept defeat. Any foe who challenges one of us will awake on the morrow to find an army at his back. This is our heritage. This is the might of Torr. Why should this not also be our calling? For we *are* fierce, and we are ready, and we will not be broken. I say that we cannot know what we might do until we try."

The faces around the circle looked greenish and queasy over their leftover fish soup. She softened her voice. "I am your queen, but I won't be your dictator. I have come to believe that making all the decisions on your behalf doesn't help anybody. We are a country, but we are also a strong fighting team, and when all voices are heard, we will be best able to make the noise that is needed. So, let us bring the matter to all. Who thinks we should make a solid plan for venturing to the aid of Torr?"

There was a pause while the settlers turned to each consider their neighbor. Then one hand rose into the air. Then another. Within moments, every hand speared enthusiastically up into the night.

Juniper leaped to her feet. "Yes! *That* is the true spirit of Torr. We shall group together and each lay out our best plans. Starting tomorrow, we shall bring order to this chaos. We shall determine what is to be done with Cyril. We shall plan our own invasion.

"But tonight? Tonight we shall enjoy the rest of this grand celebration. Tippy? Crank up the Musicker, for I've a pair of new dancing slippers and a yen to break them in."

"Are you certain?" whispered Alta. "Surely it is past midnight already."

Juniper reached out and caught the other girl's hand in a warm squeeze. "Who cares? We've no timepiece, and no schedule to drive us. We can go as late as we like."

Queen Juniper's Schedule
for Tomorrow

Unknown

Acknowledgments

STORIES BEGIN IN ALL SORTS OF WAYS, AND *Princess Juniper of the Hourglass* has roots that go especially deep. I wrote the original opening scene—a naïve, spirited princess asking her father if she might have a country for her birthday— back in 2004, as I sat in my basement office, dreaming of one day publishing a book for children.

But the heart of the story goes back even further. It goes all the way back to my own childhood: to sun-drenched summer days when I felt like a queen of my own outdoors; to the wide-spreading tree in our yard, with the huge stone wheel that leaned against it and made it just right for climbing; to my down-the-road neighbors who let my friends and me use their spare caravan for after-school play, stocking it with snacks and other goodies just right for playing house. It's got roots in my childhood favorites *The Railway Children* and *The Secret Garden* and *Little House on the Prairie*, and most especially Enid Blyton's obscure gem *The Secret Island*, about a group of friends who run away from home and set up a "house" for themselves on an island.

But the spark that took all of this from *idea* to *book* came about quite unexpectedly. None of it would have happened without a certain lunch conversation I had with my wonderful editor, Jill Santopolo. As we talked casually about royalty, then princess stories, I remembered that scene I'd written nearly a decade before. Somewhat offhandedly, I mentioned it to Jill. Her eyes lit up . . . and from there, things came together more quickly than I could ever have imagined. I'm so grateful to Jill for seeing Juniper's potential, and for her skillful guidance in coaxing her to life. I also am deeply indebted to Michael Green, for his extraordinary helmsmanship, to Talia Benamy, for her sharp eye and critical support, and to all the wonderful and talented team at Penguin for their tireless efforts on Juniper's behalf.

As always, I couldn't do any of this without Erin Murphy, my phenomenal agent; thank you for doing what you do so well. And to my wonderful critique partners and friends who have read this manuscript at various stages and offered much-needed input: Nancy Werlin, Julie Berry, Debbie Kovacs, Sarah Beth Durst, Natalie Lorenzi, Julie Phillipps, and Kip Wilson. Two separate conversations were especially enlightening and took my plot in important new directions: Thank you to Eric Luper and Nancy Hightower.

Above all, I am most grateful to Zack, Kim, and Lauren, for their unflagging enthusiasm and support. A thing's not real until I share it with you, and that's a fact. And a giant squishy hug to all the Paquettes and the Neves—what a great tribe we have!

In closing, a word about words: Astute readers might notice some unusual vocabulary sprinkled throughout this story. As anyone who knows me will confirm, I adore words. Discovering new ways to say familiar things is one of my favorite pastimes. So you'll understand what delight I found in this story's old-fashioned setting: It was the perfect excuse to seek out lists of archaic, obscure, out-of-the-ordinary words. I wove these in where they felt natural, and they make me smile each time I see them. I hope some of them might find their way into your vocabularies, too. As for me? I'm already stocking up my word list for book two.

See you back in Torr!